A Spell of Murder

A Spell of Murder

A Witch Cats of Cambridge Mystery

Clea Simon

Trade paperback ISBN: 978-1-947993-81-5
eISBN: 978-1-947993-49-5

Library of Congress Catalog Number: Data Available Upon Request

First trade paperback publication: December 2019 by Polis Books LLC
221 River St., 9th Fl. #9070 Hoboken, NJ 07030
www.PolisBooks.com

POLIS BOOKS

Chapter 1

It was Harriet's fault. It's always her fault, not that she'll ever admit it.

That was Clara's first thought as she tried to settle on the sofa, flicking her long, grey tail with annoyance. As a cat, Clara wouldn't usually have any trouble getting comfortable. That's one special skill that all felines share. But even as she tried to calm her restive tail, curling it neatly around her snowy front paws, Clara, a petite, if plump, calico, couldn't stop fretting.

Harriet was her oldest sister, a creamsicle-colored longhair with more fur than common sense. Still, despite the fluffy feline's typical self-absorption, she and Clara and their middle sister, Laurel, had cohabited with a nice enough human for almost two years without any problems, until now. Until Harriet.

Yes, Becca, their human, had begun to believe she had psychic powers. Becca, who at twenty-six usually had more sense, was training to be a witch, as if that were something one could learn from books. But to the calico cat who now fumed quietly on the sofa, the petite brunette had always seemed a harmless soul—good with a can opener. Warm. Generous with her lap. And then, last week, Harriet—who cared only for her own comfort—conjured up a pillow.

"I was tired," Harriet said, in that petulant mew that Clara knew so well, when asked why in the name of Bast she'd be so stupid. *"Becca wasn't even looking."*

"You could have moved!" her younger sibling hissed back, the grey whorls on her sides heaving with annoyance. *"And she was!"*

Harriet was taking up the sunny spot on the windowsill, as she always did that time of the morning, and Clara narrowed her mysterious green eyes to glare at her sister. Harriet was more than fluffy, she was immense, a pale orange marshmallow of a feline, whose furry bulk and predictable habits prevented her youngest sister from enjoying any of the solar bounty. Still, she probably shouldn't have hissed. Harriet was Clara's elder, if merely by a few minutes. As it was, the orange and white cat just shuffled a bit and turned her rounded back on her sister rather than responding.

Clara didn't know why she even bothered asking. She already knew the answer: Harriet didn't move unless she had to, and on a bright spring day it was easier to conjure a cushion than make the leap from the sun-warmed sill to the sofa, where Clara now fumed. The sofa where, it turned out, Becca had been trying out a summoning spell. And so now, of course, their hapless human believed *she* had pulled that pillow out of the ether.

Which was a problem because Becca belonged to a coven. Had for about three months, ever since she saw a flier in the laundromat advertising an opening for "Witches: New and In Training." That was the kind of thing that happened here, in Cambridge, where the hippies never really went away. Since then, they'd met every week to drink a foul-smelling herbal concoction and try out various spells. None of which ever produced any magic, of course. None of the humans had the basic powers of a day-old kitten, and certainly nothing like Clara and her sisters shared as the descendants of an old and royal feline line. But now, Clara feared, Becca had become obsessed, spending every waking moment trying to reproduce that one spell, while Harriet, Laurel, and Clara looked on.

"Don't you dare..." Clara muttered in a soft mew as Laurel sashayed into the room, taking in her two sisters with one sweeping gaze. Laurel was the middle one, a troublemaker and as vain as can be. Not simply of her own glossy coat—the cream touched with brown, or, as she called it, café au lait—but of her powers. That she was plotting something, Clara was certain. As Laurel glanced from Harriet back to Clara again, her tail started lashing and her ears stuck out sideways like an owl's.

"Why not?" Laurel had a streak of Siamese in her. It made her chatty, as well as giving her neat dark chocolate booties. *"It'll be fun."*

"It'll bring more people!" Clara felt her fur begin to rise. The idea of her middle sister meddling—and possibly adding more magic to the mix—made her frantic. *"Don't you get it? They'll never let up."*

The black, grey, and orange cat—the smallest of the three sisters—didn't have to explain who "they" were. That night, Becca's coven would be meeting again at their place, which, to the three felines, was bad enough. Strangers, six of them, would soon be sitting in all the good seats, with their odd smells and loud voices. What was worse was that Becca would think she had to feed them, as well as brew that horrible tea. And as the cats well knew, Becca had no money, not since she lost her job as a researcher for the local historical society.

"Redundant," her boss had told her. "What with the budget cutbacks and the advances in technology."

"That means they can get an intern to do a Google search." Becca had sniffled into Clara's parti-colored fur the day she'd gotten the news. Harriet might be the fluffiest and Laurel the sleekest, but Clara was the one Becca talked to. The one she had confided in months earlier when she found the book that had started her on this whole witchcraft obsession, a spark of excitement lighting up her face. She'd been researching land deeds, the scutwork of history, when she had stumbled on it, her eye caught by a familiar name—some old relative of hers who had been caught up in a witch trial back in the bad old days in Salem. Then, when she'd seen the flier by the coin machine at the Wash 'N Dry, she'd been so exhilarated, she'd raced back to tell Clara, leaving her sheets in the drier. And now, without the distraction of her job, Becca had thrown herself into the study of magic and sorcery, spending her days in the library or on her computer, trying to track down the full story of that great-great whatever, and sharing her fears and, increasingly, her hopes with Clara.

Maybe it was because Clara was a calico that Becca whispered into the black-tipped ears of her littlest cat. Calicos had a reputation for being more intelligent and curious than other felines. Plus, that uneven look—a gray patch over one eye and an orange one over the other—made her appear approachable. Inquisitive. Becca couldn't know that her youngest cat was often teased for her markings. "*Goofy,*" her sister Laurel said in her distinctive yowl. "*Clara the calico? Clara the clown!*" Recently, Harriet had taken up calling her that too.

Clara didn't mind, as long as Becca kept confiding in

her. The young woman didn't really think her cats understood about her being laid off, but, in truth, they were all quite aware of the straitened circumstances. Not that Laurel and Harriet always sympathized. There was that one time three weeks ago that Becca tried cutting back on the cats' food, getting the generic cans from the market instead of the tiny ones with the pretty labels. After wolfing down hers, Harriet had barfed all over the sofa. She didn't have to. She was just making a point about what she considered an affront to her dignity.

Tonight, when Becca took credit for conjuring that cushion, Clara didn't know what her haughty sister would do. Interrupt, most likely. Jump onto the table and begin bathing, if she had to, to be the center of attention. If she tried anything further—like pulling more pillows out of the ether—or if Laurel got up to her own tricks, Clara would have to get involved, she vowed with a final flick of the tail. And that, she knew, just wouldn't end well.

Chapter 2

"Bad Clara!" Becca called softly as she clapped her hands at the calico cat. "Bad girl."

The cat glanced up from her perch on the counter and blinked, the picture of innocence except for the pink petal that hung from one fang. Her harsh words softened by a gentle smile, Becca reached over and scooped up the multi-colored feline, depositing her on the floor. "Now, you know better than that!"

"Is anything wrong?" Trent appeared in the doorway, a slight frown pulling his goatee into a pout.

"It's Clara." Becca sighed, shaking her head. "She's eating the flowers."

"You have another cat?" Trent's voice was neutral, but Becca knew he'd been disconcerted to find Harriet, her largest feline, stretched out over most of the sofa.

"Three, actually," Becca admitted. "They were littermates, and I didn't want to separate them."

"Of course." He nodded, his voice as warm as his dark brown eyes. "Besides, they're your familiars."

Becca turned to hide her flustered smile, as well as the blush that was creeping up from her chest. Trent was a self-professed warlock, the leader of the coven, the small group of would-be witches she had joined a few months before. More to the point, he was devastatingly handsome, with those flashing eyes and a devilish smile played up by that goatee. And he had brought over the bouquet that her cat, Clara, had begun to nibble.

Willing her color back to normal, Becca reached into the cabinet for her one good vase. Officially, the flowers were for the table—a touch of nature to bless the May full moon, the "Flower Moon," Trent had said—but the dark-eyed warlock hadn't had to arrive early to give them to her, she knew. Besides, Becca had felt a slight charge when Trent had handed them to her, a certain warmth behind that smile.

Still, she had to get ahold of herself. Any minute now, the doorbell would ring again. The group was meeting at her place this week, as it had the last four. Partly because her apartment was central, a Cambridgeport walk-up not too far from the T. But the main reason the coven was gathering here tonight was in the hope that Becca could replicate the group's one successful act of magic thus far: the conjuring of a pillow out of thin air. She was going to have to concentrate.

"Do you feel your power?" Trent nearly purred, coming up close behind her.

"I don't…I don't know." Becca almost stuttered. "I hope so." In truth, she was beginning to despair. She had tried countless times since that day—donning the same jeans and sweater, letting her mint tea cool in the same mug beside her—as she read over the words of the spell. But she had been unable to make the magic work again. Now, Harriet was lying on the gold velvet pillow, one paw idly batting at its fringes, as if it were just another bit of home furnishing. "Maybe one pillow is the limit of my power," she said, voicing her deepest fear.

"Nonsense." Trent sounded confident—and so close she could feel his warm breath. *Maybe*, she thought, *magic of another sort was brewing*. But just then she heard the unmistakable hiss and squeal of a cat fight beginning in the other room.

"Clara!" Becca ducked around her guest, clapping her hands again to get the cats' attention. "Harriet!"

The smaller of the two felines glanced up at her, wide-eyed, and Harriet used the distraction to push Clara off the couch.

"It's the pillow," Becca said, a note of exasperation creeping into her voice. Trent had followed her into the other room with—she was glad to see—an amused half smile on his lips. "They've been fighting over it since it appeared."

"They sense its power." He sounded serious and reached down absently to stroke Laurel, who had begun to twine around his ankles. Clara, meanwhile, peered up into Becca's face, as if willing her to respond. But just then, the doorbell rang and Trent stepped back, neatly disengaging himself from Laurel, and gave Becca a gentle pat on the arm.

"Go," he said, the smile carrying through to his voice. "I'll finish up in the kitchen."

Maybe it was that pat—or the man's apparent preference for Laurel—but Clara decided to watch him and took up a position by the kitchen counter from which to observe this strange, dark-haired man who had made his way into their private space.

Sure enough, as soon as Becca had left the kitchen—with an affronted Laurel in tow—Trent began opening drawers. *Aha!* Clara thought. *I've got you.* But all he did was fish out a pair of shears and cut the blossoms loose from their wrapping.

After he trimmed their stems and placed them in the vase Becca had set out, he even cleaned up after himself, and the cat began to wonder if, perhaps, her suspicions were unfounded.

"You're so naïve." Harriet sauntered in, and although she immediately buried her face in her food dish, she must have seen how her youngest sister was watching the newcomer. *"You're not used to male attention."*

"It's not that..." her calico sibling started to argue as Harriet swiped her plume of a tail. *"It's that I don't want Becca to be hurt again."* Another swipe. Harriet didn't seem to care that their person had had her heart broken a scant two months ago. To the older cat, it was a plus when Becca began spending every night at home again. And when she lost her job, that was even better—until the incident with the store brand cans. *"We don't know this new man,"* Clara said, blinking those green eyes.

"Jealous." Even with her mouth full, Harriet couldn't stand not having the last word. But by then, other voices had joined Becca's in the living room, and so Clara followed Trent as he carried out the ever-so-tasty bouquet.

"Suzanne, Kathy, merry meet." He nodded at the two women who'd come in together, each as unlike as Clara and Laurel, whose almond-shaped blue eyes gazed up in frank, feline appraisal. Tall and slender, Suzanne had a nervous habit of running her hands over her long blonde hair that made Clara think she wanted to groom. Tonight, though, they were occupied, holding a covered loaf pan, which had Laurel sniffing delicately, dark brown nose in the air.

"Lemon poppy seed," the willowy woman was saying as she handed the pan to Becca. "To celebrate the full moon tonight, as well as our triumph."

"Oh, I didn't think to bring anything." Kathy, on the other hand, was short and as plump as Harriet, although her curly hair was penny-bright auburn and not nearly as silky as the cat's. The youngest member of the coven, she was generally considered the pet, a designation that she appeared to enjoy even as it annoyed Harriet, perhaps because of the similarity in their shape and coloring. "I mean, merry meeting," Kathy corrected herself with a giggle. "Are you sure that's okay? We all chip in for the tea and the crystals and everything."

"We have more than enough," said Becca, taking the pan and the serrated knife that her guest had wrapped in a tea towel beneath it. "But this is lovely. Thank you, Suzanne."

Kathy had already turned away. "Trent!" She chirped with a happy smile. "Now we can get started." But her progress back into the living room was stopped as she noticed the flowers.

"Oh," she recoiled, taking in the collection of pink daisies and chrysanthemums that surrounded one red rose. "A bouquet?"

"A celebration of the Flower Moon," Trent corrected her with a warm smile as he placed the vase on Becca's all-purpose table. "As well as a hostess gift. After all, we've been meeting at Becca's every week for a month now."

Before Kathy could respond, the doorbell rang again.

"Please," said Trent, nodding at Becca. "Let me."

"Thanks." She looked relieved, as Kathy trotted after him. "I forgot to put the kettle on."

Clara followed Becca back into the kitchen, trying to read her expression and understand this strange nervousness of hers.

"Becca, I can't believe you did it. I mean, I'm really

impressed." Suzanne had come up behind the cat, who sidestepped quickly to protect her tail. "In fact, I'm wondering if now maybe you can help me with something."

"I'd love to. Can you grab those mugs first?" Becca asked, filling the kettle. "I got a little behind this afternoon."

"Tea can wait." Suzanne stepped closer, as the cat scooted back to the counter. The skinny woman didn't seem like much of a threat—Harriet could probably knock her over—but she was wearing hard-soled shoes. "I've been trying to figure out what to do about something, Becca. It's…well, it's kind of private, only, it might affect all of us."

"Really?" Becca wasn't listening, as her cat could tell. Instead, she was counting spoonfuls of that foul tea into her big teapot, and so the calico emerged to brush against her, willing her to pay attention. "Oh, Clara." She paused to look down at that grey and orange face. "Did Harriet eat your dinner again too? Hang on."

Leaving off her counting, she fetched the bag of kibble from beneath the sink and poured some into the now-empty dish. But while the smallest of her pets appreciated her concern, that wasn't what she'd been on about. Nor, it seemed, was it what had preoccupied Suzanne.

"I'm serious, Becca." She leaned in, speaking softly as she toyed nervously with the crystal teardrop pendant she wore. "Especially if you can—"

"Becca, darling!" An exaggerated theatrical voice interrupted them as Larissa swanned into the kitchen, scarves trailing behind her and a plate of cookies in her outstretched, be-ringed hand. "Oh, that's a pretty piece." She reared back as she eyed Suzanne's necklace. "Is that new?"

Suzanne glanced down at the pendant, as if she'd

forgotten what she held. "I've had it for a while," she said with a nervous smile, and tucked it beneath her collar.

With a sniff, Larissa turned, once more, to their host. "What's this I've been hearing about a summoning spell?"

"A summoning?" Kathy had appeared, as if flagged down by those colorful scarves.

"It was…I'll tell you all about it." Becca looked down at the kettle, as if the burgeoning steam could explain her own reddening cheeks. "I'm not sure what exactly happened."

Turning off the heat, Becca went back to scooping tea leaves as Ande, tall and elegant with a complexion like milk caramel, entered the kitchen. The other new arrival, Marcia, must have caught her on the way in.

"Luz got a new client today." Petite Marcia had to look up to address Ande, whose dark curls added an inch to her height. "Going into private practice was the best thing she ever did, for so many reasons."

As she always did when Marcia—a paralegal with startlingly large, dark eyes—brought up her pretty Latina roommate, Larissa rolled her own eyes, heavy with mascara. "I'm sure, darling," she drawled. "But we were talking about Becca's *remarkable* success."

"I wasn't talking to—oh, never mind." Marcia shook her head, as if to free her dark pageboy, and shoved her ever-present Red Sox cap in the pocket of her overalls. "But, yeah, I want to hear about the spell."

"What spell?" Ande asked in a stage whisper before someone Clara couldn't see—Marcia?—shushed her.

"I've been trying to reproduce my results," Becca explained. "That's why I don't have anything set up, and the tea…"

"Darling Becca," Larissa's voice dripped with her usual condescension. "Magic isn't an exact science, you know. You can't expect to use the same techniques." She waved one hand and set her bangles clanking, and Clara retreated to the corner. It wasn't just the noise, though. Larissa was the oldest member of the coven, by a good ten years, and too vain to wear glasses. Thinking of this, the cautious calico pulled her tail in closer.

"Here, let me." Becca turned to take the plate and place it safely on the counter, just as a low, sleek shadow slipped in. If this crew left the kitchen without taking those cookies, Laurel would be on them in a second. The seal-point cat was as omnivorous as Harriet, only she was a better jumper.

"She's right, you know." The women all turned, making room for Trent. "We can't account for factors beyond our perception—cosmic vibrations, or even atmospheric pressure. But your instincts were dead on." His smile provoked a low murmur, almost a purr, from all of the women except Marcia. Becca's blush had deepened, and she turned away as if to hide it.

"Bother," she said, looking at the pot in her hands. "I've lost count. Now I've got to start all over again."

Chapter 3

Harriet and Laurel had already grabbed the prime seating in the living room—Laurel on Becca's overstuffed armchair and Harriet stretched out on the sofa where everyone could admire her coat. And so, Clara followed Becca once the tea was steeping and hunkered down beneath the table. It wasn't as comfy there, but she liked being close to her person. More importantly, from this vantage point, she could keep an eye on Harriet.

"So Becca has had a momentous breakthrough," Trent began once the customary invocation had been recited. "I don't know if everyone has heard."

"How could we help it?" Kathy's voice wasn't as soft as she thought it was, and from where Clara sat, she could see one of the other women—Marcia, probably, considering the high-tops—surreptitiously kick her. "I mean, it sounds so exciting." Kathy didn't sound convinced. "Oh, cool necklace, Suzanne."

"Thanks." The nervous hands suddenly appeared in the thin woman's lap, as if she'd forced them down.

"Well, I want to hear the details," Marcia piped up. "Shall I pour?"

"I rather think that's Becca's prerogative tonight, don't you?" Larissa, in her grand dame role. "By the way, Becca, did you call my friend about the position?"

"I don't have a master's, Larissa." Becca, standing, seemed to be struggling with the full pot. "And it sounds like your friend is looking for a PhD."

"Bosh." Even from under the table, Clara could picture the dismissive wave.

"I might have a lead for you." Kathy was trying to make up for her, well, cattiness. Clara lashed her tail. "What are you looking for again?"

"I did online and library research." Becca sounded tired, though it wasn't clear if that was because of the heavy teapot or the subject. "I've been hoping to finish my library sciences degree, but…" A sigh and the thud. At least the pouring was done. "I can type too, but I'm hoping to find something in my field before unemployment runs out."

"We should talk." Clara could almost hear Kathy nodding, but when she tried to poke her head up to catch Becca's reaction, she found herself blocked by a foot.

"These are good." Trent again. "Did you make these, Larissa?"

Over on the sofa, Harriet's head jerked up as if she'd been shocked. The crunch, as Trent bit again into one of the cookies, had brought her to her feet. Harriet, like most cats, could summon food, as she did with that pillow. But like that pillow, it would be pulled from the ether—with about as much flavor. And Harriet had a particular weakness for sweets. That, Clara knew, could mean trouble.

"So, this spell…" Larissa's foot swung under the table. She had those pointy-toed heels on, but Clara scooted out of the way in time, losing sight of Harriet. "I want to hear the details."

"I'm not sure exactly what I did—or did differently." Becca had tucked her red sneakers under her chair, as she did when she was nervous. Looking at all the shoes around her, Clara didn't blame the tender human. This was scary territory. And Harriet wasn't likely to make it any easier. The calico crept forward while Becca explained. "I was reciting the *Ars Advocabit*—the summoning spell—from the book, just like we've all done. And then—there it was."

"There *what* was?" Larissa's tone matched those shoes.

"A pillow." Becca's voice went soft. "I'd summoned a pillow. And before you say anything, yes, it really was a new pillow. Not anything I had in the house before. It was gold velvet and very soft."

From her new vantage point, Clara could see Harriet stretch with satisfaction, and she relaxed a little. *"And it has tassels!"* Her oldest sister was purring with pride.

"Can we see it?" Ande, ignoring the cat as people usually do, sounded skeptical.

"Yes." Becca pushed her chair back. "I left it where it was. I thought, maybe, the placement was important."

More purrs from Harriet, although when Becca slid the pillow from beneath her warm bulk, the contented rumble faded. If Becca truly had any sensitivities, supernatural or otherwise, she would have been burned by the intensity of Harriet's stare as she brought the pillow back to the table.

"It is very soft." Ande kneaded it with her long fingers.

"Let me." Harriet sat up as the pillow was passed to Suzanne and then Marcia, and finally Kathy, the cat's yellow eyes focused like lasers as it moved from hand to hand.

"Why did you summon something so tacky?" Kathy's freckled nose wrinkled as she flicked a tassel.

Harriet's ears went flat, a low growl beginning deep in her cream-colored chest as her back began to arch.

"Becca!" Suzanne sounded alarmed. "Is something wrong with your cat?"

"What?" Becca's chair scraped the floor. "Oh, Harriet! I'm afraid she's adopted that pillow as her own. It does kind of match her fur. Doesn't it?"

The murmured responses didn't sound that convinced, but Harriet seemed to accept them. At any rate, once Kathy had relinquished the pillow, she sank back down on the sofa and her ears resumed their natural perkiness.

"The problem," Becca continued, stroking the plush object, "is that I haven't been able to duplicate it. I was wondering if there was something about the moon last Thursday? Or maybe an astral projection?"

"Let me consult the chart." Trent's low voice calmed the assembled women like a warm hand on fur, and as the gathering fell back into its usual rhythms, Clara closed her eyes. Even Harriet seemed to calm down once the pillow was returned to its rightful place on the sofa. And although Becca tried reading the summoning spell several times, no further furnishings appeared, which Clara found a relief—and which left Harriet feeling rather smug.

"*Oh, please...*" Laurel extended one paw, the better to admire her claws, as the meeting droned on. "*If these humans don't move on soon...*"

Clara glared, but just then a familiar chant broke in.

"And by the rule of three, blessed be." And with that, the chairs scraped back and the coven members began to rise. Out of habit, the calico accompanied Becca into the kitchen, the now empty teapot in hand. Suzanne followed with the mugs.

"Becca." Suzanne deposited the mugs on the counter. "What I wanted to ask you about—"

Before she could finish, Larissa walked in and Suzanne turned to face her.

"Do you have something I can put the leftover cookies in?" The older woman opened one of the cabinets without waiting for an answer. "I want my plate back."

"Sure." Becca looked around. "I've got a clean Tupperware here somewhere."

"Can't you just *summon* one?" Marcia had crowded in too.

"I wish." Becca's smile was beginning to look forced. Clara, meanwhile, wrapped her tail around her forepaws. Lashing it would have fit her mood better, but with this many feet in the kitchen, she wasn't going to take any chances.

"Marcia, please." Trent, standing in the doorway, came to the rescue. "You know Becca did her best."

"She wasn't—" Ande, playing peacemaker again. "She was just teasing. You know that, don't you, Becca?"

"Of course." Becca's voice was close to cracking as she wiped off Suzanne's cake knife, taking extra care over its inlaid handle. "Oh, thanks." Ande had found the errant plastic container and was passing it over.

"Silly." A low hiss—Harriet had waddled up behind her sister. *"You could've tripped her."*

"Why would I want to do that?" Clara turned to face her, confused.

"Cookies!" Harriet's yellow eyes flashed as she crowded in. *"There were some left. It's too late now."* True enough, the plastic lid snapped shut.

"Would you like a ride too?" Trent was herding the women out. "I've got room."

"No, thanks." Not all. Suzanne was hanging back, the loaf pan and her knife clasped close. "I'll walk," she said.

"If you're sure…" Trent's voice sounded like a purr, and Clara leaned forward, eager to catch more.

"There are crumbs on the table." Laurel sauntered in, licking her chops. *"What?"* She looked at her sisters, who had both turned on her.

"I was trying to hear what they were saying," Clara nearly hissed.

"The clown was eavesdropping," said Harriet as she peered around the corner. She was peeved, it was obvious. Not only that her youngest sister had failed to trip the cookie carrier but that Laurel had found the crumbs before she could.

"I'm concerned about Becca." Clara's mew was too soft for their person to hear, she was pretty sure, but still she looked up in concern. Laurel sniffed and began to wash, removing the last trace of baked goods from her sleek tan fur, while Harriet waddled back into the living room in the obvious hope that her fastidious sister had left something behind.

"So, Suzanne, what's going on?" Becca was looking at her guest. From the living room, she could hear Trent's deep, warm voice and an answering torrent of giggles. "I should see them out."

"They're fine." Suzanne's voice had an edge it hadn't before. Shaking her head, she wiped the few remaining crumbs from the cake plate into the sink before sliding it and the inlaid server into her bag.

"Suzanne!" a voice, half laughing, called. "You promised!"

"Ande." Suzanne sighed. "I forgot. Look, Becca. I need to talk to you."

"Train's leaving the station!" More laughter, and this time it was Larissa who called. "Zany, come on!"

"Coming!" Suzanne called, loud enough that Clara flicked her ears—only to be momentarily distracted by the snuffling of Harriet as she hoovered up the last remaining crumbs.

"—not where they can hear." Suzanne had lowered her voice to an urgent whisper. "Look, I'll explain more—Saturday at my place. Noonish? Please, Becca. It's important."

"Saturday at your place." Becca sounded tired. "But if it involves the entire coven…"

"Just trust me, Becca." Suzanne turned back one final time, her face drawn. "This is—this could be—big. And, please, for the Goddess's sake, be careful."

Chapter 4

The following two days passed with no more magic, but no catastrophes either, whether feline or human. Saturday dawned with all the sunny promise of the season, and the intoxicating scent of flowers and damp new grass through the open window had all three cats' whiskers bristling. Only Clara noticed that Becca didn't seem pleased by the beauty of the day. It was hours until Becca was due to meet Suzanne, but clearly, something was on her mind. Not that she forgot to feed the cats—she'd never do that—but she did almost mix up their bowls, putting the lion's—or the lioness'—portion in Clara's multicolored dish instead of Harriet's before she caught her error. And when she committed the cardinal sin of laying down Clara's dish ahead of Harriet's, the calico stepped back before her big sister could even turn to glare, knowing that the first bites of breakfast were worth sacrificing for peace.

Once her own dish, with both her name and a golden crown motif, was set down, Harriet moved over. But Clara had barely gotten a few bites of what remained of her own breakfast before Becca set out. Worried as she was about the young woman, her pet knew she had to follow.

It wasn't hard. While an otherwise intelligent and observant human, Becca was limited—Clara knew—by the preconceptions of her species. In particular, that meant she considered the cats with whom she cohabited to be house pets, unconscious of their real powers. Being indoors was fine for most felines, especially during what had been a rainy April, and Harriet particularly enjoyed being catered to. But although Clara observed the feline rule about hiding this ability, the fact is that without too much effort, she, like all her kind, could pass through most solid objects, at least if she could get a good focus on them.

And so as soon as Becca had locked the apartment door behind her, the multicolored kitty had hunkered down and stared at the closed door. Distracted as she was, the pretty brunette was just vaguely aware of the calico's appearance as she passed through the door and manifested on the street behind her. Half in the shadows of that early spring morning and half a shadow herself, her mottled coloring adding an extra layer of camouflage, the little cat found it easy to trail Becca in her somewhat ethereal fashion. And although Clara did stop to nibble on an intriguing green—it was spring, after all—she easily caught up with her person by the time she had snagged a table at the local coffee house and settled in with a muffin and mug of something steamy.

"Maddy, over here!" Becca rose and waved, and Clara ducked beneath the table before she could be spotted.

"Becca!" A pleasantly large woman made her way over from the counter, her own mug in one hand, a slab of coffee cake in the other. "What's up? You look good. Did you find a new job?"

"No, but…" Something akin to a purr warmed Becca's voice as her friend took the seat opposite.

"Pity," Maddy mumbled, her mouth full of cake. In some ways, Clara thought, Becca's old friend resembled

Harriet. "'Cause if you find something good, I'm going to follow you. Work stress is making me eat."

Becca nodded. She'd been hearing about Maddy's work troubles for as long as her friend had been at Reynolds and Associates, a market research firm in Cambridge's Central Square.

"Reynolds has been in a mood recently. It's enough to make me start smoking again too." She took another bite of cake, as if in response. "Oh, you know it all." Her friend didn't have to be psychic to note how Becca's focus had drifted. "Wait, did Jeff call you?"

"No." The purr was gone. Becca's voice had gone flat and lifeless. "He's…that's over, Maddy. He's got some new girlfriend now."

"I don't know, Becca. I've heard that his new thing didn't work out." In the silence, Clara could almost see Becca pushing her pastry around her plate. Maddy didn't wait long for a response. "I ran into him on the bus a few days ago," she said, her tone oddly remote. "He was asking about you."

"He was?" Becca caught herself before her friend could answer. "No, it doesn't matter. It's too late. You know I couldn't take him back, even if he wanted me to."

"Good girl." The clink of a mug, and Becca's friend washed the cake down with enthusiastic approval. "He's no good for you. I was worried, because you've been so preoccupied lately."

"I know, I'm sorry." Becca shifted in her seat, scattering a few intriguing crumbs. Cranberry, Clara thought. "I've really been trying to be mindful. To be present. But it isn't Jeff, it's the coven."

"Oh, please." Maddy's chair squeaked as she sat back.

"You don't actually believe in that. Do you?"

"That's just it." Becca leaned in, excitement audible even as she kept her voice low. "Maddy, I did...something. I cast a spell. A summoning spell, and it worked."

"Becca, please. How long have we known each other? You were the best researcher in Professor Humphries' seminar, and now you're saying you believe in magic?"

"There's a lot about the natural world that we don't know." Becca's enthusiasm wasn't going to be that easily shut down.

"So become a scientist, for crying out loud!" More squeaking of chairs put Clara on alert. "I never thought I'd say this, but I think you should get back into spending your days in the library. At least then you were doing real research."

"Maddy..." Becca began to protest.

"It's those people, Becca." Her friend wouldn't let her. "They're crackpots—or worse."

"Maddy, please. They're my friends, and, well, they rely on me. They respect me."

A noise like a furball in the works caused Clara's ears to perk up. But, no, it was simply Maddy laughing.

"Besides," Becca sounded hurt, "one of them asked for my help on something."

"Please tell me you're not going to get involved." Maddy had lowered her voice, even as it ramped up in urgency. "Those women are conspiracy theorists of the highest order."

"They're not all women." Becca's own voice grew quieter. "In fact, one member of the coven is a warlock, and he really believes in my abilities."

"Oh, Becca." Her friend's tone softened. "I know you're lonely, honey. But, please. Give it time."

"I am, Maddy." Becca spoke with a confidence that made her cat proud. "And I'm exploring new interests and expanding my horizon. Just as you've always advised me to do. So, what's up with you?"

A lot, it seemed. And as Becca's buddy went on about some conflict in an office with a co-worker who sounded like a horror, the cat at their feet nodded off. Spectral travel was tiring. Besides, Becca had a busy day planned. As her cat, Clara was going to need her energy for the mysterious meeting ahead.

Chapter 5

Suzanne, it turned out, lived farther away than Becca had thought. Although still technically in Cambridgeport, her apartment was down by the river, in one of those old triple-deckers the city is known for, and Becca got well and truly lost—taking a shortcut that led her into a blind alley and then another that turned into a construction site—before she retraced her steps almost to the café and started over.

As it was, she was running late by the time she found the right street. She was tempted to blame Maddy. Her friend had kept her, going on about that nasty colleague—some woman her friend had a grudge against that she never fully explained. But Becca knew the delay was her own fault and was preparing to own up to it when she finally located the right address painted on a mailbox out front.

The bright morning had turned into a surprisingly warm day by then, and Becca was sweating slightly—her cheeks a healthy pink—as she jogged up the front steps. Someone cared for the building. In addition to that smart mailbox, the tiny front yard was neatly raked, with low blue flowers edging a lilac that had just begun to bloom, although the smell of fresh paint nearly overwhelmed that lovely, peppery scent. Somewhere, a radio was playing salsa. But the latch on the front door was old and resisted Becca's jiggling and pushing.

"Here, let me help you." A hand reached around Becca, dark with the sun, and she turned. The sandy-haired man who had come up so quietly behind her wasn't much taller than she was, but he pulled the door open easily with one hand. The other was holding a bucket full of rags that smelled strongly of turpentine.

"You're going in?" he asked, his voice soft.

She looked up. The dash of white paint on his right cheekbone made his skin look darker. Bronzed almost, with a slight glaze of sweat that added a warm and subtly spicy scent to the mix.

"What?" She blinked. "Yes, thanks. I'm looking for Suzanne Liddle. She's in unit three?"

"The buzzer should be working." He nodded into the foyer. "The electricians finished up last week."

"Thanks," said Becca, a little too breathlessly, and then turned and hurried in. Clara, who had been examining the flowers, slipped in behind Becca as the door closed. Luckily, both humans were too distracted to notice the calico, even if she hadn't cloaked her brighter orange patch in a shadow summoning that made her as grey as a Grimalkin. But though she was on her guard not to be noticed, the cat pressed close to Becca as the young woman climbed the stairs. There was something off about this building—something that even the stinging odor of that solvent couldn't explain—and although the compact cat certainly didn't want to trip her person, she did want her to be wary. Especially when her phone rang before she had even reached the first landing.

"Oh!" She paused, looking at the number, and then, taking a deep breath, took the call. "Hi."

Like the rest of her family, Clara was a witch cat,

endowed with magical abilities above and beyond the usual feline mysticism. But that didn't mean she had unlimited powers. Sure, she could pass through solid objects like doors and walls. Those powers were sort of related to how she could summon things, like Harriet did that pillow. And she could make herself more or less invisible, as all cats—even the non-magical ones—can, which is why humans trip over them so often. But although her ears were naturally more sensitive than any human's, she couldn't hear everything.

That's why she was a tad alarmed when Becca stopped walking to listen, one hand over her ear to block out the music from outside. Something about the way her brows bunched together and her teeth came down on her lower lip made the little calico's ears prick up, reminding her of those bad days two months ago. The days when all Becca had done—besides feed her cats, of course—was cry.

"Uh-huh," she said at last. Her lip still showed the marks of her teeth, but at least she'd begun walking again, slowly mounting step after step. "Yes, she told me," she said.

"No, I'm not home right now." Becca had reached the third floor. The door was slightly ajar, and she turned away for privacy. "Look, I can come by your place," she said. And then, taking another deep breath, she went on. "Okay, then what if I meet you someplace else in an hour, some place down by the river? I'm—no, really, it's fine. I'm visiting a friend on Putnam. In fact, I'm at her door now. A new friend. Her name's Suzanne. Suzanne Liddle."

At that, she straightened up, and for a moment, Clara relaxed, thinking that her person was, in fact, doing better. But then her brows came together again and she shook her head. "What do you mean, Jeff? You don't even know her. Look."

One hand went up to push the hair from her brow. "I'll call you when I'm leaving, okay? Jeff?"

The hand wiped over her face and through her soft brown curls, and with a sigh big enough to deflate her, she shoved the phone back into her pocket. And with that she turned toward the slightly opened door.

"Suzanne?" she called. "It's Becca."

She rapped softly on the door, which creaked open further. Calling a little louder, to be heard over the salsa beat, she said again, "Suzanne? Are you there?"

As a cat, Clara didn't require permission to enter any room. And while she could pass through a locked door, an unlatched one—especially one so temptingly ajar—read like a gilt-edged invitation. Only there was something about this room, this door. Something beyond the intense smell of the paint and the metallic rattle of the ladder outside.

"Suzanne?" Becca pushed the door further open and stepped inside. And so, despite an overwhelming sense of trepidation that had her guard hairs standing on end, Clara followed into a sunny room. As the door swung shut behind them and the latch caught with a click, she took in the warmth. The light from the big bay window. Two overstuffed chairs that Harriet would love crowded together on a deep plush rug, while a velvet-covered sofa, too big for the space, was pushed back against a bay window that stood slightly ajar. It was from here that the smell of the paint came in as well as the dust and the scrapings that had dappled the burgundy velvet with white.

It was also that sofa—more of a love seat actually—that had set all the cat's instinctive alarms ringing. For reclining on the dark velvet, one arm hanging low toward the floor, lay Suzanne Liddle, the inlaid handle of her serrated cake knife extending straight up from bare white flesh of her throat.

Becca froze, leaving Clara to take in the sight of the woman on the sofa, the pooled blood from the awful wound collecting at her collarbone, where it was already darkening to almost match the burgundy of the upholstery. Time stopped—for a moment—and then jarred into movement with the clang of a ladder being collapsed. A boom box cut off in mid-song.

Somewhere, outside—in a different world—work was done for the morning. And then another sound, closer, made Becca turn. A key clicked in the door. The brass knob rotated, and Clara could hear her frightened gasp, as Trent—the handsome warlock—stepped in.

Chapter 6

A purr can mean many different things. Cats purr to express happiness, of course. But they also purr to comfort themselves or others, and that's what Clara was trying to do an hour later—once the police let Becca go.

"Oh, kitties, it was horrible." Clara would have thought, after all the questions, that her poor person would have been all talked out. But as she staggered into her apartment and collapsed onto her own lovely, clean, and beautifully unbloodied sofa, she began to rehash everything that had happened.

"I had just seen her Wednesday, three days ago. She was here. She was…alive." Becca lay back with a sigh, one forearm thrown over her eyes, as the three sisters converged. Clara was a little breathless from having raced home—feline invisibility aside, she didn't think hitching a ride in a police cruiser was a good idea. "I keep thinking of her…her throat and all that blood. And that knife. I'd cut cake with that knife…" Becca repeated as she kicked her shoes off.

Clara ducked the falling footwear and jumped up to claim her place on the sofa. Laurel and Harriet were already there, Laurel cozying up to Becca's side and Harriet down by her stocking feet—and the pillow. They both turned to stare at their youngest sister, as if she were an interloper, and so she carefully mounted the back of the sofa and waited for an opening.

"I…once I realized what I was seeing, I just wanted to get away…" Becca was saying. The repetition seemed to soothe her, as a purr would, but Clara remained concerned. "They had all these questions…"

"Of course they did." Laurel reached one velvet paw up toward Becca's arm, as if she were petting her. Clara knew better. Laurel wanted to see Becca's eyes as she spoke. Even her purr had an edge to it. *"A body and all. Dead."*

"Cut it out." Clara batted down at her. Unlike her seal-point sister, Clara was trying to listen to the poor girl who lay beside them. She'd missed something in that awful room, what with her worry over Becca and the sudden appearance of the warlock, just as she'd missed the beginning of Suzanne's explanation for why she needed Becca to come visit, and she was hoping that if she paid attention, she'd figure it out.

"Oh, Clara." The movement had caught Becca's attention, and the distraught young woman reached up for the little calico. At that, Clara's prime directive—to be Becca's pet—overwhelmed any other concerns, and she tumbled onto her prostrate person and began to purr in earnest.

"Oh, great." Harriet looked up and tilted her ears back. *"Now you've pinned her down. She came back to feed us, obviously."*

"She's upset." Clara glared, but her oldest sister turned her back, fluffing out her creamsicle coat as she settled down again at Becca's feet. Laurel, meanwhile, had stretched to her full length and started to doze. If Becca wasn't going to share grisly details, the brown-tipped cat wasn't interested. Clara,

however, began to gently knead Becca's belly. Making sure to keep her claws sheathed, she kept the motion even and light, the rhythm in sync with the rumble of her purr, until she felt the tension begin to leave the girl's slim frame. Until she heard an answering purr as Becca slipped into sleep.

Only then did Clara relax and let her own eyes begin to close. She wasn't sleepy. The feline propensity toward napping aside, there were too many thoughts racing through her brain for her to give over to a catnap. No, she simply needed to focus on what she had seen and heard out in the bright world, in that walkup apartment. To figure out what had happened—and why—and how she could get Becca through it without any further complications.

A soft snort startled her, and Clara looked up to see Harriet twitching, restless in her sleep. As she watched, the larger cat muttered *"cream"* and her pink tongue darted out to moisten her nose. Then she lay still again, having satisfied her dream appetite. Laurel, as well, napped peacefully, her dark paws stretched luxuriantly along Becca's side. The two were deep in feline slumber, untroubled by anything outside their small world.

Clara watched them, willing them to stay quiet. Becca needed her rest. There was no way to explain the chaos that had exploded in that upstairs apartment. How Becca had been roused from her stupor by Trent entering the room, and how, when he'd tried to hold her, she had pulled away screaming as he sputtered some kind of explanation about retrieving something the dead girl had borrowed and a key from a house-sitting stint. How her coven leader had wrapped his arms around her then, turning her from the bloody sight until he had finally gotten her calmed down enough to call for help.

And how that had backfired as the cops had hustled the two of them out to the street and pulled Becca away from the dark-eyed warlock. How she had tried to answer all their questions until it all got to be too much and she had suddenly felt dizzy. How she had woken with an oxygen mask over her face and someone yelling. No, she had been the one yelling—it had just taken her a few moments to realize it.

"The poor girl," Clara muttered in a soft *chirrup*. Surely, her sisters could understand. *"It was a shock."*

"Shock shlock." Laurel yawned and stretched. Her claws caught the afternoon light, and she began to groom. *"I want to hear more. A body is meat,"* she said as she bit the tip of one claw. There had definitely been an edge to her purr. *"And that blood...did you taste it? Did she?"*

"No!" Clara swiveled her one black ear to check. Becca's breathing remained even and calm. *"Can't you think of anything beyond your appetite?"*

"Huh." Another bite and the seal point closed her eyes. Clara watched, unsure if her nearest sister was sleeping or simply ignoring her, then closed hers too. Whatever Laurel was up to, the little calico needed to think.

It was all because of that stupid pillow. Clara didn't know for sure why Suzanne had cornered Becca, but it had to be because of her supposed success with the summoning spell. She'd seen the way the other coven members had looked at her person. They'd all be wanting something from her now, and not just cans and cream.

As if on cue, Becca's phone rang, startling her from sleep.

"Hang on." Becca sat up, and Clara slid in a rather inelegant move down to her lap. "Maddy?"

"Are you all right?" Even from her new perch, Clara could hear the big woman's panicked tone.

"Yeah. Thanks." Becca closed her eyes as she spoke and shook her head.

Maddy must have heard the lie in her voice. "I'm coming over," she said, loud enough to earn a harsh look from Laurel. Harriet, of course, slept on.

"You don't have to." Becca's complaint was barely a mew. Clara jumped to the floor. If company was coming over, she didn't want to be caught unawares.

"Is it time for dinner?" Harriet looked up as Becca reached for her shoes.

"No," Clara rumbled softly. *"A visitor."*

"Visitors aren't bad." Harriet yawned. *"Visitors mean treats."*

"This isn't about you—" Clara broke off. Becca was heading to the kitchen, closely trailed by their middle sister. As they walked by, Harriet and Laurel exchanged a glance, and when Harriet flicked her tail, Clara cringed, wrapping her own tail around her forepaws. More magic was on the way, and that meant more trouble. With an audible thud, Harriet plopped to the floor to join Becca and Laurel in the kitchen. With a sigh, Clara followed.

"Oh, kitties! What would I do without you?" Becca sniffled as she spoke, but at least she was sounding a bit more like herself again. Clara began to relax, and then, out of nowhere, "Would you like some treats?"

Laurel turned toward her sisters with what Clara thought of as her Siamese smirk. Mind control was such simple magic, her tilted whiskers seemed to say, even though what Laurel did was more like implanting a suggestion than an actual direction. Harriet, of course, was too mesmerized by Becca to even bother to gloat.

Chapter 7

The tea Becca served her old friend was a lot kinder on the nose than what she brewed for her coven, and the almond cookies Maddy had brought were Clara's favorites. Their delicious aroma—nutty and sweet—announced her presence even before the doorbell rang.

That wasn't why the agile calico jumped up on the table, though when she sauntered over to sniff at the pot, nobody shooed her off. The day was too topsy-turvy for that, the sunny afternoon already forgotten.

Becca had begun crying again, retelling the story having brought back all the fear and the horror from earlier in the day, and Clara had wanted to check on her. Maddy, in her motherly way, was doing her bit even beyond the cookies, leaning over and patting her friend in a rather hearty manner that none of the resident felines would have appreciated.

"There, there," she kept repeating, though it didn't seem to be doing any good. "Let it out."

"What's up there? I can't see!" Harriet's plaintive meow—as close to a whimper as she got—reached Clara on the tabletop. She had thought both her siblings were napping post snack, but Harriet's gluttony knew no bounds. *"Is it cookies?"*

"*Shh,*" Clara hissed back, and immediately regretted it.

Harriet was not only her oldest sister, she could cause trouble when she wanted to—and even when she didn't, as the whole fiasco with the pillow had proved. Clara needed to stay on her good side, and so the calico leaned over the table's side to call to her, in a gentler tone. "*Come on up, if you want.*"

It was the wrong thing to say. Harriet turned away with a disdainful sniff. *"I don't jump on tables."*

Clara winced at her own mistake. Of course, the big creamsicle of a cat had never been what anyone would call athletic, and what was an easy leap for the compact calico would have been unduly strenuous for her sister. To make amends, Clara knocked one of the cookies off its plate with a swift paw strike. It flew off the table and landed with a soft thud, although that could have been Harriet pouncing on her "prey." Becca was crying too hard to notice, and if her friend saw anything, she knew better than to comment. Nobody likes to be told their pets have poor manners, especially when they've just encountered a dead body.

"So you didn't get to talk to her?" Becca was blowing her nose and looked up at Maddy's question. "Suzanne, I mean?"

"No, she was—" Becca sat up, curiosity overcoming her grief. "Why?"

"Nothing." Suddenly, Maddy was interested in the cookies too.

"No, there's something on your mind." Becca blinked, clearing her eyes, as she focused on her friend—and missed Clara taking a furtive lick at the nearest cookie.

"I was curious." Maddy reached out, picking the very cookie the cat had just tasted. "I wanted to get a sense of the chronology."

"I told you." Becca also took a cookie, but left it on her napkin. "I had trouble with the door, and the painter let me in. Then I—oh, I did forget something. Jeff called as I was climbing the stairs. I was supposed to call him back." She started to stand, but her friend put out a hand to restrain her.

"Jeff can wait." Maddy put her cookie down after one bite. A first for her, and Clara craned to see if the chubby visitor had eaten the side the calico had licked. She hadn't. "In fact… what did he say?"

"Jeff? Oh, nothing." Becca picked up her cookie again, but it was obvious she wasn't really interested in its sugary goodness. "He said he wanted to get together."

"To get together or to talk?" Her friend's voice had gone strangely low and even.

"To get together." Becca paused. "I think the whole thing was so fast—and so strange. And did I tell you Trent came in?"

"Yes." Maddy sounded strained. "Yes, you did."

"He said he was picking up something. That he had a key because he'd house sat for Suzanne before, though since she has no cats…"

"Never mind Trent." Maddy was definitely impatient. "I mean, the police spoke with him, right?" Becca nodded. "Good, let them sort him out. It's you I'm worried about, Becca."

"Me?" That cookie wasn't going to eat itself, but Clara restrained herself. Something was going on here, something that even with all her magic she couldn't understand. "What do you mean?"

"Well, you and Jeff didn't really get to talk, right?"

Becca nodded. "In fact, I should call him. I said I

would—"

Maddy cut her off. "And you haven't spoken to your ex in, what, weeks? A month?"

"Close to a month." Becca's eyes were free of tears now, but her dark eyebrows were knit in confusion. "Maddy, what are you getting at?"

Maddy looked from her friend down at her plate, and Clara shifted to the table's edge. If the visitor said anything about that cookie, the compact calico would make a break for it.

"Did he know where you were?"

Becca nodded.

"Who you were visiting?" Another nod as Becca waited for her friend to explain.

"I ran into Jeff in Harvard Square a while ago—and he was with a woman." The words rushed out of Maddy in a monotone. "A tall blonde whom I'd met before, and so I was trying to place her. I didn't think she was another programmer. He introduced her as Suzanne, and I realized that she was in your…your group."

"Coven," Becca corrected her in a voice barely above a whisper.

"Whatever," said her chubby friend as she leaned forward to take Becca's hand, pushing the plate toward the cat.

But even though the two women were definitely distracted, the feline ignored the almond treats. Instead, both her green eyes—the one in the black patch and the one in the orange—were focused on her person, on the way the color had drained from her cheeks. On the way her eyes were widening and filling with tears once again.

"You don't mean…" Becca's whispered. "*With* with?"

Now it was her friend's turn to nod. "Jeff is—Jeff *was*—seeing Suzanne?" Her question was softer than a kitten's mewl, with a little catch in it that made Clara's whiskers droop.

"That's not something you should be worried about now." Maddy patted Becca's hand once more. "What you should be concerned about is that the police don't think you knew about it. Because, frankly, if you did, you'd be a prime suspect for her murder."

Chapter 8

"I'm trying to sleep." Harriet whined, a long, drawn-out sound like air escaping from a balloon. *"Go away!"*

"Harriet, Laurel." Clara looked around at her sisters. *"Did you hear that? We've got to do something!"*

The calico had jumped to the floor after Maddy had dropped her bombshell. The horrid scraping sound of Becca's chair as she pushed it back had only precipitated her flight, and now she perched on the sofa where Harriet had settled.

"Yes, I did hear it." Laurel licked her chops, her blue eyes lighting up. *"Do you think she did it?"*

"No." Clara drew back, affronted. *"Becca is a gentle soul. Besides, I was with her."*

"You could've been napping." Laurel shrugged. She was no great hunter, but with her sleek lines, the seal-point sister fancied herself part panther. Harriet, meanwhile, was still sluggish from that almond cookie, which she'd devoured to the last crumb. Not even Becca's voice raised in outrage could rouse her.

"That's crazy!" Becca was standing. Shouting at her guest, and as much as Clara had wanted her to shake off her grief, she knew this wasn't a healthy alternative. "Maddy, they can't think that I…that Jeff…"

"Becca, please." Her friend rushed around the table to

comfort her.

"I'm calling Jeff. This is crazy." Becca stepped back and pulled out her phone.

"No, you can't." Maddy reached for it, but Becca pulled away. "You can't talk to him now."

Becca paused, looking up. "Why not?" There was an edge to her voice that made Clara lash her tail.

"Because." By comparison, Maddy sounded defeated. "The police might see that as evidence. Proof that you killed her to get him back. Or maybe that the two of you colluded."

As if on cue, the device in Becca's hand let out a chiming tone.

"Don't!" Maddy reached for the phone.

"It's okay." Becca stepped back and was already looking at the device. The commotion had finally woken Harriet, who yawned wide enough to show all her teeth and then sat up. "It's Larissa, from the group. She probably just heard."

"Becca, you don't have to—"

"So annoying!" Beside her, Laurel stretched, unimpressed by Maddy's soft pleading. *"Maybe I should get rid of her."* She stood, her tail stiff at attention and her blue eyes beginning to cross.

"Don't you dare!" Clara turned on her, a warning growl in her voice. She knew what that look meant: Laurel was concentrating. Hard. And that meant magic was brewing. Between the crazed look those crossed eyes gave her and that mental "suggestion" that cats were dangerous, the slim seal point had scared off several would-be adopters at the shelter before Clara could stop her. Clara didn't even want to guess what other thoughts her sister could implant in a susceptible

human's mind.

"Settle down." The middle sister sat and coiled her tail neatly around her cocoa paws. "*You're such a...scaredy-cat."*

"I'm practical." Clara glared at her, ears still partly back. The little calico wasn't sure what any of them could do with something the size of a person—and Maddy was a pretty big person at that. Nor did she particularly want to find out. *"Besides, anything you did would get Becca in more trouble, and then where would we be?"* Clara remembered the shelter, even if her sisters didn't.

"*We could eat her,"* said Laurel with a flick of her own ears. That got Harriet's attention, and she looked from Laurel to Clara.

"No." Clara didn't even bother trying to disguise the growl that had crept into her voice. Clara might be the youngest of the litter, but neither Laurel nor Harriet wanted to expend the energy for a fight.

"Hello, Larissa?" Becca turned away as she answered, her voice tentative. "Yes, I know, I was…I know."

Maddy looked on, glum. From the sofa, the three cats watched, transfixed.

"I…yes, you're right." Becca seemed to be listening more than talking. She looked up at her guest and raised one finger. "Here's fine. Okay, let me know. And, Larissa? I'm sorry."

A moment later, she put the phone down. "It's the coven," she explained. "They think we should meet to talk about Suzanne. To mourn, I guess," she said.

"Or because someone wants to strategize." Maddy sounded so dour that Becca grimaced.

"Oh, come on," she said in a tone rather like Laurel

might use if cats spoke the way humans do. "You can't think one of us…" She stopped and swallowed hard.

"I don't know, Becca." Maddy stepped forward again. "That's the problem. I mean, someone killed your friend just as she was going to tell you something about your Wednesday witches, right? And didn't you say the door was open?"

"That doesn't mean anything." Becca was shaking her head. Laurel, meanwhile, had tilted her blues eyes toward Clara, her whiskers raised inquisitively. This was a detail she'd forgotten to pass along.

"*Later*," Clara murmured. She wanted to hear what their person had to say.

"We're not—the coven isn't like that. It's more likely someone followed Suzanne home, or the door could have been forced." Becca was enumerating possibilities, but there was something off about her voice. "Maybe she opened it for a delivery person, or she left it off the latch. I was running late, so it could have been that she thought it was me—" She stopped, the reality of the situation catching up to her.

"Or it could have been someone she knew." Maddy finished the thought. "Maybe someone you know too, Becca. I'm just glad that you didn't get there a few minutes earlier. They might have killed you too."

Chapter 9

If Becca's friend had meant to comfort her, she'd failed miserably. After she left, Becca was as agitated as, well, as a wet cat. Even when exhaustion drove her—and the cats—to bed, she tossed and turned to the point where the feline sisters had to abandon their usual post at their person's feet.

"If she doesn't settle down, I'm going to swat her." Laurel watched from her perch atop the bureau as the morning sun crept around the bedroom blinds. *"I bet she won't even remember to feed us."*

"Really?" Harriet looked up in dismay as Becca yawned and roused. Weekends meant little to the felines—and little to Becca since she lost her job. But breakfast meant everything to Harriet. *"She wouldn't!"*

"She'll remember." Clara jumped to the floor in her role as peacemaker, and began to weave around Becca's ankles as she sought her slippers. *"If not, you can sit on her, Harriet."*

"Huh." Harriet turned away, insulted, but Laurel chortled in glee.

"Oh, no!" Becca ran over, catching Laurel around her café au lait torso. "Are you having a fur ball?"

Laurel's laugh was, at best, disconcerting. But Becca's misguided query did at least have the advantage of distracting Clara's older sisters, and Laurel obligingly hacked up a nugget of felt, which she deposited on the floor at Becca's feet. Furballs are the easiest summoning there is, which is why all cats do it, even when spring shedding doesn't necessitate it.

"*Disgusting...*" Harriet sauntered into the kitchen, following Becca, who had gone for a paper towel. "*But now that she's here...*"

Clara knew she should have interceded. Harriet had already been fed, hours before, when Becca had woken from a nightmare. They all had, but poor Becca was so distracted that when she saw Harriet sitting by her bowl, she succumbed—once she'd cleaned up Laurel's mess. Clara didn't know if her oldest sister had used any mind control tricks—that one was Laurel's specialty. That pleading look in her round yellow eyes was probably all she needed.

One thing none of them had mastered, however, was that human device called the phone. Becca's began buzzing almost as soon as the three had finished breakfast, long before what her ex-boyfriend would have called "a decent hour." The first call was from Maddy, who sounded determined to try once again cheer up her friend. And while Becca had refused the other woman's offer of brunch, hearing her old friend talking about something other than collusion seemed to do her good.

It was the other calls that began to weigh on her. Kathy had been her usual self—as bouncy as a rubber ball—when she called, acting for all the world as if the upcoming meeting were a treat. But Marcia had grown so teary that Becca had ended up putting aside her own complicated feelings to comfort her and ultimately found herself asking for Luz, Marcia's roommate, to calm the distraught paralegal down.

Becca's mother was next, and even from the other room, the cats could hear her insisting that Becca leave the city and "come home," wherever that was. Of course, any mention of moving made the felines uneasy, and Laurel took it out on Clara, batting at her as she tried to nap. Larissa—Clara believed she could almost smell her perfume over the line—had gone on so long about some personal tangent that Becca had laid the phone down on the counter and begun to clean as she rattled on. After that, Becca had turned the device off to read, pulling her notes on that old history again, the one that named her great-great-something grandmother as part of some long-ago witch trial.

It was dinnertime when Becca peeked at her phone again, muttering in dismay. "Cousin Joan? Richie? Did Mom tell everyone?" She turned the device on then, and as it rang again, she paused—open can in hand—to answer it.

"Jeff!" she squeaked like a mouse, and dropped the phone.

"Becca, are you there?" Harriet sniffed at the device with disdain. Nothing good came from separating Harriet and her can. "You never called me back." Even through the tiny speaker, the disembodied voice sounded hurt.

Becca reached for the device, only to be blocked by Harriet, who pressed her furry head into her person's hand.

"Hang on." Becca grabbed the phone and propped it on the counter before reaching for a dish. She'd been well trained—and not simply by her cats. "Sorry," she called over to the phone. "I've just been—it's been crazy."

Clara could feel the fur begin to rise along her back as the tiny speaker emitted some small, beetle-ish response, and she readied for a leap to the counter. How Becca could even be talking to her ex was beyond the little calico. Sure, he was tall and had what the young woman had called a raffish smile, but if Clara could have knocked the phone all the way into the sink, she would have.

"Wait!" Harriet's paw landed on her tail. *"Not until she fills the dish."*

"But it's Jeff." Clara rounded on her. *"He cheated on her and broke her heart. You remember!"*

"Humans." Laurel, washing her face, piped up from the corner. *"They're all like that. The males gallivant; the females accept it. Not like us."*

Clara could only stare, focusing her green eyes on her tawny sister. With her Siamese blood, Laurel affected a certain worldliness, but Clara knew that both Laurel and Harriet had to remember the bad times, after the faithless computer programmer had said his last goodbye and all Becca did was cry. There was no way they could be nonchalant about his reappearance. At least, not once Harriet got her dinner.

But Clara hadn't counted on her sisters' appetites. Once the dishes were placed on the mat, the two could not have cared less. And while their youngest sister hesitated—tempted like her siblings to bury her face in the savory pile—Becca picked up the phone again.

"Jeff." At least the break had allowed her the opportunity to compose herself. "I'm so sorry." She stopped there and bit her lip.

With a sigh, Clara turned from her dish and jumped to the counter. From here, she hoped to get a better handle on the situation, but all she heard from the other end of the line was a one-word query: "What?"

"About—" Becca swallowed. "About Suzanne."

A spurt of sound followed, and went on for so long that the calico found herself looking longingly down at her bowl.

If she didn't get to her dinner quickly, Harriet would soon be scarfing it up.

"Don't, Jeff." Becca's voice grabbed her attention back. "I know…and I'm sorry." A pause as her brows knit. "You didn't hear?"

Harriet was sitting back, demurely washing her face with those cream-colored mitts. Clara knew what was coming next and made her decision. As Becca delivered the news in halting tones—"I found her, Jeff," she said. "She was, well, she was already gone"—the compact feline hit the floor and headed for her dish. Too late: a large, creamsicle-colored mass had moved into her path.

"Harriet!" Clara tried to push by. Yellow eyes blinked back at her over a well-rounded shoulder. *"That's mine."*

"I didn't think you wanted it." Butter wouldn't melt in her mouth.

"Well, I do." Clara managed to shove past her, and nudged Laurel out of the way as well. The middle sibling had already managed a few bites, but Clara managed to wolf down the rest, ears turned back to hear Becca, who was now in the awkward position of having to comfort her ex.

"Don't use those ears with me, little sister." Harriet was waiting when Clara finally came up for air. Not to reprimand her, she knew, but to see if she had left anything over. *"I won't stand for it."*

"Fine." Clara licked her chops clean. *"I'm out of here."*

Before the calico even landed back on the counter, her oldest sister was lapping up the few crumbs she'd overlooked, leaving Laurel to watch, a particularly peeved expression on her pointed face.

"I'm sorry, I really am," Becca was repeating for the

umpteenth time. She looked over at the calico on the counter and, wonder of wonders, reached for the bag of treats. Putting the phone down on the counter, she poured several into her palm.

"I can't—this doesn't make sense." The tinny voice seemed to be repeating itself as Clara gobbled down two treats. *Take that, Harriet*, she thought. "I didn't think she was that upset."

"What?" The hand jerked out from beneath Clara. The little calico mewed in protest and her person returned it, even as she again lifted the phone to her ear. "Jeff, what are you saying?"

Clara finished the treats and licked Becca's palm before looking up with what she hoped was an endearing expression.

"No, she didn't—it wasn't suicide." More treats were not going to be forthcoming. Not while this call lasted. "What made you think…that?"

A loud howl from the floor. Harriet had seen the treats. Seen that her sister had gotten them before she did too.

"Hang on." Becca went for the bag again, putting the phone on speaker.

"I thought, maybe…" The words were breathy and hesitant, and Clara could almost connect the distant voice to the man she remembered. She had found his boyishness adorable at one point. A little rough with the belly rubs, but tolerant of the sisters' squabbling and their insistence on sleeping on the bed. But that memory was now overshadowed by another, of the gawky young man pacing back and forth as he explained to their person why he couldn't be with her anymore. Boyish—try puppy-ish—and not in a good way. It always took him forever to get to the point, as Clara recalled.

"You see," she heard him say, and Clara realized she could. He'd be pushing his too-long hair back from his forehead, a strained look on his dog-like face. "It's just that, well, you know I'd gone out with Suzanne a few times. I mean, it wasn't anything serious. But, well, what makes this all so awful is that I had just told her that I couldn't see her anymore. Becca, I'd told her I wanted to try to win you back."

Chapter 10

Becca didn't sleep much that night either. The image of Suzanne's too-white skin streaked with darkening blood might have been stained on the inside of her eyelids. Clara picked up on her restlessness and did her best to calm her, staying as still by her human's side as she could. Not that it mattered. Even when Becca finally drifted off into an uneasy rest, Harriet kept waking her youngest sister with her own grumbling complaints.

"So selfish," the big cat muttered. *"Doesn't she know I need my beauty rest?"*

Clara didn't respond. Her oldest sister could sleep anywhere—and did. But since Clara had gotten on her case about summoning that pillow out of the ether, she had made a point about what she'd had to sacrifice to live by what she called the "silly" rules. As if she didn't know full well that the number one rule of feline magic is that cats must keep their powers secret.

Despite Harriet's complaints, all the sisters knew that wasn't difficult to do. People attribute all sorts of qualities to cats. Even the most mundane of their kind is considered mysterious, as if being beautiful and incredibly limber were special skills. But while it is true that some basic physical attributes—like a feline's excellent night vision—are common to all cats, and most felines can conjure up a few supernatural tricks—that disappearing through walls thing Clara had used to follow Becca—only a few are actual witch cats. And, therefore, it was incumbent upon the three sisters to be extra careful.

Harriet sometimes said that they were descended from feline royalty, from the great Queen of Cats herself, and Clara knew that often other cats did treat them with a certain respect. But whether the claim of royal lineage had any basis in fact or was merely another of Harriet's ploys for getting the best treats, her youngest sibling couldn't tell for sure. Clara's one distinct memory of their mother was of being licked by a warm, rough tongue. However, her injunction against revealing their power had stayed with Clara, even if her sisters chose to ignore it. The loyal calico could still clearly recall their tabby mother purring it into her ear even as she sent them off to the shelter to be adopted by the young woman they now served.

"Serve indeed!" Laurel was wakeful too. Needless to say, her memories—and her understanding of the injunction—differed from Clara's, much as her ease at reading her sister's thoughts illustrated the range of their powers. *"It was pure chance Becca picked us,"* said the seal-point beauty as she leaped to the kitchen table, where Becca had abandoned her breakfast to peck away at her computer. *"I knew I should have hissed at her. Then maybe some handsome banker would have taken us in."*

"Taken you, you mean." Clara couldn't help responding. *"We were lucky to stay together."*

Laurel blinked her blue eyes demurely, which was as close to an acknowledgment as she would give, and leaned forward to sniff at Becca's cereal bowl.

Becca, too intent on her computer, didn't notice, not even when Laurel extended her pink tongue and began to lap up the leftover milk. Harriet did, though, and after a grunt of effort, landed with a thud by Clara's side.

"Is that the Fruit Loops?" She nudged Laurel aside. Some things were worth the effort. *"Are there any left?"*

"What do you mean, 'blocked'? " Becca's question didn't even merit a tail flick from the sisters, seeing as how it wasn't accompanied by any move to unseat them. Instead, her hands went to work on the keyboard in front of her. "I'll show you 'blocked,'" she muttered, typing furiously.

With her sisters occupied finishing Becca's breakfast, Clara was free to study her face. For a human, Becca was almost cat-like. Although she was significantly larger than they were, she was small for her kind, and her short, brown hair lay close to her head, much like their fur did. It was the expression on her face, however, that held Clara this morning. When she focused, as she was doing, her lips pursed slightly. If she'd had whiskers, they'd be bristling, the calico thought. Pointing forward, almost. And as if she were truly one of their litter, her intense stare made it evident that she was on the prowl—though how she could trace anything through her computer was beyond the feline who watched her so closely. True, it was warm and at times it purred, but Clara didn't think that even Becca's constant stroking and murmuring could make the silver machine give forth the kind of prey that would interest one of her own kind.

"There!" With a final, triumphant slap at the keyboard, Becca sat back, and realization dawned on Clara. Whatever kind of hunt the young woman before her had managed, using this device and her own rather closely cropped claws, she had made a successful pounce.

"So much for wanting me back, Jeff Blakey. So much

for nothing serious…" A few more keystrokes followed and then a sudden intake of breath. "Oh!" Her voice was soft. "Oh."

"What?" Laurel looked up, a rime of milk around her brown snout. *"Is she okay?"*

"Like you care." Clara rubbed up against Becca's hand, partly to comfort her and partly to gain access. As Laurel licked her chops and began to bathe, Clara focused in on the picture in front of her. Sure enough, up on the screen was Becca's ex-boyfriend, posed in front of the software startup where he spent his days. Even in this flat miniature, with none of the reassuring confirmation of scent, the calico cat recognized those floppy bangs, the broad, easy grin that her person had thought so charming. With a slow blink of her round, green eyes, Clara also realized that she recognized the woman in the picture—the one he had his arm around. Tall, blonde, slim. Suzanne.

"Oh, Clara." An arm swept the cat off the table before she could see more, and Becca held her close, burying her face in the multicolored fur. "Maddy was right. It wasn't just a few dates. Jeff even changed his status to 'in a relationship.' It was Suzanne, and I didn't even know."

Clara felt the warm wet of tears begin to seep through her fur but held still. She knew her sisters scoffed at her sometimes, but the youngest cat saw comforting their person as much of a sacred duty as, well, keeping rodents away or kicking litter on the bathroom floor.

After a few minutes had passed, Becca's sobs subsided, and she freed the cat to wipe her face. Clara stayed on her lap, though, aware of how her presence had helped. Besides, she had a great view of the computer from here, and she could see where the melancholy girl was now manipulating the image.

"April," Becca read aloud. With a tingle in her whiskers, Clara could almost feel her thinking. April had been the bad month—the month on the sofa… "So this was from a month ago. Maybe he really did break up with her…"

A few more clicks, and his page was replaced by one that featured Becca's slender blonde colleague, only in a lot better shape than when Becca had just seen her. Clara's ears pricked up as Becca began to type some more, her fingers patting at the keys as if they were catnip mice.

"That's strange." She rested her chin on the top of Clara's head, a sure sign that she was thinking. A flurry of typing followed, but the picture on the screen didn't change. "How can someone on social media have no recent photos?" Clara swished her tail in the hope that Becca wasn't talking to her. Because of all the mysteries to which the feline was privy, this was one question for which she had no answer.

***

Becca did not answer any of Jeff's calls that morning, and there were enough of them that they had become annoying.

"I could break it." Laurel sat atop the bookshelf, looking at the buzzing device. *"Just a little push…"* One dark chocolate paw rose in the air, ready to dab.

"You can't," Clara hissed. Sometimes, she felt like she was the oldest sister. *"She needs it."*

"Needs it, huh?" Laurel turned and began licking her tail. She didn't have to bathe, but she did like to show off her flexibility on the high, narrow shelf.

"You know what I mean." Clara tried a conciliatory tone. *"It's how she reaches out without having to actually go outside."*

"I thought she was trying to learn how we do that," the

seal-point sister responded, her mew muffled by a mouthful of fur. *"Get into people's minds. Like old what's his face is—at least now."*

True enough, Jeff had been calling since Becca had turned her phone back on. The voicemail kept piling up, though, and even Harriet could tell they were weighing on Becca. So, Clara at least was glad when Becca had ducked out for a run. She came back glowing and warm. And if her exuberance had been forced, at least she seemed to have an appetite finally, although Clara suspected that Laurel had a paw in that—implanting such an idea was kitten's play for the seal point, at least with a person as open as Becca.

Whatever the initial impetus, Becca poured more cereal into that bowl and topped it off with more milk as the three felines looked on. That she held the bowl and began to eat before hitting "play all" on her message app did nothing to dissuade Laurel, who circled the young woman like a shark in shallow water.

"Hi, Becca—" She paused, spoon in mouth, to hit delete.

"Bec—" Another gone. "Wait—" Gone.

Two more and she was through, but by then the poor girl seemed to have lost her appetite. Leaving her bowl on the table—Harriet and Laurel eyed each other, waiting for the right moment—she headed for the coffee maker. Before she could even fill it with water, the phone rang again. Thumping the pot down hard enough to make the sisters scatter, Becca reached for the offending instrument, a look like thunder on her usually sweet face.

"Jeff Blakey!" Her voice was at a thunder pitch too. "If you think that I—oh." She stopped so short that Laurel looked up. “Oh, I’m sorry. Yes. Yes, I understand,” she said, her righteous indignation replaced by something more like a soft worry. “The station house? Yes, I know where it is.”

Another pause. “No, no, that won’t be necessary. I want to help. Suzanne is—” She swallowed and took a deep breath. “Suzanne was my friend.”

Chapter 11

Disruption—even when it resulted in abandoned food—was not something any cat could enjoy. And this latest call, which sent Becca out of the kitchen in a rush, was too much flurry for any feline. But Laurel's latest manipulation—following as it did on Harriet's lazy summoning of that pillow—was giving Clara an idea. It started as a twitch in her tail and moved up to tickle her whiskers, before emerging as a full-fledged possibility. Since Clara and her sisters did indeed have the powers that Becca believed she possessed, was there any reason they couldn't use their particular skills to help out the human who had taken them all in?

The sisters had a quick confab on the subject while Becca showered and changed. Or Laurel and Clara did. Harriet was too interested in Becca's discarded cereal to contribute much.

"And here I thought you didn't want us using magic in front of humans." Laurel's half-closed eyes could have denoted sleepiness, but Clara knew her too well. She was watching her baby sister, hoping to catch her in a contradiction.

"I wouldn't let her see me—see us—doing anything, of course." Clara spoke softly but with what she had hoped was a contagious urgency. *"But maybe we could poke around a little. Listen in to on her friends and check out what they're doing*

when they don't think anyone is watching?"

Laurel's ears angled forward, and Clara knew that she was intrigued. *"Spy?"*

"Well, maybe not that." Clara had the classic feline sense of entitlement and knew she could enter any room at any time. That word, however, sounded a little nastier than what she had intended. *"Just…see if we can help at all. See what we can find out. Becca needs us."*

"Seems to me she's doing fine." Laurel was quick to pick up on her sister's distaste. And as the slender seal point regarded herself the most fastidious of the three felines, she decided to be insulted. Nose up in the air, she turned away from Clara—and then dipped it quickly down to lick Becca's spoon. Harriet had knocked it out of the bowl when she dove in face first.

"She's eating. We're eating." The slightest tilt of those fluffy white ears—visible above the breakfast bowl's rim—gave the sole indication that the oldest sister was listening, as Laurel continued to lay out her case. *"Am I right?"* One dark paw swiped at Harriet's broad and fluffy tail. *"And now she's rid of both her two-timing boyfriend and the little alley cat he was running around with."* Another swipe. *"Hey!"* Harriet sat up, licking her chops. "*Stop that!"*

"I was afraid you'd drowned," purred Laurel, nudging Harriet aside.

"*I hadn't,"* Harriet pouted, before beginning to wash. "*Laurel's right, though.*" She hiccupped slightly as she chuckled at her sister's joke. Cats do enjoy portraying humans as inferior felines. *"Becca's doing fine, and besides, you were so upset with me the last time…"*

Clara sighed and felt her whiskers sagging. If only she

weren't the youngest—the baby, the "clown"—maybe her sisters would take her seriously. Sometimes, she thought, that was why she cared about Becca so much. The young woman was a small creature too, in her own way. And they both needed allies. Which was why the compact calico decided to make one more attempt to win over her siblings.

"I'm not talking about physically." She worked to keep her voice even. Any hint of a growl and Harriet would be on her high horse about rank and birth order again. *"I'm worried about her emotional well-being."*

Harriet blinked. Laurel didn't even look up.

"Did you enjoy being kicked off the bed last night?" Clara was playing her last card, well aware of the reputation cats had for being selfish. In some cases, she was ashamed to admit, it was deserved. *"If Becca keeps tossing and turning, then none of us will ever get to sleep on the nice comforter again."*

Harriet's nose wrinkled up slightly in thought, making the Persian in her background even more obvious. For a moment, Clara dared to hope.

"Doesn't matter." Laurel glanced up from the bowl, her pink tongue wiping over a swath of fur. *"We can sleep during the day. And this morning, she left two bowls of cereal unfinished. Two."*

"She has a point." Harriet looked over at the bowl with longing, but Laurel had already licked it clean.

***

Neither actually refused to accompany Clara when she set out with Becca soon after. But, as if reflecting their person's mood, the day had turned grey, and the threatened rain was enough to have Laurel up on top of the bookshelf, tail curled protectively around her neat booties. Harriet, at least, sounded conflicted, and for a few moments, her youngest sister had thought the big fluffball might join her.

"I am fond of the girl," Harriet began as Becca laced up her sneakers. *"Truly. But it's so hard to dematerialize right after eating. Couldn't we wait a half hour and then follow?"*

"She's going to the police station." Clara tried to convey the urgency. *"Where they lock people up—in cages!"*

"Oh!" Harriet drew back, raising one paw as if to bat away the idea. *"Well, then. As the head of this family, I don't think any of us should be going there."*

"No, we shouldn't," Clara agreed as she watched Becca head out the door. *"But she is, and so I am too."*

Even though Clara had dismissed Harriet's excuse as unworthy, she was grateful that she herself hadn't indulged in any breakfast treats. It isn't difficult for a cat to pass through a wall, not exactly, but they do have to shimmy and squeeze a bit—just as they do through a regular door as it closes—and the atoms of a solid structure do press in an unfortunate way on a full belly. As it was, the calico had to lope to catch up with her person, and she was pleased to see that the young woman had decided to walk, despite the slight drizzle, rather than catch the bus that stopped at the end of the street.

The Monday workday had begun in earnest, for those who had jobs, and it was all Clara could do to keep up with her person as she strode rather purposefully down the city sidewalk. The hat Becca had jammed on her head before she left the house—a wide-brimmed velvet number that kept the rain off her face—helped. But the cloaked cat still nearly tripped a bearded man in a suit when she stopped suddenly to take in the scents of the damp air. By good luck, her near victim was obsessed with his cell phone and only muttered something about the slippery sidewalk as the shadowy feline slipped by.

Nerves, Clara figured, rather than timing were pushing Becca. Because when she got to the police station, the young woman stopped short. She must have realized she was early to meet whoever it was who had called her.

"That's all right," she said to the older man at the front desk. He had enough wrinkles to be a Shar Pei, but his eyes were as sad as a basset hound's. Clara hoped he'd be gentle with her poor person. "I'll wait," she said.

"You can have a seat over there." His voice sounded doggish too, a low bark without much bite in it. "I'll make sure he knows you're here."

She nodded and retreated to the bench he had pointed out. Before long, she was chewing on her thumbnail. If Clara had to bet, the dark-haired girl was thinking about Jeff and about what Maddy had said. At least, Clara hoped she was. Weighing whether or not to turn in your cheating ex-boyfriend certainly beat out fretting over his betrayal.

"Are you okay?"

Becca started at the voice. The man before her, neat in a pink-striped Oxford shirt and jeans, his damp, dark hair combed off his forehead, didn't look familiar, and she blinked up at him. Clara, of course, recognized his scent—warm, slightly spicy, with a touch of turpentine.

"What? Oh, yes." She forced a smile. "Thanks."

Human senses may not be as acute as a cat's, but even as Becca dismissed his query with a polite smile, Clara could see the realization dawning on her face.

"You're the painter." Her smile relaxed into something

more natural. "From—" And then it disappeared. "Suzanne's."

"I am." His voice was low and warm, and as he took a seat on the bench beside Becca, she looked away flustered. "Nathan," he said, holding out a tanned and calloused hand. "Nathan Raposa."

"Becca Colwin." They shook, and Becca's brows knit as the question begin to form. "Are you here because of… because of Suzanne?"

He nodded. "I let you in. Remember?" His voice sounded kindly, but its effect had worn off. Becca's slight blush faded to something close to green. "Are you sure you're all right?"

She nodded. "That was the first time I've seen—well, a body," she said. "And you?"

"Oh, I didn't go in!" He rejected the suggestion with a grimace. "But I was working there all day, and so I guess I'm as close to a witness as they've got."

"Did you see who did it?"

He shook his head, freeing a lock of hair that, as it dried, was slowly returning to sun-bleached blond. "I was around back, probably. And with my music playing…well, I get into the zone. I told them that, but they kept insisting, like maybe there was something I'd overlooked."

Becca waited.

"I told them all I could." He paused, that grin was looking sheepish. "And that was that I was working there all morning, and I didn't see or hear anything. At least, not until you came by."

Chapter 12

Becca didn't like the sound of that. Clara could tell by the way her forehead furrowed as she took in a quick breath. But before she could respond—or even let that breath out—her name was called by the man behind the desk.

"You'll do fine." Nathan reached over, as if to place one hand over hers, and pulled back just in time. "Just tell them what happened."

"Rebecca Colwin?" An older man in a rumpled brown jacket was looking around.

"Here, before you go." Nathan pulled his wallet from his back pocket. "Why don't you give me a call after," he said, extracting a card. "It might help to talk about it. I'm not going to be able to work today anyway. And, besides, maybe we can salvage something good from the whole experience."

"Ms. Colwin?" The man in the brown jacket was coming toward her.

"Here." Nathan pressed the card into her hand as he rose. "Good luck."

"Thanks." Her voice cracked as she, too, stood and turned toward the disheveled man. "I'm Becca—Rebecca—Colwin."

"Well, Becca Rebecca," he said as the edges of his mouth twitched into a grin. "Why don't you come with me?"

Becca turned back, but Nathan was already walking toward the door, and so, with a sigh that probably no one but Clara could hear, she followed the older man in.

***

Fifteen minutes later, she looked like herself again, neither too pale nor too pink. The older man—Detective Abrams—had gotten one of his staff to bring her coffee and take her sodden hat. But even without the extra fortification, she had done her best to recall everything she could from that morning. The detective's questions had helped, prompting her along when she couldn't seem to remember some of the details.

Although she'd been dreading it—her response to the handsome painter had made that obvious—the entire experience seemed to be doing her some good.

"Yes, that's true." She was nodding enthusiastically as the detective read back her description of the room. "That's it exactly."

He had seemed tentative, as if he didn't trust his own note taking, and Becca was eager to help.

"The door was definitely unlocked when I came in."

"Unlocked, but was it closed or open?"

She paused. "I am pretty sure it was slightly open. I mean, I knocked, but I wouldn't have opened it unless it had been off the latch. That's not me."

"Of course not, Ms. Colwin." The detective looked tired, his face as wrinkled as that jacket. But his manner was gentle and his voice soft. "So you heard a voice?"

"No." Becca looked lost in her memory. "I just—the door opened, and I stepped in, calling for her."

"Because you sensed something was off?" The detective sounded genuinely curious, his head tilting like

Laurel's did when she was listening to something she didn't quite understand. "Because of your power—what did you call it, a sensitivity?"

"No, I don't…" Becca looked flustered. "Oh, you mean the summoning? No, that was—I don't know what that was." She almost laughed as she shook her head. "I just wanted you to understand how Suzanne and I know each other. We're not—we weren't—friends, exactly, though maybe we could have been, if it weren't for… Anyway, we know each other from our group. *Knew* each other." She swallowed and fell silent.

"Your coven." The rumpled man waited a moment before offering the word, pronounced so carefully, as if he had never heard it before. At least, thought Clara as she watched him, he was being respectful.

"Well, that's what we call ourselves." Becca looked down, slightly abashed. "I don't even know if I believe in any of it. Only the last time we all got together, things were a little crazy because, well, because I think I did summon something."

The man opposite her looked so confused Clara almost began to wonder about his intelligence.

"I thought I explained," Becca said. Obviously, she was wondering too. "I was trying out these spells. And, well, I summoned a pillow out of the ether—out of nowhere."

"Ah, of course." A nod of understanding at last as a smile reconfigured those wrinkles. "So you do have power of some kind, and did Suzanne?"

"No, I don't think so." The memory made Becca stop and think. "I was the only one who had had any success. At least, thus far."

"So you were special to the group." He was speaking slowly, as if he were trying very hard not to miss anything again. But something in his tone was beginning to make the fur along Clara's back rise.

"Well, I wouldn't say that…" Becca must have heard an off note too. She had turned away from the man, but Clara could see the hot dark splotches that now stained her cheeks.

"Still, it must have been very gratifying, to have a spell—a summoning spell—work. Especially when none of the other women in the coven had managed that." He appeared to be reading his notes, but Clara could tell that he was watching Becca. Watching her color rise.

"We're not all women." Becca faced him again, eager to set the record straight. "We're equal opportunity."

"Ah." The detective sat back, waiting. A broad grin began to spread across his worn face.

"Our coven leader, Trent, is a man," she explained. "I mean, we're very egalitarian. That's one of the tenets of Wicca, of what we do. But it just so happens that Trent is the most experienced and, well, he's a man." She sounded like she'd run out of steam.

"One man in the coven." The detective seemed to find that interesting. "But even he can't do what you can. That must be extremely gratifying, especially since you've lost your job. Your boyfriend too, I believe. Having a power like that must have made you feel special—especially to this man, this Trent."

"No." Becca's voice was full of scorn. Too full, Clara thought, remembering those flowers. "It's not like that."

"No, of course not." The kind, fatherly face beamed right back at her.

"So tell me, how long were you stalking the victim?"

Chapter 13

Despite her sisters' reservations, Clara knew that they would have responded. Laurel would have attacked that detective, claws out. Harriet would have bristled, at least, fluffing up her bulk to ottoman-like proportions. Clara simply wanted to get Becca out of there as soon as possible. Luckily, the young woman seemed to be on the same wavelength.

"What? Are you kidding me?" She stood up, her voice rising along with her. "Stalking?"

"Now, now." The seated man raised his hand as if to stop her, his tired face looking just as gentle as it had all along. "Please, miss. We understand how emotions can run high. Your boyfriend was stepping out…"

"But you don't understand." She hesitated, and Clara feared she was going to sit again. "I wasn't stalking anyone."

"You knew that the victim was seeing your ex-boyfriend? You've said that you were to meet her at noon. He tells us he spoke to you at half past, which leaves a half hour unaccounted for. We've also heard that you were quite upset."

"Jeff?" Her voice ratcheted up again. "He said that?"

"We've had several people in to talk with us," the detective continued.

"What about Trent?" Even as Becca said the name, a look of horror came over her. "Wait, he had a key…"

"We're speaking to several people," the detective repeated.

"But you think I…" She reached for the back of the chair, this time to steady herself as she suddenly went pale. "That I could…?"

The tired-looking man did not answer. Instead, he pushed his own chair back with a scraping sound that made Clara—her fur already on edge—jump. "This is an ongoing investigation, but I'm sure all questions will be answered in time," he said as he rose with a tired sigh. "In the meantime, we'd appreciate it if you remained available to answer any further questions."

***

Clara had to hold back as Becca left the suddenly airless room. As much as she wanted to brush up against her person—to give her the feline equivalent of a hug with her soft fur and the gentle pressure of her warm body—the little cat had to keep in mind that she was, for all intents and purposes, invisible to Becca. If she showed up here, she'd be as likely to startle her as comfort her. Besides, the young woman was so distracted that even if Clara were as big as Harriet, she'd be at risk of tripping her person as the detective escorted her down the hall and out.

"Becca!" At the sound of her name, the flustered young woman looked up. The day had cleared, but she didn't appear to feel the warm sun. Instead, she blinked, blind as a new kitten, as a man approached. "Are you okay?"

"Yeah, thanks." She stopped and focused. It was the painter, only he had rolled up his shirtsleeves to reveal sinewy forearms and his hair had dried. "I'm sorry—Nathan?"

"Yeah." He smiled, his teeth white against his tan. "I

thought I'd wait around. And, well, I'm glad I did. You look a little out of it. They didn't make you look at photos, did they?"

Becca shuddered. "No. No way. We just…talked."

"Ah." Nathan nodded, comprehension dawning. "That can be worse. Hey, would you want to get something to eat? I know I could use some coffee and a muffin."

"Yeah." She sounded tentative, but then repeated with more resolve. "Yes, I would. I think they think…I think that maybe…" She swallowed hard. "I need to talk this all over with somebody."

As Clara followed them to the coffee house, she grew increasingly grateful that her sisters hadn't come along. For starters, Harriet would have gotten so excited by the idea of a muffin that she might have materialized right there, which would have caused no shortage of confusion. Laurel, meanwhile, would have been so intrigued by the sun-kissed painter with his spicy scent that she'd be twining around his ankles as he walked—unless she'd have already rejected him as competition for Becca's time and attention, in which case, who knew what havoc she would wreak. Although the housecat in Clara understood both impulses, she had more discipline than either of her siblings and prided herself on her calico ability to hang back and weigh a situation before acting.

As she slipped in the closing door and waited by the one empty table, Clara tried to focus on what Becca needed—and what one small feline could do for a beleaguered human.

"Here, drink this." Nathan had insisted that Becca sit—choosing the same table Clara had picked out—and returned a minute later with a large, froth-topped mug. "You've had a shock."

"Thanks." A sound rather like a purr emanated from

Becca's mouth, and she licked away a foam moustache with a gesture Laurel would have been proud of. "I really need—what is this?"

"Mocha cappuccino." Nathan put his own mug down and went back to the counter. By the time he returned, with muffins, Becca had begun to look more like herself, the warmth, milk, and sugar augmenting the caffeine in her recovery.

"I figure you've been through an ordeal." He raised his own mug to drink, but Clara could see he was watching the young woman who sat opposite him. "Were they brutal?"

"It was one man—a detective—and he was, well, full of questions," Becca said, reaching for the closest muffin. "Though he seemed to know a lot." She broke off a piece and nibbled at it absently. Clara, who enjoyed her food almost as much as her sisters did, thought she wasn't really tasting it. "What did you tell them about me?"

"About you?" Nathan's eyebrows rose. "Just that I let you in."

"Did you tell them what time?" But the man seated opposite was shaking his head.

"No, I'm sorry. I wasn't really keeping track." He had the decency to look abashed. "And they asked, and so I had to tell them that you looked distracted. But, then, I went around the back again, until, well, until you started screaming."

"Did you at least tell them how brief my visit was?" Becca broke off another piece, but only crumbled it between her fingers. "I mean, you must have only gotten back to work."

It was not to be. "Sorry. I had my music playing, and I was really done with the painting for the day. It being Saturday and all, I'd only come by to do another coat on the trim. But, well, I'd noticed you." He looked down at his mug and thus missed seeing the blush climbing into her cheeks. "I'd seen you coming up the street and I'd been kind of hoping you'd come out soon, and so I was taking my time, cleaning up, until I heard—well, you know. And then I ran around front and saw that other guy holding you, hustling you out of the building. I was ready to jump in. But just then, I heard sirens and the cops were pulling up, and I realized I should stay out of the way."

Becca blinked up at him.

"Until you'd been taken care of, of course." The painter's eyes opened wide. They were blue, Clara noted, but a more grey-blue than Laurel's. "By the EMT, that is. Then I came forward—anyway, I'm sorry. Finding your friend like that must have been awful."

"Yeah, it was. Thanks." Becca held her mug close as color drained from her face to leave her sickly pale. "But Suzanne and I weren't friends. Not exactly."

"Ah." Now it was his turn to look thoughtful. "Work colleagues?"

"We're in a cov—a group. A discussion group. We *were*," she corrected herself as her color returned to something like normal. "We had just had our weekly meeting a few days before, and she'd asked me to come by."

"And she called you that morning, right?" He bit into his own muffin while he waited for her answer.

"No." Becca shook her head. "She'd asked me when we last met. Why?"

"Huh." Another bite, and his face grew thoughtful as he chewed and swallowed. "That's strange. I heard her on the phone earlier that morning—maybe an hour or two before you showed up. She sounded like something was on her mind.

Honestly? Maybe even angry."

Becca nodded. Clara didn't have to be as psychic as Laurel to know she was thinking of Jeff and of what he'd told her. "So you did hear some things," she said, and Clara looked up with pride. Cats don't tend to think of their humans as successful hunters. They know the average biped is far too inept. But this girl was sharp.

"I was working right outside her apartment at that point." Nathan spoke as if it were no big deal, but Becca was on it like a kitten on a catnip mouse.

"And I assume you told the police that her living room window was open?"

Clara held her breath, every guard hair on alert.

"I'm sure they know." Now it was his turn to look away, flustered. "And they had people all over that apartment. I haven't been allowed back to finish, or even get my gear."

"You haven't—" Becca tilted her head, as if she'd heard a whistle far away. Maybe, Clara thought, she was thinking of keys—and access to a young woman's apartment. "How well did you know Suzanne?"

"Me? Not at all." He shook his head. "We said hi a few times." His sadness seemed genuine, but Becca pushed on. "I didn't know any of the tenants."

"So then who hired you, Nathan?"

"Some management company." He was staring at the door, like Harriet at a cabinet full of treats. "I get referrals. Why are you asking—you don't think that I..."

"I don't know what to think." Becca said, speaking slowly. "I've never been involved in a murder investigation before."

Chapter 14

Becca was on her phone as soon as she left the coffee house.

"Maddy, I've had the weirdest morning, you wouldn't believe who I just had coffee with." She sounded breathless, and Clara didn't think that was due to her pace. Nor did she give her friend a chance to answer. "That painter I told you about?"

Late morning, and it was easy for the shadowing feline to keep up, the rush hour crowds she'd battled earlier having all dispersed to their various daytime destinations. As Becca walked, holding her phone to her ear, Clara realized that her friend was one of those office drones. That would explain why her person was sharing her news over the phone rather than at one of their customary confabs. It might also have explained the friend's mood, which—from Becca's face—was not improved by the news that Becca had shared a snack with this particular young man, no matter how solicitous he might have seemed.

"Maddy…Maddy, wait." Becca actually stopped, raising her hand as if her friend could see her. "This wasn't a date. I know he was there. We ran into each other at the police station. Look, we talked about it. I asked him a bunch of questions, and they did too. No, he's not a suspect." She lowered her voice on that last word, but Clara's ears pitched forward to catch it all. "I was down there answering questions too, Maddy."

After she hung up, Becca walked the rest of the way in silence. That gave her pet a chance to mull over what she'd learned—and what she could infer. This Nathan, for example, was not previously known, not even to Becca's more gossipy friend. That he seemed to like Becca was obvious, even without that rather flattering admission.

To her cat, this made perfect sense. Clara knew Becca was an attractive young woman. Her coat was smooth and glossy, and she always smelled nice to the little feline. Plus, as her pet well knew, Becca hadn't had any suitors since Jeff had broken her heart. And while Trent had seemed promising—those flowers had been good enough to eat—he hadn't made any moves that a friend wouldn't. Well, if you bought his line about the bouquet being a hostess gift, that is. It didn't take any magic to see that Becca liked the painter as well, perhaps because of his pleasant pine-y aroma. And while Becca had been appropriately skeptical, asking some good questions, Clara had witnessed that blush.

But the conversation had taken a dark turn once Becca had brought up the ongoing investigation. For all that the cute painter had claimed not to have kept track of the time, he did seem to keep adding details to his recollections—details that might implicate Becca. And when Becca had asked about his work—about who owned or managed Suzanne's apartment—he'd become as skittish as a kitchen mouse. Clara could tell that Becca was disconcerted when the handsome painter had excused himself rather suddenly and left. What she didn't know was whether her human had been more upset by the questions he had left unanswered—or the ones that he had failed to ask her.

Perhaps it was too much to expect some peace in which to ponder all these variables. Too much to expect a quiet afternoon once the two got home. Not when they'd left Laurel and Harriet behind. After all, Clara had tried to get them involved, and she should have known that both her sisters took a while to get started in the morning. But Becca and Clara returned to find the apartment a wreck—all the cushions off the couch and the mauled remains of Trent's bouquet spread across the floor.

"Oh, kitties!" Becca immediately began gathering the scattered blossoms, most of which were broken or shredded past recognition. They had been fading anyway. Now, however, they were beyond recall.

"What were you thinking?" Clara found Laurel and Harriet on the sill, reclining in the sun. For once, Harriet wasn't hogging all the space, and their calico sister jumped up to join them, squeezing in between the two. *"Isn't she having a hard enough time without this?"*

"We were…investigating," said Laurel with a faint purr. *"I'm not sure I trust that Trent fellow."*

"I'm not sure I do either," Clara had to admit. Men, she was beginning to realize, were often a complication. *"But…"*

"I thought about cleaning it all up." Harriet looked up, blinking, and Clara realized her oldest sister had been asleep. *"But you threw such a hissy fit last time."*

"That was diff–" Clara caught herself. No good ever came out of arguing with Harriet.

"Besides," the oldest sister said as she began to bathe, *"Jeff wouldn't want to see some other man's flowers here."*

"Jeff?" Clara turned her head and caught it. The vibration. Someone was coming to the door. With a thud, Harriet landed first and waddled off, but Laurel and Clara quickly caught up as she headed toward the door.

"What the—kitties?" Becca looked up, broken stems in her hand, just in time to hear the buzzer. "Jeff!" She opened the door, reaching up reflexively to smooth her hair, and only succeeded in dropping some pale pink petals in her brown curls.

"Here, let me." In lieu of a more traditional greeting, Jeff leaned over and picked out a few blossoms as Becca sputtered. "Cats got at the flowers again?"

"Yeah, they can't seem to resist." Becca turned toward the kitchen, where she dumped the ruined bouquet rather unceremoniously in the trash.

"I don't know why you bother." Her ex followed, stopping only when he saw the vase, where the one rose had somehow survived. "Oh," he said, the reality dawning. "You didn't…"

"A friend brought them." Becca focused on cleaning up the rest of the debris. "Just a thank you gesture."

"Silly girl," Laurel mewed as she leaned her tan side against Jeff's shin. *"We got him to notice them, didn't we?"*

"Becca doesn't play those kinds of games." If looks had claws, Laurel would have felt Clara's. *"So that's why you trashed the place."*

"Huh." Harriet sat staring up at Becca. To her, a human in the kitchen meant only one thing: food. *"She just attacked them because she could."* Of course, the bouquet had been on a high shelf. Becca has grown rather used to the cats' tricks, at least, the non-magical ones.

"With everything going on, I took the day off," Jeff explained as he extricated himself from Laurel and reached out to Becca. "I wanted to see you. I mean, that—it—must have been so awful for you."

"Yeah, it was." Becca fussed a bit more with the dustpan, chasing the last few petals with the brush as they skittered away like so many moths, before giving up. Standing, she turned to face her ex. "Saturday was possibly the worst day of my life, but today hasn't been great either."

"Oh, honey." He reached to embrace her.

"Don't!" Her raised hand stopped him short. "Jeff, you can't—I didn't even know about you and Suzanne before… before Saturday. You can't just waltz back in. Not now, that she's…"

"Becca, it's not like that." His arms had dropped to his sides, but he showed no sign of retreating. "I told you. I'd broken it off with Suzanne. We were over."

"Yeah, well, that's not what the cops think." Her voice had an edge that set Clara's ears back.

He shook his head as if bewildered.

"They accused me of stalking her," Becca said.

"Oh." That one syllable was enough.

"Jeff?" It was the warning voice. The one Becca used with the cats when they got too close to a candle.

"It's just—" He paused and his boyish face assumed a hangdog look. "They came by to talk to me this morning. They had a lot of questions, and they seemed to know we'd, uh, gone out a few times. They seemed to think it was somebody Suzanne knew and, so, well… Anyway, I'd told them that Suzanne had been freaked out recently. That she was worried that someone was following her. I didn't know that they'd think it was you."

"So that's why you took the day off. I think you'd better start at the beginning, Jeff Blakey." Becca nodded toward the living room, but from the way she was standing, arms crossed, she wasn't thinking of her guest's comfort. "And this time, don't leave anything out."

***

"I didn't mean to get you in any trouble." Twenty minutes later, they had moved to the couch, though Becca was keeping a cushion—*the* cushion—between them. At some point during Becca's retelling of what had happened and Jeff's apologies for what he'd said, Harriet and Laurel had given up and gone to seek out real moths, leaving only Clara to listen in. "It was all that stupid group—your witch group." His voice dripped with contempt. "The coven she was so proud to be part of."

Becca held her tongue, but a more sensible man would've noted her expression.

"I mean, who believes in magic in this day and age?" He was digging himself in deeper.

"What do you mean?" Clara saw the effort it took for Becca to keep her voice level. Maybe Jeff did too, because he sighed and pushed his hair back before trying to explain.

"Well, like, Suzanne told me there were some issues. I guess she'd gone out a few times with someone in the group? Anyway, he'd given her this necklace. You know, that glass thing she always wore?"

"The crystal teardrop?" Becca had only seen it briefly, but she could visualize it. Her hand moved up and she touched the hollow of her own throat.

"Yeah." Jeff nodded as he watched the movement of

Becca's hand. "That's the one. She was really careful about taking it off before you guys met, though. Said it would bring down bad juju or something. What kind of craziness is that?"

"Really." Clara knew there was more to this. Becca did too, from the way she stared at her ex. "Bad juju?"

"I don't know. I thought maybe it was a jealousy thing. You know, 'cause she'd dumped the guy. Then I thought, well, maybe it was some other ex. But the group is mostly women, right?"

She nodded. "So you told the cops that I was stalking your new girlfriend. Making me the prime suspect for her murder."

"Oh, Becs, I'm sorry." His arm went up on the sofa back, so Clara jumped to the space between them and settled in. One couldn't be too careful. "It was just the first thing I thought of—I never meant for them to suspect you."

Becca shot him a look Laurel would have been proud of but held her tongue.

"Really," he said, leaning over Clara. The cat yawned and stretched to her full length. "I meant what I told her. I've really missed you."

"So you keep saying." Becca stood and walked to the door, arms once again crossed across her body. She didn't need Laurel to suggest that it was time for Jeff to leave. "And maybe it's even true. But all that means is that maybe you had reasons of your own to get rid of Suzanne."

Chapter 15

"And I left my hat at the police station too!"

Becca was leaning on the door, having just ushered Jeff out. But all her resolve seemed to crumble once her ex was gone, and she collapsed on the sofa with a wail that brought her three pets running.

It wasn't just the hat, of course. Even Harriet recognized that, as much as she had liked to sit on the velvet topper—when it was dry—and who now offered her bulk as comfort. It's hard when your heart has been broken, Clara figured as she rubbed her head against the prone girl. It's harder still when your ex suggests you have a motive for murder—and you realize he might have done it himself.

But the Becca who sat up, dislodging Harriet, and wiped her face seemed more clear-eyed than the love-struck girl of only a few minutes before. And after she blew her nose, she pulled her laptop computer toward her and began typing.

"I don't know if Jeff meant to get me in trouble," she said, glancing over at the calico cat who had sat beside her, grey tail coiled neatly around her white paws. "But he's forgotten that I'm a researcher. If someone really was stalking Suzanne, I bet I can find out who."

Her typing was interrupted by the phone. Not that she answered it—not right away—but she did reach for the device.

The observant feline watching her could tell by the way she bit her lip that she was considering letting it go to voice mail—yes, cats know about such things—before, on the sixth ring, she picked up.

"Hey, Kathy. I mean, merry, uh, meet?" She made the effort to put some cheer in her voice. "What's up?"

In the pause that followed, her shoulders sagged.

"No, no news." Her assumed cheer was drooping as well. "I answered some questions for them, and I guess they talked to—well, they're talking to some other people as well. Look, Kathy, I was in the middle of trying to research something—" A pause, and she sat back up. "You do? Wow, that would be great. With everything going on, I could use some good news. Thanks."

An hour or so later, the bell rang and Becca jumped to answer it. Despite having hosted the coven only five days earlier, she'd spent much of the time since the phone call cleaning up—as if the tufts of fur her pets had placed so carefully in the interim were something to be ashamed of.

"Kathy, come in!" Becca ushered in her guest. "I guess I should say merry meet, but…"

"Darling, don't worry about it," said the redhead, whose all-black outfit seemed somewhat at odds with what had become a bright spring afternoon.

"Thanks. Is that…" Becca hesitated. "Are you in mourning?"

"Of course," said Kathy, who plumped down on the sofa right in Harriet's spot. Clara looked around for her oldest sister, but she and Laurel had made themselves scarce, which was odd. Laurel, in particular, usually relished a chance to adorn black clothing with her lightest brown body fur. "Oh, you mean—all black?"

Becca nodded and took her usual seat, while Clara made herself comfortable on the arm rest.

"I just came from work." Kathy shooed the word off like a pesky fly. "I want them to respect me there."

Becca nodded again, as if this made sense to her.

"Do you have, like, a glass of wine or something?" Kathy leaned forward, her voice becoming conspiratorially soft. By force of habit, Clara looked around. Laurel had appeared in the doorway, tail up inquisitively.

"Oh, sure!" Becca retreated to rummage in the kitchen, while Clara leaped to the floor to fill her sister in.

"Something about a job," she mewed, ever so softly, in her brown-tipped ear. *"Though I think this one wants to gossip."*

"I know that." Laurel glanced sideways at her sister, her blue eyes looking deceptively innocent.

"Oh, look at your cats!" Kathy called into the kitchen. "They're head-butting each other."

"They are?" Becca appeared with the glasses and the bottle of Chardonnay she'd opened on a whim two weeks before. "Usually, they fight."

"Cats." The redhead reached up to take the bottle with an exaggerated shrug. "Who can tell? Anyway, I've been meaning to stop by and see how you were doing. I've been thinking about you. How awful that must have been—finding her and then being interrogated by the police."

"Told you," Clara whiskered to Laurel as the guest shivered dramatically.

"Well, not interrogated, actually." Becca stared into her wine. "They just asked me about what I saw and how I know her, and everything."

"Horrible." Kathy shook her head. Her mouth was pursed in concern but her eyes were wide with interest. "What you must have seen…"

In response Becca only nodded and took a swallow. When she started to choke, the other woman jumped up to pat her back.

"Sorry." Becca wiped away the tears from her coughing fit. "Yeah, it just brought it all back."

"I can only imagine." Kathy eyed her own glass, then appeared to think better of it. "They don't have any suspects yet…do they?"

"I hope not." As her guest blinked, Becca rushed in to explain. "I mean—I don't think so. Only I'm worried they might think I was involved."

"Oh, they can't!" Kathy protested, reaching for Becca's hand.

"They called me back in this morning to answer more questions." Becca sounded glum, even as Kathy held onto her. "And they said they might have more."

"Well, we know there's nothing in that—and we're all here for you. Here." Kathy topped off her glass, and lifted her own in solidarity. "Interesting." She examined the bottle.

"It's been in the fridge for a while." Becca admitted.

"It's fine." Kathy waved her off and took another swallow, wrinkling her freckled nose at the taste. "After all, you've had quite a shock. But anyway, that's not why I came over." She raised her glass in a salute. "I've got a job for you!"

"Yes?" Becca actually shifted to the edge of her seat. Kathy grinned and almost shimmied with satisfaction as she took another sip.

"She's toying with her." Laurel's tone made her sister turn. She was staring at Kathy as she choked down the wine. The expression on the feline's face was a little hostile but also a bit respectful, and Clara didn't think it was because of their visitor's ability to drink.

"How dare she!" Clara could feel her ears going back.

"No, it's okay." Laurel raised one dark chocolate paw, ready to bat her younger sibling. She was leaning in and listening—using her skills to hear the thoughts behind the words. *"She's dragging it out to make it last. She wants to bond. Like we do."*

Clara lashed her tail, unsure of that, and Laurel wisely lowered her paw.

"It's not a glamorous position," Kathy was saying. "And maybe you wouldn't even want it. Only, well, I know how tough it is out there." Now it was her turn to lean in, and her voice got softer. "You know what a hard time I had after Joey and I broke up," she said. "How I fell into a depression."

"I don't think I knew you then." Becca's voice was gentle, and when her guest didn't respond, she kept talking. "I'm sorry it was hard for you."

"Thanks." Her friend looked down into her glass, her voice unusually quiet. "The coven really saved me. We witches have to stick together."

"Definitely." Becca smiled, though Clara could see the uncertainty around the corners of her mouth. "If only I could be sure we're really witches."

"You're not?" The redhead's eyes went wide in surprise. "I thought you, of all people…"

"Well, I'm hoping." A faraway look came over Becca. "You know, I did some research on my own family, and it does look like there was at least one wise woman—a 'wyrd sister'—in my family tree, back in the 1760s. In fact—"

"Well, don't tell Eric that when you speak to him!" Kathy interrupted.

"Eric?"

The brassy curls bounced as she nodded. "Eric Marshfield, my supervisor. They're looking for someone to handle data entry. They want to modernize the system, make it so you can see comparables. I think that's not your thing exactly, but the company's growing…"

"I'll call him tomorrow." Becca grabbed a pad and began making notes. "I can do systems, and, frankly, I need a job. Thanks, Kathy. After all that's happened…"

"I know." Kathy tried the wine again, with only a small wince this time. "It's just unbelievable, isn't it?"

Becca swallowed, going slightly green. Clara made a mental note to knock the wine bottle over if she got the chance. "Yeah."

"You didn't hear what the trouble was with her and Ande, did you?" Kathy seemed not to notice Becca's discomfort. Then again, she'd finished her own glass.

"No." Becca shook her head. "Suzanne said she wanted to talk to me about something, but I never got to hear about what."

"Trent gave us all a ride, and there was definitely something going on with those two. Larissa noticed it too. You know," Kathy leaned close. Clara's ears pricked up. Laurel might be right about the desire to bond. That didn't mean the calico wanted to miss out on anything. "I hear they were both into the same guy. I wonder if the police know about that."

"The same—" Becca recoiled, her eyes as wide as

saucers. "Ande was seeing Jeff too?"

"Who's Jeff?" Kathy tipped her head to the side. "I'm talking about Trent."

Chapter 16

"I knew that man was up to no good." It was all Clara could do to keep from spitting.

Laurel stared at her sister with her blue eyes wide, the feline equivalent of raised brows. *"Really, Clara?"* Her normal mew sank to a near purr as her whiskers perked up—more a result, Clara had to believe, of her being right than in glee over Becca's disappointment. "*You are such a kitten.*"

"But you were the one who suspected him..." Clara closed her eyes, thinking of the ruined bouquet. Laurel always did try to misdirect attention from her appetites.

When she opened them, her sister was still there. As was that Kathy. Though, to do the shorter woman credit, she looked just as upset as Becca.

"You didn't know?" Her mouth made an O of concern.

"Someone may have suggested…a while ago." Becca shook off the exaggerated response. "But I'd heard that Suzanne was seeing my ex, Jeff."

"Oh." Kathy sat back and seemed to take that in, her round face growing serious. "I'm sorry. I don't know anything about that."

"But you're sure about Suzanne—and about Ande?"

A shrug. "No, I'm not *sure* sure. Not really. But that's what I heard."

"Where'd you hear it?" Clara tilted her ears forward. This seemed a legitimate question to her, the kind an inquisitive cat would pose.

"I don't really remember." Kathy looked at her wine glass, but then seemed to think better of it. "Maybe from Larissa? Anyway, it probably doesn't mean anything—Trent's, well, you know." A shy smile brought out her freckles. "He's Trent. Anyway, I should get going. Get in touch with Eric, though, and let me know what happens, okay?"

Becca walked her guest to the door in a daze and stood, her forehead leaning on the doorframe, for several minutes after she left. Clara circled her ankles in solidarity and allowed the young woman to heft her to her shoulder.

"How undignified!" The calico looked down to see Laurel staring up at her.

Harriet joined her seal-point sister a moment later. *"Does this mean we'll get treats?"* she asked, before Laurel swatted her, and she plodded off. Becca, meanwhile, had collapsed back on the sofa, her lids closing in exhaustion.

"I need to talk to Ande. If only I could just summon her." Becca was talking to herself; Clara knew that. Still, she glared down at her sister in alarm. Had Laurel suggested this stupid idea somehow?

But the slim feline flicked her tail and turned away dismissively. She didn't have to be psychic to read the angle of Clara's ears, but, clearly, she was having none of it. Clara didn't think either of her sisters could actually implant a totally new thought in a person's mind, only suggest a direction. Then again, she was the youngest and not at all sure of just how much power they each had. As it was, Becca had let her smallest cat slide to her lap, and with a deep sigh, reached for her phone. "I should just call her," she said, her voice flat with fatigue. "Tomorrow." She put the phone down. Just then, a yowl sounded. Harriet—from the kitchen.

That roused Becca as nothing else could, and Clara jumped to the floor. Laurel was already on her way to see what their oldest sister was up to.

"*I'm hungry!*" Harriet complained once her audience had assembled, her yellow eyes wide with pleading. Of course, her request sounded like a plaintive mew to Becca, but because the chubby creamsicle of a cat was standing by her empty dish, it wasn't hard to figure out her meaning.

"Oh, kitty! I'm sorry." Becca reached for the cabinet where she kept the cans. "It is your dinner time, isn't it? Only—" She paused, and it hit Clara: she knew why Harriet had disappeared moments before.

"*You didn't!*" She hissed. Partly out of surprise. Harriet never let anything get in the way of her creature comforts. "*But why?*"

"*Yow.*" It was a non-answer as she turned her round eyes on her youngest sibling, her whiskers spreading into a supremely self-satisfied smirk.

"I could've sworn I had…" Becca paused, staring at the empty shelf and shaking her head. Seeing her dismay and evident fatigue, Clara concentrated, trying hard to will the young woman to keep looking. The little calico knew that while her sister could summon items out of the ether, it was harder to send them back. Besides, odds were that those cans had simply been moved to another shelf. Clara couldn't imagine Harriet would ever really risk having no food in the house.

But any feline's magical power has its limits, and Clara

lacked Laurel's particular ease with human thoughts. And so instead of doing a thorough search for those missing cans, within a minute Becca was cursing her own carelessness and muttering promises to her pets that she would return soon—with provisions.

"I wouldn't let my girls starve!" She sounded so earnest it hurt Clara to hear her. "I know you depend on me."

Harriet's low, self-congratulatory "*thrrup*" was the only response. Clara didn't even make eye contact with her sisters as she followed their person out the door. She knew they were up to something, but it was more important to the compact calico that she watch out for Becca than she grill her siblings. Besides, being the youngest as well as the smallest, she didn't have much leverage. She wasn't a tail biter like Laurel. And the one time Clara had tried to actually push Harriet, as opposed to reasoning with her, her big sister had responded by sitting on her. Her whiskers weren't right for months.

Taking advantage of the deepening dusk, the little calico was virtually invisible even without a masking, her stripes and splotches blending in with the shadows as the after-work crowd filled the sidewalks. And as Becca made her way to the local grocery, Clara began to wonder if she'd made the wrong choice. Maybe Laurel and Harriet had merely wanted to get her out of the apartment. It didn't take much to imagine what they might be up to, back there alone, and she was just about to turn around when Becca stopped short.

"Ande!" Clara looked up to see a tall, slim figure about to enter the store. The woman paused on hearing her name, and Clara could hear Becca whisper to herself: "Did I summon her?"

"Becca, blessed be." The dark-haired woman managed

a smile as she walked back toward her coven mate. But it was a weak one and didn't touch her eyes. "What's up? You headed to the Superette?"

Before their person could answer, Clara turned with a hiss. *"Harriet!"* Only instead of her fluffy sister, she saw a pair of almond-shaped blue eyes. *"Laurel?"* Clara corrected herself as the other cat took shape. *"Don't you see that Becca is going to think she made Ande appear? You knew she wanted to question her. How could you?"*

"I was curious," her sister purred. *"Weren't you?"*

"No!" Clara stopped. *"Well, yes, but..."* It was too late. First, Laurel's brown ears and tail faded into the shadows, and then her tan torso, until finally she closed those mischievous blue eyes and disappeared entirely.

Clara still sensed her sister's presence and knew she'd be lurking somewhere, listening. But the youngest cat was in damage-control mode now. Drawing closer, she focused on the conversation between the two young women.

"I know, it's just so horrible. I can't imagine…" Ande spoke softly as the stream of post-work shoppers flowed past them. As she did, she shook her head, as if she could rid her mind of the last few days.

"You don't want to." Becca's voice was somber, and Clara had to fight the urge to go to her. As much as the little cat wanted to comfort her person, she knew that materializing in front of the Superette would not have the desired effect.

"Ugh." Ande put her hand over her mouth, as if she could block the image. "That's right. Are you okay?"

Becca shrugged, staring off into space as if she were a cat or simply done with the conversation. And then, just as Clara had begun to hope that maybe this would be it—that her friend's sympathy would stir in Becca a desire to talk about anything *but* the events of the previous Saturday—Becca took a deep breath and turned to face her elegant friend.

"In fact, I was wondering." Becca was holding her voice steady, but Clara could hear the tension vibrating within her. "I gather you and Suzanne were chatting about something—after the coven meeting?"

"Oh, it wasn't important." Another wave, as if the question were a pesky fly. "Not in light of what's happened."

Becca's voice dropped. "Ande, are you dating Trent?"

The other woman flushed, a deep red infusing her caramel-colored cheeks, and her long, dark lashes sank to shield her eyes. "I went out with him a few times. But I wouldn't say we're dating."

"So that wasn't what you wanted to talk to Suzanne about? I remember you calling to her—that she'd 'promised' you something?" Becca's voice was gentle, but there was something in her expression that her cat recognized. It was the look she got when she was hunting down an elusive reference—as intense as what Clara had seen on Laurel's face that one time a mouse had gotten into the apartment.

Ande didn't take refuge under a nearby refrigerator, however, or even duck inside the store. Instead, she stood straighter, emphasizing the good six inches she had on Becca. She had an imposing presence anyway, and as she squared her shoulders, two separate shoppers held their grocery bags closer as they made their way around her.

"What? No." She dismissed the question before launching her own. "Is that what Larissa is saying?"

"I—never mind." Becca tended to look down when she was embarrassed, and she began to stare at the sidewalk, as if unsure whether the gathering dusk would soon obscure whatever she found so fascinating there. "I just…"

"You can't think I…over a man…" Ande's face froze in horror as the implication of Becca's question hit home. "No, he and I—it was never serious. In fact—"

She stopped so short, Clara peered around to see if either of her siblings had grabbed her tongue.

"In fact?" Becca dared a glance up, as curious as a cat waiting to hear what the taller woman was about to say.

"In fact, Suzanne and I were kind of working on something together."

Becca nodded, waiting for the other woman to continue.

"Okay, this is going to sound crazy." Ande crossed her arms and leaned in. "You know I'm an accountant, right?"

Becca's curls bobbed as she nodded.

"Well, the coven actually has a bank account. Silly, I know, but that's how Larissa set it up, back when we started, for our monthly tithing and anything else that came up. And a few weeks ago, she asked me look into something. I think she got whacked on taxes this year. Anyway, she wanted to know if we could apply for nonprofit status." Ande rolled her eyes. "I mean, she has a point. We probably should come under the religious exemption, as practicing Wiccans, but that requires a whole lot of paperwork that I'm not sure we want to get into—or that I want to do gratis." A wave of one of those elegant hands, as if she were summoning the seafood department to come out to greet her.

"But anyway, when I was looking at the statements, it was pretty obvious that some money has gone missing. We don't have a lot, but it's added up over the years, and even with Larissa's carelessness—her bookkeeping is positively reckless—we're down a couple of thousand dollars."

Becca didn't say anything. She didn't have to. Even in the fading light, her confusion showed on her face.

"Crazy, right?" Ande chuckled. "When Larissa started it, I think it was more like a personal account—a way for her to put some money aside. She provided the seed money for expenses—you know, the fliers and the tea. And, well, she has the bucks, so why not? But the balance is definitely not what it should be, especially since we've all been ponying up our five bucks a month. Though it could just be that awful tea is more expensive than any of us knew."

Becca's lips twitched with the hint of a smile. "The witches' tea?"

"Awful," Ande repeated. "But anyway, I told Larissa that it would be really complicated to apply for a change in our status and that if she wanted to pursue it, I was going to have to find out what was going on with the accounting, you know? Larissa told me to forget about it. Said it didn't matter, she'd make up the difference, and went on about how the cohesion of the coven was what really mattered. Our trust is our power, and all that. She's got more money than the queen, so I'm fine with that. It was Suzanne who wanted to pursue it."

"How'd she know about it?"

Ande had the grace to look sheepish. "I might have mentioned it when we were all getting our coats a week or two ago. She said she'd found something—and that she thought more of us should know—and promised to tell me. Only I never got to find out what it was. I thought she'd tell me on the ride home, but no luck."

"And you didn't follow up?"

A sad smile as she shook her head. "Frankly, I didn't

think it was a big deal, though it seemed to matter to Suzanne. I mean, we're kind of Larissa's pet project, and so if she didn't care about making up the difference, why should I, right?"

"I guess." Becca sighed. "I wasn't aware of any of this."

"Well, you've been dealing with your own stuff." Ande's voice was gentle. "We all know about the breakup and your job…" She didn't have to say more. Becca's eyes had already begun to fill again.

She blinked back the tears as Ande kept talking.

"Besides, it probably wasn't anything," she was saying. "Larissa thought Suzanne was just being paranoid. She'd taken to calling her 'zany Zane,' like she had gone utterly nuts. I thought that was a bit harsh. Honestly, it made me wonder if maybe Larissa had it in for poor Suzanne."

As soon as the words were out of Ande's mouth, she tried to backtrack.

"I don't mean it like that," she said, waving her hands again, as if she could clear the air. "Larissa wouldn't. She's not a killer. But she is a drama queen, and I thought maybe she was embarrassed that I saw how sloppy her bookkeeping was—or even that she was enjoying, well, pitting us against each other."

"She does like to be the center of attention." Becca looked thoughtful. "And when I found Suzanne, her door was open."

"Her door?" Ande sounded confused and gasped as the import of Becca's statement hit her. "You mean, like she opened it for someone? Oh, you can't mean…Becca, no."

"Did the police talk to you?" Becca answered Ande's question with her own, a curious look on her face. "Because they should really know about this."

"No." Ande started backing away. "They haven't. And why should they? I mean, all I can really say for sure is that Larissa is careless with her bank balance and she doesn't want anyone to know it."

"I don't know what to think." Becca laughed softly. "Because I told the police that Suzanne was my friend too, and they're still asking questions about me, Ande. They think I might have done it."

Chapter 17

"That's ridiculous!" Ande rejected the idea that Becca could be considered a suspect. "It had to be a stranger. She must have just opened her door to someone she didn't know."

Clara watched Becca as she listened to her colleague's increasingly heated protest. Ande's words echoed what Becca herself had said, her pet knew, and yet the focus visible on her person's face suggested that her own dear person wasn't accepting her own answer so readily from the other woman.

That focus seemed to grow sharper—and almost catlike—as Becca narrowed her eyes and pressed for more detail about the coven finances. If Becca had whiskers, Clara thought, they would have been bristling as Ande continued to stonewall.

"It's silly, really." The accountant fluttered those elegant hands as if she could dispel the thought. "Larissa doesn't care, so I don't even know why Suzanne bothered. Larissa is the one putting the money up." But when Becca pressed her about what else might have been worrying the dead woman, Ande only shook her head.

"She and I weren't that close," she kept repeating. "I mean, she asked about my work—she had only recently started some new job herself, something Larissa helped set her up with, so I think it was just conversation, you know?"

Knowing how limited human senses could be, Clara snuck up to the other woman at that point, sniffing at the accountant's chic boots to see if she could pick up on anything more than general distress. This close to a grocery store, such a task could be a challenge: the aromas of meat and fish, herbs and produce were as distracting as fireworks to acute feline senses. Before she could get a good take, Becca appeared to give up on the financial thread and instead began insisting that Ande inform the police about her conversations with Larissa. At that, Ande grew so distraught that she abandoned her errand, leaving before she had even begun her shopping.

But although the calico briefly wondered if Becca's mission would be similarly derailed, she soon realized she hadn't counted on her person's loyalty and focus. No matter what else was on her mind, Becca wasn't going to come home empty-handed. Of course, the flicker of fur Clara caught out of the corner of her eye as they entered the grocery might have had something to do with that. Clara didn't think either Harriet or Laurel could influence Becca's thoughts that much, but she was pretty sure they had found a way to keep both "cat" and "food" in the consciousness of their impressionable person.

"Don't you have any of the turkey treat?" Becca was evidently under Harriet's influence. The fluffy marmalade adored poultry flavors, and the shelf in front of her was fully stocked with Clara's favorite tuna feast.

"I'll check, miss." The harried-looking clerk took off, leaving Becca standing there. Clara did her best to concentrate.

"I wonder if the missing funds were really what was bothering Suzanne?" She reached and—yes!—took two of the tuna cans from the display as she mused. "But if there was something else going on, why wouldn't Ande tell me about it?"

She absently reached out, putting two more cans in her basket, and Clara began to reevaluate her own powers of psychic suggestion. "Just because they both dated Trent…"

By the time the clerk re-appeared, a case of the horrid turkey treat in his arms, she'd loaded up on Clara's preferred flavor. "Here you go." His smile looked a bit forced as he held the opened case out to Becca.

"Oh." She looked into her basket and back up at him. "Thank you," she said, taking two cans. Clara was grateful her distracted human couldn't see his expression as she turned toward the checkout.

"Maybe I should reach out to Larissa." Becca might have thought she was talking to herself as she paid for the cans, but Clara wondered if her person sensed her presence nearby. After all, she was missing an important element—the cat's concern over the direction her thoughts were headed.

"I mean, the police would never understand about the coven and why it matters," Becca mused as she loaded up her bag. "They'll just think she's a Cambridge flake, starting up a coven of witches in this day and age. But if there is something hinky with that bank account, and Suzanne found out, that could be something. As it is, they're only looking at Suzanne and Jeff, and if they find out Ande had gone out with Trent too, and Jeff tells them about Suzanne's necklace—"

Almost out the door, she stopped short, causing a businessman on his cell to bump into her. "Watch it, lady!"

She let him walk by in silence, a look of horror on her face. "If they look at my search history and see I was trying to find out about her…" Hiking her bag higher on her shoulder, she began to walk again, faster than before.

Chapter 18

Even if looks couldn't kill, Clara knew that by rights she should be singed hairless. Harriet was not happy with the selection that Becca unpacked, and from the way she glared at her baby sister, Clara knew her creamsicle sibling had sussed out that the little calico had made her preference felt.

"Honest, I was only listening." Clara protested in vain. *"I only wanted to keep her out of trouble."*

"Like you want to be the only one who can use her power," Harriet grumbled even as she played up to Becca, rubbing against her shins like she hadn't seen her in a week. *"Like you're the only one with any magic."*

"I didn't use any—" Clara stopped herself. *"I only passed through the door."* The little calico was fundamentally honest, but she knew better than to add that Laurel had been there too. Harriet was angry enough as it was. *"And I did remind her why she had gone shopping. She was getting distracted."*

"Right." Harriet grunted when she ate, which she did as soon as the first dish was placed on the mat. She might not like the tuna feast, but that didn't mean she was going to pass up a meal.

"You can make the other cans re-appear tomorrow." Clara tried to make nice. *"Besides, I'm worried about Becca.*

She thinks she needs to help the police solve Suzanne's murder."

"Not a bad idea." Laurel appeared with a yawn, as if from a nap in some other dimension. *"And she may have a chance to do some hunting tonight too."*

"Hunting?" Clara glanced up at Becca. She was listening to a phone message, a furrow appearing in her brow. *"But she's just come in. She's exhausted."*

Laurel only lashed her tail in dismissal, and so Clara turned back to their person. Becca was standing and staring at the phone, as if it had just bitten her. When it began to ring again, she jumped.

"Hello?" She sounded as breathless as if she'd just come in from a run. "Oh, Trent." She sagged against the wall. "I'm sorry, I just got your message. All of this with Suzanne, and now the police…" She paused. "It's a long story. I'm sure I can clear it up. You haven't spoken to them today, have you?

"Well, that would have been too easy." Even her voice was weary. "But how can I help you?"

Clara's hearing was as acute as any cat's, and the magic helped. Still, even with her black-tipped ears tilted forward to catch every sound, she couldn't hear more than a tinny voice saying something about "dinner."

"Tonight?" Becca winced. "Well, to be honest, I'm kind of wiped out. And Larissa said we're going to have our regular coven meeting on Wednesday." More talk that the cat couldn't hear. "Of course, you're right, Trent. I do have to eat."

Clara listened with rising panic as Becca's voice went softer and lighter both. "The River Café? Sure. That would be nice."

Beside her, Laurel purred and licked her chops as

Harriet scarfed up the last few crumbs of food in her dish and began to eye Clara's. But the youngest of the three cats blocked her sister out of habit, barely noticing as the orange and white fluffball flounced off. Because Becca had hung up, and turned toward the two cats who remained in the kitchen. For a moment, Clara almost thought Becca could see her concern.

"Well, kitties, I'm going out to dinner with the man who seems to be in the middle of this mess," she said, her voice growing thoughtful. "So now maybe I'll be able to get some answers." Clara knew then that her person hadn't understood her at all, and she looked at her sister in alarm. But Laurel only turned in that dismissive way that all Siamese have and began to bathe.

"I wonder what I should wear." Becca wandered out of the kitchen, not even noticing that Clara's dinner had barely been touched. "And if there's a spell that might help me decide."

Chapter 19

The hissing commenced as soon as Becca opened her closet.

"I cannot believe you want her to dress like that." Clara's fur had expanded in her rage. She was a small cat, but fluffed out like this, she could have covered the stretch velvet mini that lay on the bed. *"He might be dangerous."*

"Silly little girl!" Laurel spat back, her dark ears flat on her head. *"Don't you see? She could control the situation, looking so slinky."* Her blue eyes took in the velvet frock, although whether she wanted to scratch it or roll on it, her sister couldn't tell. *"If she brought him back here, we could question him. Only you—you—"* Her rage devolved into wordless spatter, and she turned her back on her sibling and proceeded to wash.

"You!" With one last exhalation, more sigh than hiss, Clara began to calm down. At least she had stopped her sister, slapping her on her chocolate nose just as Laurel had begun to work on Becca. Clara didn't know if it was because Laurel's powers were limited or her sister was simply lazy, but she did know that the other cat's ability to implant suggestions in others' minds was vague at best. If Becca hadn't already been considering her upcoming dinner a sort of date, Laurel might not have been able to steer her toward that short velvet number.

Still, it was a close call, and Clara wasn't able to relax until her person left the house in a flowered frock that fit her—and the occasion—more comfortably. If it were not for that well-placed bonk, Becca might have wiggled into that stretchy dress—and into more trouble.

"Spoil sport." Laurel muttered as she bathed. *"Now we're both going to miss the fun."*

Clara deflated, her fur settling in despair. It was true, her squabble with her sister had kept her in the bedroom too long. Without any idea where Becca had gone, she was at a loss—unable to follow. And so with one bound, she leaped to the windowsill. Nudging aside Harriet, who was napping again, she settled in to watch and wait for Becca to return.

***

"Merry meet, Becca. How are you doing?" Even giving the coven's ritual greeting, Trent's voice rumbled deep and confidential, and as his questions turned personal, Becca felt her color rising in response. "I've been so worried about you. I didn't want to wait until Wednesday."

Despite the melancholy motive for this get together, the setting felt distinctly intimate. Maybe it was because the waitress had led her to a booth in the back, rather than the open seats at the counter. Maybe it was the nice shirt the warlock was wearing, open just enough for her to see the glint of gold nestled in the dark hair of his chest. As he leaned forward, it bobbed, and she found herself staring—and wondering once more if she should have gone with the sexier outfit. She blamed her slight buzz. She should probably have objected when he'd ordered the pitcher of margaritas. She definitely shouldn't have taken such a big swallow, even if it was the house special, strawberry, her personal favorite.

"Thanks." She bent once more over the menu, hoping to hide her face, which felt as rosy as that drink. She was having trouble concentrating, and she didn't think it was just the alcohol. "I'm okay. It's just been exhausting."

"Of course," he said, his voice warm with understanding, and Becca relaxed. It would have been too odd to try to explain that she kept thinking about her cats. They were home, safe, and she was the one out. But even though she was sitting here—at the River Café with Trent—she kind of wished she was with them. At home. Snuggled up on the sofa. Trent, however, was doing his best to be solicitous. "You've probably spent way too much time with the police these last few days."

She nodded. "I know they're doing their job—and I want them to. Only they had me come in this morning, and it was, well, weird."

"I can imagine." His voice as soft as a purr. "They must have had a lot of questions."

She nodded. "They did." The margarita had been a bad idea. But he was waiting, his dark eyes full of concern. "They were asking about the coven and, well, about the man she was dating."

"Suzanne was seeing someone?" A note of excitement—or could it have been regret?—tightened his voice.

The effect must have been contagious, because all of a sudden Becca found it hard to swallow. "My ex." She choked out the words. "But I think that was over."

Thoughts of Jeff and of that last phone call on the stairs of Suzanne's apartment, and suddenly it all came back. Her voice caught in a sob, and Trent leaned forward, reaching across the table as if to embrace her. It was too much. Becca felt like a fool and drew back, embarrassed, even as she found herself staring once more at his chest—and at the gold medallion that had swung forward from inside his shirt.

"Is that…?" Becca stopped herself from stretching out her hand for it, silently blaming the margarita once more.

"A witches' knot." To her relief, he glanced down and grasped the gold medallion himself, holding it still to allow Becca to see the intricate looped design on its front. "You have a good eye."

His own eyes twinkled as he smiled, but Becca only shook her head, confused.

"It has charms on it, and not everyone would see it right away." His voice was low and conspiratorial. "But we already knew you have power."

"I guess." Becca turned away. Bad enough that she was out alone with Trent—a member of the coven who had romanced several of their colleagues already—she'd been caught staring at his chest. They were supposedly going to talk about the death of one of their own too.

"I'm so sorry," he said. Though if he meant in general or for reaching for her, Becca didn't know.

"Me too." She looked up into eyes that were shadowed and deep set. Could those be tears as well? Now it was her turn to reach out for his hand. "Were you and Suzanne close?"

A slow, sad shake of the head. "Not anymore," he said. "She'd been going through something, I think."

Becca nodded, her last conversation with the dead woman coming back to her mind. "I know she had questions." She bit her lip, unsure of how much she wanted to reveal. Trent was a friend, but still… "I think she was worried about money."

"Money?" Trent pursed his lips in thought. "Do you know why?"

Becca considered. "I'm not sure. You don't think that's why she was…" She swallowed. Hard.

"No, no." Trent rushed to correct himself. "I mean, I don't know. But, well, Suzanne had been acting odd for a while now. And you saw how skinny she was."

"Skinny?" She was sounding like a parrot. That margarita.

"Not an ounce of flesh on her." He had her hand now. His thumb brushed over hers. It was all too confusing. "Speaking of—should we order?"

Only then did Becca notice the waitress standing beside them, pad in hand. From the smile she suddenly dropped to the way she straightened, she must have been there for a while.

"Oh, sorry." Becca was too flustered to consult the menu. "I'll have a salad?"

"How about nachos for the table?" Trent leaned in with a conspiratorial smile. After that comment about Suzanne being skinny, his suggestion sounded flirtatious.

"Sure." Becca pushed her menu at the waiting server and eyed the margarita glass. "And, uh, a Diet Coke?"

She pretended not to hear the waitress's snicker as she walked off, instead steeling herself for the task at hand. "So, what have you heard?" As soon as the words were out of her mouth, she regretted them. She wasn't after gossip.

"Nothing concrete." Trent leaned forward again. "Just enough so that I was worried about her."

"Oh?" The server plunked down her new drink with a thud as Becca took a few moments to reorganize her thoughts.

Jeff had hinted that Suzanne and the warlock had had a brief romance, and Kathy had confirmed it. Trent seemed to be denying this. Or was he? Pushing the sticky strawberry glass aside, she took a swallow of the soft drink. More caffeine—that's what she needed.

"Poor Suzanne." When she put the glass down, she saw that Trent was shaking his head slowly. "I'm sorry I didn't pursue it."

Now she was getting somewhere. "Pursue it?" She waited.

"She was troubled." Another slow sad dismissal as the waitress slid a plate of nachos onto the table. "I should have—well, I knew something was bothering her. It was selfish of me not to get involved."

"Selfish?" That parrot again.

Trent didn't seem to notice as he pulled a chip free of the sticky cheese. "Her being so skinny and all. I don't know anything for sure." He looked up, his dark eyes as melting as that cheese. "But I was wondering if she was on drugs."

Their entrees arrived before Becca could respond. And while she tried to focus on her salad, the nachos were as tempting as all the unanswered questions that kept popping up.

"Drugs?" With her mouth full of cheese and chili, that was the best she could manage. "Did you tell the police that?"

"I didn't want to, how do they say, muddy the waters." Trent took a bite of his veggie burger and waited for her to answer. "You didn't notice anything?"

Becca thought back. "Only that something was bothering her."

"You see? I knew it."

That wasn't what she had meant. Only now, sitting

here, she had to wonder. Had Suzanne wanted to confess to a problem? Is that why she wanted to get Becca alone?

"Poor girl." Trent chewed thoughtfully. "I knew she was hard up for money too. So that might all be connected. I mean, I don't think she'd have asked you because we all know about your job and all."

Becca began to respond—to share what Ande had said—and then caught herself. She wasn't sure, but she suspected that the tall accountant had told her about the missing funds in confidence.

"What?" Trent's question caught her in mid-thought.

"Suzanne did want to speak with me, alone," Becca confessed, reaching for the nachos. "That's why I went over to her place on Saturday. You know, when I found her?"

"That's so sad." He shook his head. "I don't think you should bring this up when the coven gathers. Let her have her dignity."

Becca started to protest—Trent was the one who was suggesting the dead woman had a drug problem. But another thought interrupted. "And the police didn't ask you about any of this?"

"Nope." Trent's answer was cut short as he bit into a nacho. She didn't want to tell him about the string of cheese that had just caught in his beard. "Why muddy—"

He must have noticed her gaze, as he paused to fish out the cheese. "Sorry." His smile was charming.

"So what did the police ask you?" The caffeine was definitely kicking in.

"The usual." He waved the question off. "You know, how I knew her. Why I had her key. I gave them the parking receipt from the city meter, so they knew I'd only pulled up to her street after you arrived, so…"

His explanation ended in a grin. A guilty grin, Becca realized, as it seemed to focus suspicion back on her. "I was only there a few minutes earlier." She didn't like how defensive she sounded.

"I'm glad!" Those eyebrows again. "Maybe you got lucky. I mean, in the grand scheme of things."

Becca swallowed hard, the chip stuck in her throat. "Lucky?" The word came out as a croak.

"I mean blessed, of course. Beloved of the goddess. Think about it, Becca. We don't know if it was her dealer or just some random crazy off the street." Trent leaned in, his dark eyes aglow. "But if you'd been there a little earlier, Becca, it might have been you."

Chapter 20

"I can't believe you went out with him!" Clara's powers tended to accentuate her hearing, but even an ordinary cat could have heard the yelling over the phone. Becca's ex, Jeff, sounded like a tomcat whose tail had been stepped on. "He's a person of interest. Becca, are you nuts?"

Despite her own annoyance—she couldn't help but agree with the angry man on the phone—the calico was doing her best to soothe her person. Becca had slept badly again, even with her obvious exhaustion. And although Jeff's call had woken her from an early nap, she'd been plagued by scary dreams. That—and his apparent concern—had prompted her to tell her ex about her outing the evening before. At least, that's what Clara hoped had brought about the confession. As the little calico began to knead, working on Becca's shoulder as her person slouched on the couch, she looked around for Laurel. Her sister was definitely capable of using anything to provoke some interesting jealousy.

"Jeff, I was just telling you where I was." Becca's eyes were closing again. Clara could feel her fatigue and increased the pressure of her massage, hoping to relieve some of Becca's tension. "Ow, wait—"

She sat up, moving away from the calico. Across her

lap, Clara caught a glimpse of Laurel's smirk as her seal-point sister settled down beside their human. Drawing her own paws under her creamy chest, Clara considered. She didn't know if her sister was simply enjoying the drama or had an ulterior motive. Jeff had always been quite complimentary about Laurel's sleek markings. Clara glared at her sister, and felt her ears begin to flatten in anger. But then Becca began talking again, and Clara turned to listen in.

"It wasn't a date." Becca was using a particularly flat tone of voice that Clara recognized. It was the same tone that she used when she was pretending she didn't have any more treats. The man on the other end of the line seemed to recognize it too. Even before he began to speak again, she felt as much as heard the intake of breath that presaged an argument.

"Look." Becca must have heard it too, as she cut him off. "I'm involved in this. Suzanne and I were friends. Besides," her voice dropped to a near whisper, "she wanted my help, Jeff. That's why I went over there."

Laurel's ears pricked up as Jeff answered. Laurel always did have an instinct for scandal.

"This had nothing to do with you, Jeff." Becca, on the other hand, preferred her life to be straightforward, whether it really was or not. It was one of the reasons that Clara felt protective of her. "At least, I don't think so. Trent said—" The young woman paused, clearly gathering her thoughts. Across her lap, Laurel's eyes closed in pleasure. "Trent agreed that something else was bothering her. So if there's anything that we can tell the police—"

Another burst of noise from the phone. Clara was leaning in, but lost the thread as her oldest sister landed hard beside her.

"Are we having treats?" Harriet pushed by Clara on her way to Becca's lap. *"Why didn't anyone wake me?"*

"I was here first." A hint of a growl from Laurel, but Becca was too distracted to notice. To the cats' dismay, she stood up and began pacing. And while Laurel and Harriet stared at each other from opposite ends of the sofa, Clara jumped down to follow their person around the apartment.

"Yes, I know what you told the police, Jeff." The note of tension made Clara's spine stiffen. "But that just made them suspect me, and I know I didn't want to hurt her. She is—was—a friend, and I found her. So, yeah, I want to help."

She stopped so quickly that Clara nearly bumped into her. It was only the round little calico's feline grace that allowed her to swerve in time to brush by her person's ankles instead.

"What are you talking about, Jeff?" Becca's voice had gone cold, and Clara peered up, trying to see her face. "Why would I need a lawyer?"

***

"You're not the one who needs a lawyer." Maddy showed up soon after, bearing scones and sympathy. Although Clara wasn't sure exactly how it worked, it was obvious that Becca's furious typing on her laptop had communicated the latest. Still, it was Harriet who had first spotted Becca's old friend—or at least the bakery box she carried—and jumped heavily from her window seat to greet the plump young woman with a purr. "Oh, what a nice cat!"

Maddy bent to stroke the fluffy marmalade's back as Harriet reached up to nose the cardboard box.

"You can't think that Jeff…" Becca turned back toward

the kitchen. After a night tossing and turning, she trod as heavily as Harriet. "That he would…"

"I don't know what to think." Maddy stood, to Harriet's dismay, and followed her friend into the apartment. "But they had been seeing each other, and Suzanne wanted to talk to you. And now he seems to be keeping tabs on you awfully closely." She placed the box on the table and pulled up a chair.

"Maybe she found out something about him. Maybe he's lying about breaking up with her. Maybe she dumped him, and he didn't want it to end."

Becca winced, and even Harriet looked up. Although that, Clara realized, could have been because her fluffy sibling was hoping the shock would result in a dropped scone.

"Maddy." Becca slumped into her own seat.

"I'm just saying…" Maddy opened the box and suddenly, Harriet was staring daggers at her. "I never really liked him."

"Drop one. Come on!" Harriet was muttering, a low rumbling that could almost be mistaken for a purr. *"You're feeling clumsy…"*

"Hush, I'm listening," Laurel responded, appearing under the table. Becca would say "out of nowhere," Clara knew. But that was Clara's special skill. Laurel simply had an appetite for gossip that matched her older sister's taste for sweets.

"You didn't?" Becca stopped, plate in hand. "Really?"

"He always thought he was too good for you." Maddy took the plate and opened the box. Two scones. Harriet's ample bottom began to twitch as she readied for a jump.

"No!" Clara's paw came down on her sister's tail, and Harriet turned, too affronted to protest. *"Sorry."* Clara pulled

her paw back. *"I want to hear. I'll owe you,"* she hastened to add.

"You sure will." Harriet flicked her tail out of reach, secretly grateful—Clara suspected—that she didn't have to try for the tabletop.

"He didn't." The hurt in Becca's voice made both cats look up.

"I wouldn't have said anything if you'd stayed together." Maddy broke off a piece of one scone, and Harriet licked her chops. "And, hey, maybe I was wrong."

Becca was slumped in her seat. "No, Jeff never wanted us to be serious." The accent she put on the last word made Clara's fur bristle. "He said we weren't ready."

"Good riddance." Maddy kept eating. "Because if 'being serious' is what happened to that other woman? I'd say you're better off."

Becca nodded, not even objecting to the circular logic of her friend's argument. "I guess," she said. "I mean, no, Maddy. Jeff's not a…a killer."

"There's a lot about that man you don't know." Her friend popped the last bit of pastry into her mouth and glanced up at the clock. "Hey, I should be getting to work."

"Wait, what do you mean?" Becca reached for her friend's arm. "What aren't you telling me, Maddy?"

"Oh, honey." Maddy bit her lip. "Let him go, okay?"

"Maddy." Becca was growing more insistent.

"Look at the facts." Her friend leaned on the table. "This is a man who would throw you to the wolves. Why else is he keeping such close tabs on you?"

"Because he wants to get back together?" Becca's voice faded out even before she finished—and brought her friend in for a hug.

"That makes no sense. I'm sorry, Becca. I really am, and I feel awful about leaving you like this. My boss…well, you've heard it all." She said it apologetically, though whether that was because she was leaving her friend in no better mood than she'd found or because she still had a job, Clara couldn't tell. "Do you mind?"

Harriet began to whine, and Clara turned in dismay. But her sister's golden eyes were riveted on the table above them. Maddy had stood and was reaching for the box. Becca hadn't touched her scone and pushed the plate toward her.

"No, you take it." Becca forced a smile. Beneath the table, Harriet lashed her tail. Clara was going to have a lot to make up for.

***

After her friend left, Becca fetched her laptop, settling on the sofa with the same resigned posture Clara was growing accustomed to. Torn between jumping up beside her—she didn't think her person was beyond distraction—and trying to find out more, Clara turned toward her sisters and blinked, the feline version of an invitation to chat. But, whether because they were her older sisters or simply because of the nature of cats, they resisted.

"Why?" Harriet was still staring at the kitchen table, the lost treat a personal affront.

"So we can figure out how to help Becca," Clara explained. *"I think she's worried about Jeff, and you know how she is. Even if he did try to set her up, she's going to want to clear his name."*

"By looking into a murder?" Laurel was intrigued, but Harriet simply glowered. In this state, she'd likely pin it on

Maddy.

"She is our charge." Clara hoped the appeal to Harriet's vanity would ease the way.

"I should just make a knife like that one she used on the cake, and let Becca find it," the long-haired sister grumbled. *"Only I'd want to put it in that scone stealer's back. Who brings treats and then takes them away again?"*

Clara held her tongue. Harriet had a point, but Laurel came to the rescue.

"The calico clown is right." She rolled the R as if she were purring. *"The way she's going, Becca's not going to be good for much soon. And besides"*—the Siamese paused to lick her paw, a purely dramatic move—*"if we can get her out of this slump, she's more likely to bring home a new man. A new man who wants to win our approval."*

The way she stretched out that last word made her intentions unmissable. Laurel wouldn't stop at using her powers of suggestion, but Clara couldn't argue this time. Especially since Harriet had come trotting over.

"Maybe I should make a knife appear—someplace convenient, like in the kitchen." She tilted her head to better take in their person, who was still typing away. *"That might make her do a thorough search. Pull things out of cupboards, and the like."*

"*No, please."* Clara turned from one sister to another. *"The police probably have the real one and any others will just confuse things."*

"Suit yourself." Harriet began to bathe, working on one fluffy hind leg as if it were a drumstick. *"But you said..."*

"I know." Clara sighed. *"But I worry that anything so... creative will only make things worse for her. Becca is so down*

already."

"If I could've gotten her into that outfit..."

"That wouldn't have solved anything." Clara cut her sister off. It was time for drastic measures. *"Hang on. I want to see what she's searching for with that machine."*

Leaping up beside the seated girl, Clara willed herself to be if not invisible then at least not easily detected. That went against the grain for a cat, and she could feel her two sisters eying her with curiosity. But unlike the usual morning, when Clara would be the first to rub her head against the young woman's arm and try to cheer her up with a rousing purr, right now, Clara wanted to pass unnoticed. Better that Becca should keep on with whatever she was typing, so Clara could figure out what to do next. Clara knew that cats can't read, per se, but they can get a lot from the images on a screen—even without psychic powers. But just as Clara crept close enough to focus, Becca closed the laptop and reached for her phone.

"I'm just being silly," she said, turning toward the cat. "And I've got you kitties depending on me."

Clara looked on in mute sympathy as Becca dialed. "I'm calling for Eric Marshfield." As she spoke, she sat up, her posture as crisp as her diction. "Mr. Marshfield," she said a moment later. "Thank you for taking my call. I'm contacting you about the open position? I couldn't see a way to submit a resumé on your site." The voice on the other end caught her up short. "I gather it's data entry, but I can promise you that I—" Another pause. "I'm sorry, a friend told me about it. I gather it hasn't been posted yet. Shall I send you my resumé anyway?" This time, Becca was holding her breath. "Well, then, thank you again for your time, and I'm—"

She stared at the phone as if the device had bitten her.

***

"Nexus?" Clara muttered to herself, sounding out the word she had heard her person mutter only moments before. Then the screen changed, and she understood. Becca still had the library access she had used in her last job. Good, the calico thought. Becca was good at research, and it made her feel better about herself. But the next screen that came up only made the little cat's whiskers sag. Becca wasn't reading up on criminal law or even the forensics of a stabbing. No, as the branching chart materialized in the screen in front of her person, Clara knew the situation was dire. Becca was once again tracing her own lineage in the futile search to uncover the magical roots that, in truth, led to Clara and her littermates.

"This is worse than I thought." Clara jumped down as soundlessly as she had ascended, ready to address her sisters.

"Oh?" Laurel flicked her tail. Harriet, Clara noted, was already curling for her mid-morning nap.

"Becca thinks she can do this by herself.." Clara turned back. No, the young woman was still at it. *"She thinks she can do it with magic."*

"Fine, let her." Harriet wasn't going to forget that missing scone. *"What do we care?"*

This time it was Laurel who swiped at her. Though whether that was out of sympathy with Clara or simply because she enjoyed provoking her fluffy sister Clara didn't know for sure.

What she did know was that Becca needed her. Needed them all, actually. That was why they'd been placed with her. And although her sisters seemed to believe that such placement was random—much as Becca voiced the opinion that she'd "adopted" all three cats of her own free will—Clara knew better.

"Hecate, come to me!" While still seated on the couch, Becca had raised her hands from the keyboard. Head back, she opened her arms, as if readying for an embrace.

"Oh! That's my cue!" Harriet wiggled her plump bottom, readying to jump.

"No!" Once again, it fell to Clara to restrain her oldest sister.

"What's the matter?" The marmalade cat turned, her pique evident in her flattened ears. *"You don't want me to materialize anything? You said it yourself, Becca needs help."*

"I don't want you to encourage her." Clara's voice sank to a hiss. *"She's not a witch. We've got to stop her from thinking she is."*

"Huh." Harriet turned and began to groom. It was a dismissal, but Clara was grateful that her sister wasn't going to put up a fight. *"We could end this once and for all,"* Harriet muttered, her mouth full of fur. *"I could summon a knife and place it at that scone stealer's apartment, and Laurel could get the police to go look for it, I bet."*

"That wouldn't solve anything." Clara had given up arguing with Harriet and simply stared at their person. She was trying desperately to think, and her sister's interruption wasn't helping.

"She's right, of course." Almost soundlessly, Laurel had joined them on the rug. *"The clown, that is. We send Becca after the wrong person and, if we're not careful, she'll get killed too."*

The Siamese didn't seem too distressed by that thought, but Clara turned to stare at her, her own fur standing up along her spine.

"*What*?" One syllable was all she could manage.

"*Someone is out hunting.*" Laurel looked up, her blue eyes cool and inscrutable. "*Who's to say that our little Becca wouldn't be next?*"

Chapter 21

That question was only one of the many Clara was still mulling over when Becca finally gave up, forty minutes later. By then, she'd tried a scrying spell, an incantation supposed to make the hidden known, and fifteen words of power guaranteed to grant wisdom.

As Clara or any of her sisters could have told her, none of them had a chance of working. Human tongues are simply unable to give the spells the proper feline pronunciation. As it was, the calico had gradually grown grateful for her person's distraction. As she sat on the sofa, entranced by Becca's gestures and strange pronouncements, she had had time to run through her own list of possibilities—many of a more mundane kind—searching for an answer.

"I should just implant the idea that she drop the whole thing." Laurel had woken from her nap and now stretched, extending her claws dangerously close to Becca's leg. *"This obsession is becoming quite dull."*

"No." Clara resisted the urge to bat at her sister. It wouldn't do to provoke her. *"You were right, what you said. I'm worried that she's in danger."*

Laurel tipped her head, regarding her baby sister anew. *"Really?"* Her voice dripped with something akin to skepticism. *"You care about her that much?"*

"Of course!" Clara's response was automatic, and then she caught herself. "*You do too. Don't you?"*

Laurel gave the feline equivalent of a shrug, the velvet fur of her shoulders twitching as she rearranged herself on the cushion. She would never, Clara knew, admit to having bonded with a human. Still, she had to love Becca, didn't she? Becca had taken them in. She was their person.

"She's competent," Laurel said, a bit begrudgingly, and Clara bit back her own reply. From her sister, this was high praise. Besides, Becca was finishing up.

"It's no use, Clara." She addressed the little cat with a sad smile. "Maybe all the magic I have was used up on that one pillow. Only, you'd think…" She closed her laptop and stood with a sigh. "I mean, this is important."

Clara butted her head against Becca's thigh. Her jeans were soft and warm, and the hand that came down to fondle her ears gentle. "You guys probably just see me as a walking dispenser of treats," she said. Across the room, Harriet's ears pricked up. "But I know what happened. I have power, and I should be able to use it. I mean, someone killed Suzanne, and I'd like to think it wasn't someone in the coven…"

The hand on Clara's head froze, and before she knew what was happening, Becca was typing once more. "Maybe, it wasn't us. Ande said something about a new job…" The hopeful tone had the calico purring, only to stop as suddenly as Becca did. "No!" One word, exhaled in a start.

Before Clara could even figure out what had happened, Becca had risen once more. Grabbing her phone, she began pacing. "Come on. Pick up!"

But the young woman's invocations to the cell gods had

no more power than any of her other spells, and soon she had dropped onto the couch again, the phone still and silent in her hand.

"I can't," she said, turning to the cat beside her. "There's no way to leave a question like that in a message."

Clara stared up, feeling as blind and powerless as most mere mortals must. All she could do was blink in support, but Becca didn't even seem to notice. In fact, the young woman was staring into space with such intensity that Clara found herself compelled to follow her gaze. No, nothing there. Nothing one small cat could see, at any rate.

"Larissa." Becca mouthed the name of the coven's oldest member and then bit her own lip as she read the images she had summoned. "Could she know?"

Clara was itching to understand. If the older woman knew more about the murder, wouldn't she have shared it? As she watched, wide-eyed, Becca stood once more and reached for her phone.

"Larissa?" Becca's voice sounded too light, like she was forcing herself to sound happy. "I'm so glad I caught you. I know we're meeting tomorrow, only I was wondering if I could talk to you privately first. What about? Oh, that position you mentioned to me, and some other things. Would that be okay?" She paused, and appeared to hold her breath. "Great!" The word rushed out as if in relief. "I'll be over in a few."

Clara watched as Becca grabbed her jacket and threw her laptop into her bag. The calico followed her gaze as she took in Harriet, dozing on the windowsill, and Laurel, whose complete unconsciousness was revealed by her most undignified sprawl. Just to be sure, Clara dabbed at her tail, one leather paw pad gently brushing the guard hairs along its edge.

In response, the appendage flicked, and its owner shifted, one dark foot extending up into the air, as she rolled onto her back. Out cold, good.

"Bye, kitties." Over by the door, Becca called softly. A plaintive note in her voice alerted Clara to her slight unease. No, this wasn't a social call. Her person was going hunting, or some version of the same. Using her real down-to-earth skills, Clara realized Becca was trying to uncover the truth. And once more, Clara was going with her.

***

Becca didn't take the T, and for that her cat was grateful. Using her powers and the mottling of her coat to fade into the few shadows of the bright spring day, Clara could have followed her person anywhere—even down into the subway and beyond. But like all cats, Clara detested loud noises, and even as Becca strode past the station entrance—the shaded calico hard on her heels—she could hear the roar of the steel beast below. As Becca kept walking, Clara felt herself relaxing, her open-mouthed pant subsiding once more and her tail perking up, as the roar of the city gave way to the quieter streets down by the river. This was better, she thought. Almost as if Becca were a cat herself.

That thought faded as the young woman approached a gleaming tower as threatening as a trap and as out of place in the quiet neighborhood as a dog in a cattery. Becca herself seemed to have a moment of doubt. She stood, head back, examining the looming modern structure that reflected the glare off the river, her hands knotted together in what Clara recognized as the human equivalent of a self-calming groom. Then, as if the caress had indeed given her courage, she strode down the concrete approach, pulling open a steel-and-glass door so heavy it nearly swung shut before Clara could slip inside.

"Larissa Fox." A doorman blinked at her, his face impassive. "17 F, I think?" Becca added, and he shoved a book toward her to sign. While she did, Clara scoped out the lobby. Two plants, in the corner, wouldn't offer much in the way of protection. She lowered her head, willing herself to become more deeply cloaked, and then trotted along behind the young woman as she headed toward the elevator.

***

"Becca, you poor dear! Blessed be!" Larissa ushered the younger woman into her apartment so quickly, Clara barely had time to follow. Once she did, however, she found plenty of cover. The lobby of the high-rise might be modern and spare, yet Larissa's space inside it was anything but. Potted plants clustered around a freestanding bookshelf that served to separate the entranceway from a large living room. Hanging lamps inset with stained glass cast colored shapes on the rugs, which overlapped, almost tripping Becca as her host led her to a wide, low-set couch covered with bright, patterned throws. More lamps at either end were dimmed by shawls, their fringe so enticing that Clara forced herself to turn away.

By then, Becca was seated, her slight form almost disappearing in deep, plush upholstery. An image of Harriet kneading those pillows sprang into Clara's mind, and she willfully dismissed it. As much as she knew her sister would adore a setup like this, Clara had more important concerns right now.

"Please." Larissa was handing Becca a saucer, on which stood more colored glass. Green this time, with a filigree pattern. Clara's discerning nose sniffed at the steam that rose from its gold-rimmed edge. This wasn't the usual foul brew. "You must be distraught."

"Thanks." Becca took a tentative sip. "Peppermint!"

"It's healing." Larissa settled next to her, one hand brushing her long, dark locks out against the cushions in an almost feline fashion. "How have you been, my dear? Not taxing yourself emotionally?"

"I don't think so." Becca had to struggle a bit to lean forward but managed to place her glass on a brass tray that rested on the nearby footstool. "Thanks for seeing me. I mean, alone." She made another attempt to sit up and only succeeded in sinking deeper. "I was hoping you could tell me more about that position?"

"The job with Graham? My old friend—mentor, really—he's so much older than me, of course. But are you really ready to talk about this, my dear? It's been such a trying week! I was thinking we should gather and do a cleansing circle for you. For dear Suzanne too, of course."

"Of course." The smile on Becca's face was as strained as that tea. "And, well, that's part of what I wanted to ask you about."

"Oh?" Larissa's hands fluttered like busy moths, rearranging the throw on the back of the sofa.

"I gather Suzanne was concerned about the coven's finances." Becca stopped at that, though by the way she was biting her lip, Clara could tell she wanted to say more.

"Dear Suzanne." Larissa's musical laugh sounded a bit forced. "She worried so, and about nothing. And you're so sweet to ask. You know, I do believe there's a reason you found dear Suzanne. You've always been the most gifted of our little coven. You and Trent, of course. But then, he's special in so many ways."

"Trent?" Even Becca's all-too-human ears must have picked up the off note in the older woman's voice. "How do you mean?"

"Well he's our very own warlock, of course." Larissa's kohl-lined eyes cast down, as if following the pattern in the throw, before darting up again. "And, of course, he does like to do a little outreach, doesn't he? You must know something of that, my dear."

Becca was too unworldly not to flinch, although in the dim light the color rising to her cheeks was probably not immediately apparent. "He's been concerned about me after… after Saturday. And, well, he cared for Suzanne too."

"Of course." Larissa sat back. "We all did. Now, would you like me to talk to Graham for you?"

"I was hoping you could give me an introduction." Becca managed to sit up straight finally, propping herself up on the pillows. "Just to get me in the door. I'm guessing that's what you did for Suzanne, because she'd recently started a job that you'd referred her to as well—a position at Reynolds and Associates. Didn't she? And it turns out my friend Maddy works there too."

Chapter 22

"Come on, Maddy, pick up." Becca was back on the sidewalk less than an hour later. Her visit with Larissa had raised more questions than answers. The older woman had laughed off her earlier referral—"Graham does run through his worker bees!"—despite Becca's attempt to shock her into any kind of revelation. And despite three more distinct attempts to raise the issue of the coven finances, she'd been unable to get any kind of proper response to those questions either. In truth, the older woman's defense—that their accounts mattered little and had no impact on the coven's weekly functioning—had begun to sound increasingly sensible, supporting Ande's assertion and leading Becca to wonder if Suzanne had indeed wanted to speak to her about something else entirely.

Maybe, Becca mused, she simply had finances on the mind. Although the older woman had promised to call this mysterious Graham for her, Becca was no more convinced than she'd been earlier that she had a lead on a new job. In fact, once Becca had realized that Larissa's "old friend" must be the same grumpy Mr. Reynolds she'd been hearing Maddy complain about, she was less likely to pursue a position—especially one that, as she already knew, called for qualifications she didn't possess. Still, she was intrigued as to why neither Larissa nor Suzanne had ever mentioned this particular connection. Or, for that matter, why her old friend had never said anything about working with the dead woman.

"Maddy, it's me." Becca made an effort to hold her voice steady. "Call me, please? It's important."

While Larissa had brushed off her earlier referral of the other coven member as a mere triviality, referring vaguely to the intimacy of their world and the necessity of distributing what she called "patronage" among those she knew, the question had seemed to upset her. She'd spent the rest of the visit fussing with the upholstery and avoiding any direct questions about her supposed friend—or mentor, as she'd begun to term him—whom Maddy had always described as a bitter old man, his mind—and office demeanor—stuck in a century or maybe two prior. Somehow, Becca couldn't reconcile that with what she knew of Larissa, and that left only her friend to explain.

As Clara watched from underneath a forsythia in full bloom, Becca stared at her phone. That she could no more will it to ring than she could summon that pillow only made the little cat's heart ache for her person. It must be so hard to lack power over the world, she thought. If only…

"Becca?" The cat and the girl she loved turned at the sound of a male voice, warm and friendly. The blond painter, almost unrecognizable in a sport jacket, was striding up the walk, a wrapped bouquet in his hands. "What a surprise!"

"Nathan." Becca smiled despite herself, and tucked her phone into her pocket. "Hi." But as she took in his clothes and the flowers, her cat heard her gasp. Disappointment, waiting to happen. Before she could say anything, the painter was talking again.

“It’s good to see you again. I was hoping to hear from you—or run into you.” That smile seemed at odds with the nice clothes. The flowers. “I know this is a small town, but I’m sorry I ran out yesterday. The whole thing must have gotten to me more than I’d admitted to myself.”

Becca nodded. “Me too.”

“I’ve been thinking I was a fool for not getting your number yesterday.”

Becca held her breath once more, this time with anticipation, and Clara looked on with concern. Those flowers… “You don’t…you don’t live here, do you?”

“Me? No.” Nathan chuckled at the idea. “I was visiting someone—a relative. And you?”

“Same. I mean, visiting. Larissa Fox.”

“Ah.” He nodded, a sly smile tweaking the corners of his generous mouth.

“You know her?” Becca saw it too. “She’s…well, she’s part of a group I’m in. We meet once a week to discuss, well, paranormal events.” She looked down, and so didn’t see his smile spread into a grin.

“And let me guess.” Whatever humor was behind that smile now gave his voice a lilt. “She finances it—or some part of it—and thinks that her money gives her special rights over all of you?”

Becca recoiled slightly. “I…that’s not entirely fair.”

His brows went up.

“Well, maybe a little.” Their eyes met, and for a moment, Clara felt a tingle of magic in the air.

“Hey.” He broke the silence. “If I don’t get these flowers up soon, I’ll be in trouble. May I call you?”

“Yeah.” Becca was beaming. “Yeah, I’d like that.”

She was still humming to herself as she hit the street, and it wasn't until she had turned the corner that she stopped short. "He didn't take my number." But the dismay on her face quickly resolved into a chuckle. "Small town," she repeated, and walked on, so lost in thought that she almost didn't hear her phone.

"Maddy?" She stopped and swallowed. "Look, Maddy, we really have to talk."

***

Both Laurel and Harriet were at the door when Becca and her feline shadow returned. And while their sister wasn't sure if their restless circling had more to do with the approach of dinnertime or their person's anxiety, Clara joined them in circumambulating her feet.

"What's gotten into you three?" Becca caught herself. Laurel was, as always, graceful, but Harriet's decision to stop short and wash her face had nearly sent their person flying.

Still, their mobile presence served its purpose. Two purposes, actually. Becca dropped her bag and immediately went to fetch their cans, prompting a smirk from Harriet. *"See?"* She mewed over her shoulder as she led the way into the kitchen. *"I can make more than a pillow appear!"*

"We didn't get any answers out in the world, but something's up," Clara warned her siblings, even as she waited for her dish to be lowered to the floor. Laurel turned toward her, her blue eyes skeptical.

"Don't mind her," Harriet muttered as she ate. Out of habit, Becca fed her first, having learned that the big marmalade would take the first dish set down anyway. *"She's just trying to distract us."*

"No, I'm not!" Clara rarely got angry at her siblings,

but Harriet was being particularly obtuse. *"Don't you see? Something's wrong."*

"Yeah, we still don't have the good flavor," Harriet mumbled as she lapped.

"That's not..." Clara gave up and sat, looking anxiously up at her person.

"You don't want that?" Harriet didn't wait for an answer, and Clara ceded the space in front of her dish, following Becca, who was pacing around the apartment. Not that her person noticed. In fact, twice Clara had to jump out of her way as a foot came dangerously close to her tail.

***

None of the activity served to distract Becca, however, and the calico grew increasingly worried about her person, whose unsettled behavior led to another fitful night. By the next afternoon, Becca's edginess had agitated all three cats. It was bad enough that she had tossed and turned in bed, but as Wednesday progressed, Becca wouldn't even sit still with her computer. Instead, she seemed to be avoiding the warm machine, and that meant naps for her pets were limited as, by silent accord, they kept watch, circling her until Becca, in her preoccupation, actually stepped on Harriet's tail.

"I'm going to make a tree house for myself!" The fluffy feline licked the appendage furiously, more because of the insult than any real injury. *"I'll climb way over all your heads!"*

"Harriet, please," Clara pleaded.

Laurel only rolled her blue eyes. *"The day you climb is the day I eat a bug."*

Clara opened her mouth—and quickly shut it. Laurel prized her reputation for finickiness, and it would do none of them any good for Clara to point out that her seal-point sister had done just that last summer, when a particularly tempting moth had gotten inside.

When the doorbell rang late in the afternoon, Clara breathed a sigh of relief. Any interruption had to be better than this ongoing nervous activity. At this rate, Clara thought, they'd all be hissing at each other by nightfall.

"Maddy." Becca sounded a little breathless, the result of all that pacing, Clara reasoned to herself. "Come in."

"Becca." Her friend seemed tired too, and dropped her bag on the floor before slouching onto the sofa. Done with her dinner, Laurel came over to investigate, sniffing delicately at the leather bag. Harriet, Clara noted with a touch of dismay, was still in the kitchen, cleaning up the crumbs of the other cats' meals.

Becca settled beside her friend but didn't relax. Clara didn't know if Maddy could tell, but to a cat, it was easy to spot the tension in her person's posture. "So, you knew Suzanne," she said.

It wasn't a question, but Maddy nodded slowly. Becca drew her feet up beneath her. If she could curl up into a ball, she would, Clara thought, and jumped up beside her. "Maddy?" Her voice was tight, as if she needed to swallow. "Is there something you want to tell me?"

Her friend turned to her with a look of such horror that a slight moan escaped from Becca's opened mouth. "No, Maddy. You couldn't have…" She shook her head slowly, as if to ward off the awful truth. "The cake server…"

"I couldn't? Oh, no!" Maddy reached out to grab her friend's hands. "No, Becca. No matter what I felt, I, well, it was almost like I forgot."

"You forgot?" Becca was breathing easier, but her brows were knit in confusion.

"I'm sorry." Maddy didn't look any more comfortable. If anything, she seemed to sink further down on the cushions while her friend waited. "I wanted to tell you."

"What, that you worked with a member of my coven? Jeff's new girlfriend? The woman who was killed?" Becca tried out the options, rejecting each in turn. "But you couldn't have known what was going to happen—so, why didn't you say anything?"

Maddy twisted in her seat as if she could avoid Becca's gaze. "I told you I kind of knew who she was, when I ran into them in the Square. But it was before that—before I realized who she was—I mean, in your little crew…" Taking a deep breath, she began to talk again, and as if a dam had burst, this time, the words rushed out. "It was right after she started, in February. She was standing in the lobby when I went for my lunch break and I thought I'd ask her to join me. Just to be friendly. Only there was something about the way she was standing, kind of fussing with her hair before she put her hat on, and I realized she was probably waiting for a date. Well, I hung back for a minute—just to see—and, sure enough, her date showed up."

Maddy fell silent, as if the flood had left her exhausted. "It was Jeff, Becca," she said at last. "She was waiting for Jeff."

"But…February? We were still…" Becca sputtered. "Maybe they were friends. I mean, they probably knew each other."

Maddy's face told the story. "Knew each other? Becca, honey. He was a creep. I always felt something was off about him, but I didn't know what to say."

"Maddy, you don't know." A note of desperation had crept into Becca's voice.

"I know you don't kiss your casual acquaintances." Her friend delivered the coup de grace. "Not like they did, anyway."

***

Maddy left soon after. She would have stayed—had wanted to comfort her friend, it was clear to see—but Becca shooed her off. "I can't," she said as she pushed Maddy's bag back into her arms. "I need to process this, but I can't—not now."

Maddy had protested. "Come on, kiddo," she'd said. "Let's go to a movie. Or better, to that cupcake place in the Square."

"No, I've got…an appointment." The way she stumbled over the word had Maddy looking at her funny.

"You're not doing that witch thing tonight. Are you?"

"We…we need to meet. To talk about Suzanne—and to figure out what's going on," Becca confessed. "I mean, for closure and everything."

"Becca, honey."

"Please, Maddy. I've got to get ready."

Maddy looked like she'd swallowed a bug, and not a very tasty one at that. Still, she allowed herself to be hustled out the door with a final protest. "Call me, Becca?"

Only then did Becca allow herself to collapse, throwing herself on the sofa with a sob.

"Jeff." One word said it all, and Clara brushed her head up against the hands that covered Becca's head, hoping to offer the comfort of soft fur. A slight thud behind her alerted her to

Laurel's arrival. For once, she was pleased to note, her sister didn't dish up any snark and instead stretched out alongside the crying girl. Before long, Harriet joined them, landing with an audible grunt. Despite—or perhaps because of—her hogging of their dinner, she accepted the remaining position, by Becca's feet, lending her warm bulk to the sisterly effort.

This wasn't their usual mode of magic. But Clara could feel the purr as it rose between them, and if the three felines couldn't right all the wrongs of the world—or of a certain faithless boyfriend—they could at least set a certain cosmic vibration in order. In their presence, Becca went from tears to silence and then, Clara suspected, a short nap. When she sat up, about an hour later, her breathing had returned to normal. And although her eyes would be swollen for some time, as she wiped her face, she glanced around with clarity and maybe even, Clara thought, a new purpose.

She also, on seeing the clock, began to panic. "Seven thirty!" She jumped up, discomfiting the cats.

"Ungrateful," grumbled Harriet. Becca had been careful not to kick the plump cat as she rose, but she had straightened out the cushions behind her, which Harriet had arranged for peak comfort.

"Typical," noted Laurel as she stretched. The Siamese sister knew what all the fuss meant and was readying herself to be admired.

Only Clara remained silent. She saw how their person bustled about with renewed purpose and considered herself amply rewarded. *What's the use of power*, she thought to herself, *if it can't be used to comfort those we love?*

Chapter 23

The doorbell interrupted all their musings—as well as Becca's last-minute attempts at soothing her reddened eyes. Drying her face with a washcloth, she called out a greeting. A moment later, she was opening the door to Larissa and Trent, both of whom reacted to her appearance.

"You poor dear." Larissa pushed her way past Trent in a swath of multicolored silk and kissed the air beside both of Becca's damp cheeks. "You must be absolutely bereft. I wanted to get here early to give you a hand."

She followed this embrace with a pointed look at Trent that seemed to demand an answer. "I'm sorry." His handsome face appeared drawn with concern. "I guess we both had the same idea. Merry meet, Becca."

"Merry meet." Becca managed a wobbly smile. "It's good to see you both. Come in."

Larissa took charge, as usual, ushering Becca into the kitchen with a sweeping gesture that released a cloud of patchouli.

"I'm sorry." Becca did her best to summon a smile, even as she blinked. Clara, at her feet, sneezed quietly, while Laurel winced and stalked off. "I haven't put the water on or anything."

"Nonsense, dear." Larissa craned around until she saw

the kettle, then gestured Becca over toward it. "Would you? My sleeves."

Clara watched as Becca complied. Having something to do certainly seemed to settle her person, but the calico couldn't help but wonder at the older woman's apparent helplessness as she ordered Becca around.

"No, dear, fill the pot with hot water, then pour it out. You don't want to brew your tea in a cold pot." With a flick of those sleeves, she herded Becca toward the sink, then followed to stand close behind her. "I wanted to speak with you before the others arrived."

She turned theatrically as if she could see through the wall to the foyer and the door beyond. When she began to speak again, her deep voice was abnormally soft.

"I don't think it would be healthy to mention our chat yesterday." Even muted, her suggestion had an air of command about it. "About Graham and all. You are one of my favorites, but it wouldn't do to sow dissent."

"Of course." Becca's open face showed her confusion. "But…you've encouraged me before. Right here, last week, and if you did the same for Suzanne…"

Larissa's sleeves fluttered as if she were patting down an animal. "There are too many factors, my dear. Things might be misunderstood."

"But—" Becca paused, her brow wrinkling in a look of intense concentration. It was almost as if her whiskers were bristling, thought Clara. If Laurel had looked like that, it would have meant prey was about—and in danger. But whatever observation Becca was about to make was cut off as Ande rushed into the kitchen.

"Oh, dear! How are you?" She hugged Becca, who was

still holding the kettle. "I mean, blessed be—and, please, let me."

Unencumbered by flowing clothing, Ande took the kettle and set it to boil, freeing Becca, who turned to Larissa once more. But the older woman simply raised one manicured finger to her lips and then left the kitchen as dramatically as she had entered, a sweep of her long sleeves wafting patchouli behind her.

"Phew, what's that smell?" Ande's nose wrinkled up. "It's not the cats, is it?"

***

As this was not their usual meeting, Larissa had not brought her special tea. Instead, Becca was pleased to find the scent of a spicy mint mix—akin to what they'd enjoyed the day before—soon filled her small apartment, almost drowning out the older woman's perfume.

"To promote healing," Larissa explained once they were all gathered around the table. "And to ease our dear sister's spirit onto the next realm, of course."

"Of course," Kathy echoed as she reached out to pat Becca's hand. "That should be our main goal."

Becca managed a tight smile that even from over on the couch Clara could tell was forced. Her human colleagues appeared to notice this too, as Ande and Marcia exchanged a look that could only be described as weighted.

"I was thinking a sunset circle." Larissa addressed a space somewhere above the gathering, and Clara tilted her own head back to see if perhaps a fly had gotten in. "By the river, perhaps."

"A circle?" Becca broke into the other woman's reverie.

"To concentrate our energies," Marcia explained. "You

know, because we won't be at the funeral."

"We won't?" Becca was full of questions.

"Oh, dear, I guess you hadn't heard?" Larissa turned toward their host. "Poor, dear Suzanne's parents are having her interment back in Connecticut." Her crimson lips formed a moue of disapproval. "Such negative energy."

"Oh." The small, sad sound made Clara long to leap into Becca's lap. "No, I hadn't heard."

"We haven't wanted to burden you. I spoke with her employer, of course." Larissa blinked, as if holding back her own tears, which was probably why she didn't notice Becca lean forward. Clara perked her ears up, waiting for Becca to speak. "More tea?" Larissa got there first, and Becca sat back again, holding her mug close.

"Well, since there's no great urgency, shall we wait for the solstice?" Trent, Clara noticed, had been strangely quiet until now. "That might be auspicious." He looked around at the coven, moving from Marcia to Ande to Kathy to Becca before pausing, it seemed, at Larissa, to his right.

"That's a bit of a wait." Ande sounded doubtful—and Clara saw her turn toward Marcia.

"It's too long," Kathy responded, before tiny Marcia could. "That's more than three weeks from now. Better to do it sooner. We need to let her move on." She might have been speaking of Suzanne, but she was looking at Becca, who slouched back in her seat.

"Darling, are you all right?" Larissa reached for her, but Becca pushed her chair back.

"I need a little air." Leaving the table, she walked into the kitchen.

Laurel and Clara followed, and found Harriet waiting.

"Treats?" The big marmalade rubbed her considerable bulk up against her leg, and then grunted as Becca hauled her up into her arms.

"What a pretty kitty." Ande had followed her in. "May I?"

Harriet accepted the gentle pet as her due, while Laurel looked on. Becca, however, just stared out the window.

"I just can't stop thinking about her," she said, her voice barely above a whisper.

"Of course." Ande bit her lip. "But you can't think that you…"

Becca shook her head. "I was just wondering about what you told her."

"What was that?" Trent had appeared, but Becca only shook her head. "Are you okay, Becca?"

"Yeah, thanks," She released Harriet, who shot an evil glance at the warlock. "It's nothing."

Without offering up any treats, she rejoined the table, where Kathy, Marcia, and Larissa were deep in conversation.

"Luz thought it was probably random," Marcia was saying as Ande and Trent took their seats. "A robbery gone bad."

"I don't want to suggest anything." Kathy's voice suggested anything but. "Only, do you think, maybe, it wasn't an accident that Becca found her?"

"What?" Her person's uncharacteristic squeal made Clara's fur stand on end. Even Harriet looked up. "Me?"

"I mean, because of your conjuring." Kathy scanned the table for support. "Maybe if you make something appear, then you also…well, you know."

"Now, Kathy." Trent was the voice of reason. "That's

not how the rule of three works. If one of us does something malicious, then that will come back three times. I don't see how a mere pillow–"

"I'm sorry." Becca pushed back from the table again. "I don't think I can do this—not tonight."

"Of course, it's all my fault." Kathy went to her and reached to draw her into an awkward hug. "Trent's right. I shouldn't have said anything."

Obviously, no further planning was going to be done. And although Harriet looked up expectantly—fewer of the cookies had been eaten than usual—Clara felt for her person. She was glad when Larissa signaled the end of the meeting, shooing Ande and Marcia off with the mugs and the teapot. Becca watched as they cleared the table and excused herself to follow. She found the two huddled over the sink, rinsing dishes, as Harriet, who had followed the food, stared in rapt attention.

"This isn't the time." Marcia seemed incapable of speaking softly, but her tone implied a confidence, even if her volume—quite audible over the running water—didn't. Neither was paying much attention to the fluffy feline at their feet, or to the two other cats who sauntered in to join her.

"Excuse me?" Becca, however, wasn't so relaxed, and her voice was sharp enough that even Harriet's concentration was briefly broken.

Marcia and Ande glanced at each other before Marcia turned the faucet off. "I'm sorry," said Ande, dishtowel in hand. "I spoke out of turn."

"If either of you know anything, you really do need to come forward." Becca studied the faces of the two women. When Ande dropped her eyes to the floor, she turned to Marcia. For once, the petite Sox fan was silent, her lips tight set as she reached for a towel to wipe her own hands dry.

"Ladies?" Larissa, calling from the front of the apartment. "If you're done with clean up…"

"Coming!" Marcia hung the towel over the faucet and leaned over to give Becca a quick hug. "Thanks, Becca." Neatly sidestepping the three cats, she left.

"Ande?" Becca leaned in, cutting off the taller woman before she, too, could escape. "What was that about?"

The remaining guest folded her towel in her hands and peered ruefully toward the living room. "I can't," she said.

"If this has to do with the money that went missing…"

"No, it doesn't." She shook off the idea, running one hand over her face as if to wash it. "And really, Larissa just wants to forget about the finances. I shouldn't have said anything."

From the living room, the sound of laughter, and Larissa called again: "Hulloo!"

"Ande?" Becca wasn't giving up.

"Look, it's not my secret to share." Ande forced a smile. "It's just—well, I guess it's true that you never really know what's going on in someone else's relationship."

"Is this about Trent?" Becca's voice squeaked. The warlock's deep voice could be heard by the front door, warm and jocular. Clearly, the general mood had recovered. "I mean, the cops spoke with him too."

"I can't believe you two." Kathy stood in the doorway, her freckled face unexpectedly stern. "Trent doesn't need money."

"I didn't…" Becca closed her eyes and sank back against the sink in exhaustion. "We weren't…."

Clara rose to go to her. It was quite apparent that some

feline comforting was needed. But Laurel had one brown bootie firmly on the base of her tail.

"Hang on," her sister hissed. *"I want to see how this plays out."*

Clara glared, but in that moment, Ande had gone to Becca in her place, draping one arm around Becca's shoulders. "There, there, honey." She pulled her close, murmuring like a mother cat.

"Did you know the red-haired one was listening?" Clara nudged Laurel as the two looked on. Harriet, sensing that no cookies would be forthcoming, had padded back into the living room.

"Just the last bit." Laurel shrugged and lifted her paw. *"I wanted to hear more too. That grooming behavior..."*

"I know," Clara agreed, grateful to have her tail released. *"Do you think she feels guilty?"*

"Becca's been through a lot, Kath." Before Laurel could answer, Ande had turned back to the redhead. "Let's cut her some slack, okay?"

"Of course. I'm sorry, Becca." Kathy reached out with both hands. "I can't imagine. I guess we're all on edge."

"Thanks." Becca choked out the word as the redhead drew her into a hug. "I just need to get some sleep."

"Valerian," Kathy pronounced sternly. "And, Ande? We should get going."

"Will you be okay?" Now that she wasn't being questioned, Ande seemed reluctant to leave.

"Yeah, thanks." Becca pushed off the counter. "It's just been a long week."

"It's Wednesday," said Kathy, earning a poke from Ande. Becca didn't respond, beyond holding on to that sad, tight smile as she walked her guests to the door.

Minutes later, she was stretched out on the couch. "Oh, I'm sorry."

She moved her feet as Clara jumped up to join her. It had been a stressful visit, and the little calico was as tuckered out as her person. For once, she had Becca—and the end of the sofa—to herself. Harriet, still annoyed about the missed opportunities in the kitchen, was prowling about, muttering about cookies and treats and the stupid, ungrateful creatures with whom she was forced to cohabit. Laurel, meanwhile, was lingering by the door, though if it was because of the residual patchouli or some other trail, Clara couldn't tell. As Becca's breathing slowed and deepened, the tired calico felt her own lids start to close and she fought to stay awake. So much had happened that she needed to ponder, but it had indeed been a very busy couple of days.

The gentle tap on the door woke Clara first. Stretching, she peeked over the arm of the sofa to see Laurel staring expectantly at the knob. From the way she lashed her chocolate tail, Clara knew her sister was expecting that door to open.

"*Who is it?*" Clara landed as soundlessly as a cat can and kept her mew soft as she approached her sister. Laurel's blue eyes remained riveted, as the knock was repeated, a little less softly.

"*Maybe if you'd paid a little more attention...*" The tail lashing quickened, as if the Siamese were readying to pounce.

"*To what?*" Clara sat beside her, wrapping her own tail neatly around her front paws. "*I was focused on Becca.*"

"*You weren't the only one.*" Almost a purr, this time, as the knocking grew louder and more insistent.

"Hang on." Clara's whiskers sagged. The sound

had woken Becca, who was now shuffling toward the door. "Trent!"

Clara turned as her person straightened up, one hand going to her hair. Beside her, Laurel gave her a knowing sidelong glance. *"See?"*

"I'm sorry." The warlock's voice was as warm as his dark eyes. "I woke you. I could tell how exhausted you were, but I thought maybe…" He dipped his head shyly.

"Please, come in." Becca stood back to let him enter. "Yeah, I fell asleep." She rubbed her face. Clara couldn't understand why her person should sound so apologetic. Napping was not only healthy, it was the appropriate reaction to many things, stress being one of them.

Trent passed by her and entered the apartment.

"I'm sorry." There she was, apologizing again. Clara was beginning to get as agitated as Harriet. "Did you forget something?"

"Only my manners." The dark-haired warlock turned to her. "I'm the one who should be apologizing. This whole evening." He looked around, as if their coven were still assembled. "I know that it's important to talk about what happened and to plan a memorial. But it was too soon. I should have known."

"It's fine, really." Becca perked up a bit in the warmth of his gaze. "Would you like something? More tea?"

A soft laugh. "Please," he said, "I don't think I could. I only wanted to make sure you were all right."

"Oh." A soft mew of disappointment. Laurel, meanwhile, was leaning against the visitor's shins so aggressively that he almost stumbled as he tried to step forward. "Please, won't you sit for a minute?"

"Well, if I'm not interrupting."

Now it was her turn to chuckle. "I think I was just kind of overwhelmed. Who knew not doing anything would be so exhausting?"

"Who said you're not doing anything?" Sidling around the feline, he took a seat on the sofa. "Living the self-directed life—being freelance—takes more energy than simply punching a clock."

"But I'm not freelance. I'm just unemployed." Becca settled in beside him, and for once, Laurel did not insert herself. Instead, she sat back and, when Clara approached, swatted her sister. *"Stop that!"* The hiss as swift as the paw.

"That's still stressful." Trent sounded as if he knew. "And, of course, you're still processing the grief and the shock, I would imagine."

"I guess," Becca acknowledged. At their feet, the two cats faced off.

"What are you playing at?" Clara's murmured question only earned her a fierce stare.

"Just...watch." The low yowl was unmissable.

"Your cat makes such a funny sound." The two felines looked up to find the guest watching them. "They're sisters?"

"Yeah." Becca nodded. "I know it's odd, but littermates can have different fathers, and Laurel's definitely got some Siamese in her. They're, well, more talkative than other cats."

Trent nodded, as if he understood. Laurel blinked at him slowly. Even if he couldn't make sense of her vocalizations, thought Clara, surely, he would get that the slinky feline was flirting with him.

"Kind of like some of our coven mates." He turned toward Becca, a hint of humor softening his words.

"Oh, they're not so bad." Becca was looking at her hands, Clara noted. And while they were very clean, gentle hands, the calico could not see what made them so interesting at that moment.

"I don't know." Trent must have admired her hands too. He'd reached over to place his own over hers. "They were a bit much tonight. Admit it."

His tone begged for a response. "Well, Larissa can be a little demanding," she conceded, peeking up at him.

"Tell me about it." He chuckled softly. "But I was thinking more of how you were attacked in the kitchen."

"I wasn't attacked." Her demurral as soft as Clara's mew. It didn't matter. Whether it was the word or some latent gifts that Clara didn't understand, Harriet had heard her and came trotting into the room. *"Did someone say 'kitchen'?"*

Those wide yellow eyes turned from her two sisters to take in the humans seated so close as to be almost cuddling on the couch—and became almost saucer-like as Becca pulled back.

"Actually, I'm glad you came back, Trent. Because I realized I still have some questions…"

"I have some questions too," Trent interrupted, his voice soft as velvet, as with one finger, he turned her chin to face him.

Becca gave a slight squeak, as if a mouse were hiding in the depths of her throat, and blinked as if transfixed. Clara looked on in dismay, wondering if she should interrupt. There was no way Harriet would put up with being so ignored.

"Becca?" Trent's voice was soft and insistent as he leaned in, apparently unaware of the hefty marmalade who had bounded up onto the sofa.

Neither was Becca, it seemed, an oversight that Clara could not comprehend, as her plump sister had landed beside her with a noticeable thud. But even as she opened her own mouth to mew a warning, she heard a soft growl of warning.

"Don't you dare." A hiss as soft as a sigh. Laurel, her blue eyes glowing with anticipation.

And suddenly, Clara understood. Finger still beneath her chin, Trent had lifted Becca's face and leaned over to gently kiss her lips. The sound she made in response—as faint as a kitten's whimper—seemed to encourage him further. Shifting on the sofa, he leaned forward to pull her close. The gold amulet swung from his open shirt, almost as if it too wanted to make contact with the person Clara most loved.

For a moment, that gold pendant was the only thing moving, swinging back and forth in the space between the two humans as they kissed. It was mesmerizing, Clara had to admit. That steady motion. The glitter as the engraving caught the light. Beside her, on the floor, Laurel had begun to purr, the rhythmic sound matching the back and forth, back and forth.

And then everything changed. Trent shifted, moving one arm around behind Becca as if to draw her closer still. But Becca pulled back, ever so slightly, to address the dark-eyed man. "Wait, Trent, I need to know—"

Before she could finish her question, a sound like the grinding of gears caused them all to turn. Harriet had had enough. And whether she growled because of her annoyance over the lack of cookies or other treats, or whether the hypnotic swing of the amulet had been too much for her subjugated hunting instincts, Clara didn't have the chance to inquire. As her complaint modulated into a high-pitched whine, the plump marmalade launched herself over Becca and onto Trent's lap, landing with a thud that made the young couple flinch.

"Ow!" Trent jerked back. Of course, thought Clara, Harriet would use her claws. But whether it was her size or lack of agility that had made her dig in, it did Trent no good to pull away. Those yellow eyes were focused on one thing—the glittering toy that had swung so provocatively only seconds before. And with one fat paw—Harriet's fluffiness extended even to her white mitts—she swiped at her prize, knocking the shiny piece off its chain and sending it flying across the room.

"Harriet!" Becca was off the couch, even as Trent squealed. "Bad girl. Bad! I'm so sorry." Trent pressed his hand to his pillaged chest. "Trent, are you all right?"

"I think so." He glanced down to check his fingertips.

"Are you bleeding?" Becca returned to the sofa and nearly climbed into her guest's lap to check.

"No, I'm fine." To Clara's surprise, he retreated. "It's just a scratch."

"Here." Becca bounced up again. "Let me get you something to put on that. Her claws must have gotten stuck in the chain or…something." Her words trailed off as she ran to the bathroom. Clara could hear her rustling under the sink.

"She could just say fur." Laurel leaned in, apparently amused by the whole adventure. *"He has a thick pelt."*

"She's distressed." Clara contemplated going after their person, but she had emerged, cotton balls and a bottle of rubbing alcohol in hand. *"He's a guest."*

"Could've been more," Laurel purred. But the romantic mood had definitely been dispelled.

"No, really!" Trent backed up as Becca approached, holding out one hand as if to ward her off. "I'm okay."

In truth, Clara could almost understand. The rubbing

alcohol smelled foul, its stench so sharp and biting that the three cats retreated to the window. That might have been why the man had stood and was stepping backward, but when he suddenly fell to all fours, the calico grew concerned. Straining to see, she stood as tall as she could. Luckily, at that moment, Becca closed the noxious bottle and, as the fumes began to disperse, got down on her knees beside her guest.

"I'm so, so sorry," she said again as they prowled around. "Harriet's got quite the swing."

Clara waited for Trent's objection, but heard none. Perhaps he hadn't time, because within a minute, Becca called out, "I think I've found it!"

Harriet's swipe, it seemed, had sent the amulet across the room, where it must have slid beneath the overstuffed armchair. Unless… Clara turned to her older sister, but the plump marmalade only glared, her yellow eyes as poisonous as the stink from that bottle.

"Where? Oh, I see it." Trent crawled over toward the chair, nearly knocking Becca over in his rush. "I think I can reach it." Beside her, Clara felt Harriet shift and wondered if her sister was going to jump down in order to reclaim her prize. But either the effort wasn't worth it, or the man on the floor was too quick. Even as Becca was reaching out—one arm extended beneath the chair—he managed to snag it.

"Is your amulet okay?" Becca sat back on her heels. Clara thought she would want to inspect it, but Trent had already shoved it in his pocket after the most cursory of inspections.

"Yup. Dandy." He spoke as if he'd reassure her with such jolly words. But if Becca thought that all had been set right—and that her visitor would pick up again from where he had left off—she was in for a rude surprise. Leaning on the chair, Trent pulled himself to his feet, and although he did offer Becca his hand, he made no effort to draw her close again. In fact, he seemed to recoil a little when she stepped forward.

"I think I need to call it a night." He smiled as if offering an apology, and some of the warmth came back to her face.

"Of course." Becca nodded a bit too enthusiastically, Clara thought. "I'll—well, I'll see you at the next coven meeting, I guess."

"See you then." He slipped out almost as quietly as Clara would, leaving his hostess dumbfounded. And the three cats muttering on the windowsill.

"*Well, that was interesting.*" Laurel began to wash.

"That was my toy. Mine." Harriet stared after the departed visitor, her orange-tipped tail lashing in delayed fury. *"I never liked that one,"* she said.

Beside her, looking on as their person stared vacantly at the door, Clara could only agree.

Chapter 24

Despite another night of tossing and turning that discomfited all three of her cats, Becca faced the day with a new determination.

"It's not my place to figure out what happened to Suzanne," she told her pets as they gathered around her in the kitchen. Neither Harriet nor Laurel were listening, their gaze fixed instead on the can opener she was wielding. But Clara's ears perked up as their person kept talking. "And I'm not going to waste any more energy on Jeff, either. I don't care about his excuses anymore. He and I are through."

That resolution, as much as the assurance in Becca's tone, set the calico purring as the three bent to their breakfasts. Even Harriet seemed to have a good appetite, despite her dislike of the infamous tuna treat. Still, Clara couldn't but be a bit distracted as Becca left the kitchen without preparing anything for herself. When she heard her open her laptop, she looked up in concern.

"You going to finish that?" Clara felt the nudge of a wet nose and looked over to see her biggest sister staring down at her can. *"'Cause, if you're not..."*

"All yours." Clara lowered her head, blinking slowly as a sign of affection and submission. She'd eaten enough, and she owed her oldest sister. Besides, right then, Becca was her

priority.

Even before Harriet could finish what remained of her food, Clara was beside Becca, perched on the arm of the sofa as her person typed on the keyboard.

"Dear Mr. Reynolds," Becca read aloud to herself as she pecked away, which made things easier for Clara. "I'm writing on the recommendation of Larissa Fox…"

"What's going on?" Laurel landed beside her and immediately began to groom.

"I'm not sure," admitted Clara. *"I think she's looking for another job."*

"Too bad." The Siamese extended one dark chocolate paw. *"She needs to focus more on us."*

Before Clara could respond, their person had stood. Reaching for her phone, she punched in numbers and began to pace.

"Mr. Reynolds? Thank you so much for getting back to me." A pause. Despite her sister's assumed nonchalance, Clara could tell that Laurel was listening too. "Why, yes, thank you. I would love to come in tomorrow for an interview."

"Now you've done it," Laurel snarled as she and Clara watched Becca head off to shower and start her day.

"What?" Clara didn't understand her sister's pique.

"Pushing her to be all proactive. To go outside, and all." As she spoke, Laurel stepped down onto the sofa cushion their person had just vacated, carefully arranging herself in a perfect circle. *"If she'd kept that handsome Trent here, she wouldn't be running off."*

"That wasn't me." Clara bristled at the injustice. *"It was Harriet who went for that pendant he was wearing."*

"But you've been following her, and I know she senses

your presence. Pushing her to ask questions and uncover every little thing." Laurel was beginning to doze off, which was never her most logical mode.

"Besides, if Becca were still in bed, then we wouldn't have had breakfast." Harriet had finally joined them, licking her chops.

"I don't think it's bad for her to go outside." Clara knew she was in the minority, and the sidelong glances of her sisters confirmed this opinion. *"Besides,"* she added as a way of making peace, *"I doubt she's leaving right away."*

"You heard her." Harriet was in a mood, and Clara kept silent. Most cats live in the present, which makes the idea of "tomorrow"—or of any appointment, really—hard to grasp. Luckily, it also keeps them from worrying too much about the future or even holding on to a grudge for too long. Indeed, by the time Becca returned, showered and dressed, and sat back down on the sofa, Laurel and Harriet had seemed to forget their earlier pique. As Becca typed, it was Clara who grew concerned. Surely, it wasn't good for a healthy young woman to spend an entire sunny spring day indoors. Not even a sweet one who had been through the mill recently, both personally and professionally.

"What are you complaining about?" Laurel's fangs showed as she yawned, and her claws unsheathed as she stretched. *"This is perfect!"*

"I don't know." Clara didn't want to leave Becca's side. Still, she found herself pacing as the morning passed. She was even grateful when Becca picked up the phone again, as poor a substitute for fresh air and real contact as it might be.

"Hey, Maddy." Becca sounded happy, at least, and willing to forgive her old friend her well-intentioned lapse.

"You wouldn't believe what I just found in the genealogy archives. A woodcut of my great-great-whatever. Oh, and I've got an interview! Call me?"

Harriet was asleep on her pillow by then, and Laurel halfway there, her dark-tipped tail lashing languorously across the sofa. Clara, however, found herself intrigued by Becca's message, and when she jumped to the back of the sofa, she realized why. There—on the screen—was a picture. All lines and in black and white, it took a moment for the cat to make sense of it. An image without a scent is only half what it should be to most cats. But as she stared, she had the most profound realization. There, on the computer screen, was a print of her great-great-great-great-great-grand dam. The witch cat of Salem! Standing next to a nice-enough looking lady. A woman who—Clara leaned in to get a better view—kind of looked like Becca, if Becca had grown her hair long and then tied it all back in a knot.

"Laurel, check this out." Clara nudged her sleepy sister. *"It's Grandma."*

"It's a box." Laurel stretched and rolled over. *"A box you can't even sit in. Though it is warm..."*

"No, look—" But before Clara could convince her sister to try to make sense of the flat, odorless image, the phone had rung again, and Becca, reaching for it, had closed the electronic device.

"Maddy? Oh." From the way she straightened in her seat, Clara could tell that her person was surprised. Not unhappy, though. "Hi, Nathan. I was expecting…someone else."

Clara angled her ear and was able to pick up the voice of the painter, if not his pleasant pine scent.

"I realized I should take the initiative." A nervous edge—or maybe it was the connection—pitched his voice high and brittle. "I know you've been through so much, but I was hoping we could get together, if you've got time."

Poor connection or not, Becca's face lit up as he spoke, in a smile that warmed Clara like a purr—at least for the few moments before her brows drew together in consternation. "Wait, how'd you get my number?" There was a sharpness to her voice that made Clara take note.

"I have my ways." Clara heard Becca's quick intake of breath. "I'm sorry, not funny." Apparently, Nathan had too. "I got it from Larissa." The answer came quickly and easily, his tone calming down to what the little cat remembered. But something about the way Becca had tilted her head—her lips tightly closed—made her pet think it wasn't sufficient. "I mentioned meeting you to her the other day, when we ran into each other."

"Uh-huh." Becca wanted more.

"She seems to think we should get to know each other." He laughed. "I know, pushy, huh? But you can ask her. I gather you're getting together for a memorial tonight?"

"Tonight?" Becca started and then caught herself, as if the man on the other end of the line could see her. Then she paused, and to her cat she appeared to be wrestling with a question other than the one she had just answered. "Look, Nathan, can I get back to you? This is an odd time."

Clara couldn't help but feel a bit disappointed when she rang off and, instead, began fiddling with her phone, tapping away at the device with her thumbs. While it was true that none of them knew this young man, the plump feline had liked his scent. Even more, she had liked the way he had treated Becca, taking her out for treats after that disconcerting meeting with the police. But Becca wasn't Harriet, and if she had doubts, they were probably sensible, the pet reminded herself.

Still, the little cat looked up hopefully when the phone rang again. Becca was no house pet to spend all her time on the sofa.

"Maddy?" She'd grabbed up the phone without glancing at it.

"Sorry." Even before she saw Becca's shoulders' drop, Clara knew. It was her person's ex.

"Jeff." No greeting, nothing cordial, and a new note—defiant—had crept into Becca's voice. "What do you want?"

"Look." His voice had an edge of panic. Or maybe it was desperation. "I'm sorry, all right? I was a lousy boyfriend and I'm sorry. I really—I guess I was afraid of the commitment, or of how I felt about you." Laurel couldn't have rolled her eyes any harder. Jeff must have heard something because he suddenly broke off. "Look, Becca, don't hang up. I'm sorry, okay? I mean it. And when I told you that I'd broken up with Suzanne, I meant I was going to. That going out with her was a mistake, and even before she found out I was your boyfriend, I was going to end it."

"So she was the one who ended it." The words leaked out as sharp as Laurel's claws. "Of course."

"I was going to stop seeing her. Really." She didn't respond, but before he could hang up, he tried one more time, his voice pitched high and desperate. "You've got to tell the cops that, Becca. I mean, I had no reason to want her dead."

Chapter 25

"Excuse me?" Becca's default mode was polite. "I, wait, what?"

"Just, don't take our relationship stuff to the police, okay? This is serious."

Polite, but still furious. "Jeff Blakey, if you think that I've been airing my personal laundry to the police…" She stopped with a sputter. Her outrage was convincing, but Clara could tell that, for the moment at least, the angry young woman standing before her was concerned that she'd done just that.

Luckily, her ex didn't know her as well as her cat did. "I'm sorry, Becca, but I think someone's been telling them things, and, well, you're the only one who makes sense."

"Oh?" She leaned back against the sofa, waiting.

The answering sigh would have been audible, even to non-feline ears. "I thought I was in the clear, but then I was called in to answer some more questions about Suzanne, and it was kind of obvious they came from someone in your, you know, your group."

"The coven?" Becca straightened.

"Uh-huh. There was a lot about if I knew how often you guys got together, and what was my involvement. I told them I didn't know anything. That you and I had broken up before you got really into all that Wicca stuff. But this one cop, he kept pushing. Asking me why I was, you know, seeing two of you, and what that meant."

"What that meant?" Becca pronounced the last word as if it tasted bad, and Clara licked her whiskers in sympathy.

"You know." The man on the phone was at a loss to explain. "What was it about your witchy stuff that attracted men. Whether you girls had some kind of competition going."

"Uh-huh." Becca bit her lip. "And you think that this means that they suspect you?"

"What else?" His voice was cracking. The fatigue had broken through into desperation. "They questioned me for more than an hour."

"Uh-huh." The way Becca was nodding, Clara knew she was digesting his words slowly, as if they were a bit of gristle. "Maybe you're right, Jeff. Maybe they were trying to get you to confess to being something more than just a nasty cheat." A sputter came through the line, but Becca kept talking. "But if you ask me, what they're doing is something else entirely. I think they're asking you about me and my friends for a different reason. I think they suspect one of us in the coven."

Jeff had the grace not to sound too happy about that idea. Or maybe, Clara thought, the callow young man simply lacked the sense to follow Becca's reasoning. All she could tell for sure was that despite some vague protests, Becca was able to get him off the phone fairly quickly. And if Clara had worried about her person's lack of drive before, now she faced the opposite fear. Instead of settling back on the sofa, where Laurel was snoring gently, Becca became a whirlwind of activity. Picking up the few dishes she'd used, she muttered to herself like a discontented cat, until, finally, she disappeared into her bedroom and began throwing clothes around, emerging at last in an all-black outfit that seemed at odds with the beauty of the day.

"Okay, kitties." Laurel had woken and joined Clara in staring at their human. Even Harriet roused herself to look up. "I'm going to be out for a while, but don't worry. I'll be back in time for dinner."

"Really?" Laurel yawned and began to groom, her spirits if not her fur unruffled by the turn of events. *"Do you think she expects us to respond?"*

"I don't know," said Clara as she checked her own tail and whiskers. *"But I fear she's going hunting, and not for the kind of prey that would feed any of us."*

***

Her coat neatly groomed, Clara waited by the door until Becca left, slipping out only after the dark-haired girl, so as not to cause her concern. But as she followed her person's rather hurried steps, the little calico began to have apprehensions of her own. Becca was upset, that much was evident. That she had felt spurred to action by the phone call—or maybe both phone calls—was also evident. What Clara wasn't sure of was what her person intended to do about it.

Surely, the cat thought as she trotted to keep up, Becca wasn't going to meet Jeff. Nor would she likely be heading back to the police, not after what she'd said on the phone. Cats may not understand the ins and outs of law enforcement, but they tend not to believe in closed doors of any sort, as anybody who has cohabited with a feline knows.

Still, the determined young woman marched on, her slight stature giving her an edge as she wove through the workday crowd. For her cat, it was a bit more difficult. Keeping herself semi-shadowed meant she had to be more careful of feet as she ducked and dodged down the crowded city sidewalk. When Becca turned off the busy main street, her pet breathed a sigh of relief. Even magical cats have a hard time out in the world. But as Clara looked around, the realization of where her person was headed made her catch her breath in a way no near miss by a pointy toe could.

Suzanne's apartment. The triple-decker with its fresh coat of paint looked as cheery as could be on this sunny day. Still, Clara was grateful when her person stopped short of walking up to the clapboard building and mounting its three white steps. Not that she was easy with the way Becca stood on the sidewalk opposite, considering.

"I wonder who lives downstairs?" Becca voiced her thoughts. "And what they heard?"

This, her cat knew, could not end well. Surely, if the police were talking to Becca's ex, then they must have interviewed the neighbors as well.

Of course, being a cat—and a shadowy one at that—Clara could check out the two lower apartments. In fact, she realized, it wouldn't be difficult to slip inside the front door and at least take in the scents of the inhabitants.

The first floor, she could tell right away, was the home of an older woman. Even from here, she could sense that simply from the combination of aromas: peppermint tea and the sharp tang of a muscle rub, leavened with the not unpleasantly musty smell of old books. The couple on the second floor were likely academics, she figured, from the amount of paper rustling in the slight breeze that made its way inside. They'd been gone for several days, Clara gathered from the dearth of any other sound, as well as a certain stillness of the dust. Probably since Suzanne had been found there, she realized. Cats, like most humans, have an aversion to violence, but the parti-colored feline couldn't quite understand why people would leave *after* an attack. Surely, that young couple—French, she decided, from some faint herbal quality to their kitchen—must have realized that the violence above them was over by the time they took off.

All she would have to do would be to cross the street. Clara took a deep breath. Cloaked as she was, no car would see her. Dare she risk it? For Becca she would, she decided, and glanced up at her person, only to see that she'd extracted her phone from her pocket.

"Hi, Nathan?" Startled, Clara sat back down on the sun-warmed sidewalk. "It's me, Becca. I was thinking and, yes, I'd like to get together," her person said. But all the time, the cat at her feet could easily see, the young woman was staring at the building before her.

Chapter 26

Nathan had been right. The coven had voted not to wait for the solstice. "None of us want to rush you, my dear, but it simply wouldn't do to put off the inevitable," Larissa had said when Becca reached her that afternoon, in response to the flurry of texts. "We need to focus on the goddess."

"Too long to wait," Maddy had interpreted, when Becca had explained to her friend why she'd be busy later. "She wants to get back to being the center of attention."

"I gather everyone else agreed," Becca protested mildly. Marcia, sequestered in her law office, had been particularly keen on acting sooner, Larissa had told her, and as soon as Marcia had spoken up, Ande and Kathy had chimed in too. Trent's opinion wasn't cited by the older wiccan, but Becca certainly wasn't going to reach out to him after what had happened. If Larissa said they were all on board, she'd accept that.

"Like they had a choice?" Maddy snarked.

"You've not even met Larissa." Becca didn't really disagree with her friend's assessment of the situation, but she did feel honor bound to speak up for the older woman. "That is, unless she works with you too."

"Very funny!" Her friend had been wise enough not to take offense. "Just don't stay out too late, okay? I want you to bright-eyed and bushy-tailed for your interview with old Reynolds."

***

In truth, the sun had barely begun to set by the time the coven had gathered. However, the lengthening shadows did make it easier for Clara to follow as her person made her way to their meeting place by the river. The setting, the little cat had to admit, was perfect. Although cars roared by as commuters made their way home from work, the gently sloping bank was grassy and fragrant from the sprinkling of wild flowers along the verge. Already, the water reflected as much orange as blue, the surface broken only by the wake of a single sculler passing by, silent as a water bug.

"Becca." Larissa had, as anticipated, taken charge, and was greeting each member of the coven as she arrived. Despite the usual handicap of draping sleeves and an impressive manicure, the dark-haired witch had already set up a small folding table with a jug of what looked to be cider and a plate of cookies that Harriet would have made quick work of. "Kathy." The older woman nodded as the redhead came down the path. "Merry meet."

"Merry meet," Becca responded, spotting Ande over by the river's edge. The tall accountant had her hands in her pockets and appeared to be staring at the reflections that wavered and took on new shape in the water before her. As Larissa began to fuss with the refreshments, Becca took a few careful steps down the sloped bank to join her, shuffling a bit on the slick grass to avoid losing her footing.

"Hey." Ande turned from her reverie, and Becca had the oddly unnerving realization that she and the taller woman were eye to eye. "I mean, merry meet."

"Hey, Ande. Merry meet to you too." Becca took a deep breath, emboldened by this new equality. "I hear you voted for having the memorial tonight, Ande. I mean, as opposed to waiting for the solstice."

"Well, yeah." The glowing light warmed Ande's skin, and she stared over the water as if she were remembering a good dream. "I mean, life goes on, right?"

"'Life goes on?'" Becca searched the other woman's face. "No, Ande, something's going on, but you can't just dismiss it that easily."

"What are you talking about?" Ande snapped to focus suddenly. "Becca, I know how horrible this has been—I mean, you found Suzanne."

"You know it's been horrible, but you're not doing anything to help." Becca spoke with quiet urgency. Up by the path, Larissa was getting louder. She wasn't the most patient woman. "No, worse. You're obfuscating things."

"Obfuscating?" Her brow wrinkled.

"You know, making things muddy."

"I know what obfuscating means." Ande sounded sad rather than wounded. "I just don't get what you mean."

"You keep saying that Suzanne only wanted to talk to you about the coven finances, but that there wasn't anything real there." Becca fought to keep her voice low, even as her frustration mounted. "And you won't come forward and tell the police about it. Meanwhile, I think they suspect me."

"No, that's ridiculous." The tall accountant had the temerity to smile. "You're…you're so nice."

"Thanks, I guess." Becca wasn't having it. "But Suzanne was seeing my ex, and they've heard that someone was stalking her, so…"

"Okay." Ande raised her hands, signaling her to stop. "I'll talk to the cops, I promise. I just really don't think I have anything to contribute."

"Thanks." Becca turned to go when another thought stopped her in her tracks. "There's not any reason you wouldn't want to go to the cops, is there?"

"Me?" Ande smiled, her dark brows rising in mock surprise. "You mean, because I'm black?"

"I wasn't…" Becca struggled, a bit flustered. "I just think there are too many secrets. Like, what's going on with you and Marcia?"

"Me and Marcia?" Maybe it was the dimming light, but Ande appeared genuinely confused.

"You two are hiding something." The conversation in the kitchen. The shared glances. Becca was sure of it.

Ande didn't argue. "It's—look, I can't tell you. It's not my secret to share. But yeah, Marcia has taken me into her confidence about something—and no, it's not about Suzanne—"

"Ande, where were you last Saturday?" The question burst out of nowhere. Ande's response—a startled laugh—surprised Becca even more.

"Saturday? I was with Marcia. She and Luz had me over for lunch. We were probably talking—even as…dear goddess, there was no way to know."

"No, of course not," said Becca. "So Luz was there too?" She hated herself for asking.

The taller woman tried a smile, but it didn't reach the sadness in her eyes. "Yeah." She nodded. "Yeah, if you need confirmation. She was there."

"Hey, you two." Kathy stood on the top of the bank.

"What's up?"

"Just thinking." Ande turned for one more look at the river, where the orange was spreading over the blue. "Remembering."

Becca nodded. "Isn't that what we're here to do?"

"Well, yeah." Kathy turned back toward the main gathering.

With a sigh, Ande began to climb the bank, her voice sinking to a conspiratorial level. "Though I think Larissa has something a lot fancier in mind."

Becca reached out to give the other woman a hand up. "I'm sure—and shouldn't we get started soon?"

"You're right." Ande looked back once more at the calico reflections. "The sun is beginning to set."

***

She was right. Already the light was changing, splashing the pale blue sky with orange and pink. For Clara, the increasing darkness was a blessing. Out here in the wild, she tended to be more cautious. A domestic cat could get in trouble, and besides, she didn't want to give her person a scare. But although the tall weeds by the water's edge stopped far short of the path, the play of shadows had given her an increased freedom, and even as her person returned to the cropped grass, the shaded feline lingered close to Becca's feet. Close enough to pick up a tension that had not been alleviated by Ande's capitulation—or her alibi.

"Finally!" Larissa's growl would have done Harriet proud.

"Shouldn't we wait for Trent?" Kathy looked around as the two joined the main party. "I mean, he is our leader."

Larissa, raven brows lowered, shot her a look that by

rights should have pushed her into the river. Only the sight of the bearded warlock, jogging down the path, stopped her rebuttal. "There he is, the little scamp," she said.

"Sorry—ah, merry meet." Breathing heavily, he forced a smile. Becca, Clara could see, was eying him carefully as the coven gathered and joined hands.

So was Larissa, who scowled as his hand went up reflexively to his open collar. "You're not wearing your amulet," she said, forgoing the usual greeting.

"No." His long fingers played over the dark curls as if feeling for the missing piece. "I—the chain broke, and I have to get it fixed."

"Ah." Larissa sniffed, and for a moment Clara wondered if she could smell the blood that Harriet's claws had drawn. "You should be careful with a piece like that." The smile was back, only a slight rebuke in her voice. "It has power, you know."

"I know." His smile wasn't quite as wide as usual, but before Clara could approach and attempt to sniff out anything about the man, Ande and Marcia had joined hands. For a moment, Becca seemed about to address them—the question in her eyes—but instead she turned toward Trent, and Clara had the distinct impression that she was going to apologize, yet again, for Harriet's indiscretion. Only then Kathy reached for her hand and drew Becca in, linking her to Larissa and the others. Trent completed the circle, joining Becca and Ande, and Larissa began to speak.

"We are here today to celebrate our sister, Suzanne." She looked around, her gaze taking in each of them in turn. "To remember her magic, and to return her to the stars."

"Oh, brother." Kathy's whisper was audible to all.

"She was our sister in the mysteries we share." Even as she kept talking, Larissa silenced the coven pet with a glare. "Mysteries that evoke the mysterious secrets we all share." Becca, conscious of her status as the newest member of the group and suddenly very conscious of Larissa's eagle eyes, held stock still as the older woman droned on. Beside her, Kathy struggled to contain her giggle.

"And as we watch the sun descend, so too we bid farewell to this stage of our sister's being." With the last of the light, Larissa seemed finally to be winding up. "Farewell, Suzanne," she intoned in a voice that must have carried to the water's edge and beyond. "Farewell!"

"Thank the goddess." Ande's exhalation was audible, even if its meaning was open to interpretation. And as Larissa turned toward her, she girded for the rebuke. "I mean, goddess be praised," the other woman said.

"Goddess be praised." Becca echoed the sentiment as the circle broke its bonds.

"What was that about?" Marcia sidled up to Becca as Trent wrestled with the bottle of cider Larissa had brought, her attention on the flamboyant pair. "I thought this was supposed to be focused on Suzanne."

Becca couldn't bring herself to disagree. "I'm beginning to realize I never really knew her."

Marcia's large, dark eyes peered up at her as she once more donned her cap.

"She wanted to talk to me about something," Becca explained. "That last meeting. I never found out what it was."

"Oh, I know." A surprising smile. "She wanted to do a casting out."

Becca's jaw dropped in confusion.

"Because of your summoning spell. You know," Marcia explained. "She was hoping you could help her."

"In her personal life?" Becca couldn't help thinking of Jeff. Casting out spells were to rid oneself of negative influences—or people.

"You mean, like she had mice in her apartment?" Marcia was in an exceedingly jolly mood despite the occasion.

It was contagious, and Becca found herself chuckling at the idea. "If that were the case, she wouldn't need a witch. She could have borrowed my cats." That was so close to an oxymoron that Clara's tail twitched.

"No, I don't think so." Marcia leaned in again, her voice growing soft. "I think she was talking about the coven. Something—or someone—who wasn't, well, right."

"Trent!" Larissa's shrill command cut through the growing dark, and Marcia rolled her eyes.

"I can think of a couple of candidates," she whispered.

"A couple?" As soon as the words were out, Becca regretted them. "I'm sorry, I didn't mean…"

"No, it's fine." Marcia dismissed her slight cattiness. "I wasn't just thinking of our queen bee. I mean, look at Trent. Doesn't he seem to think he's our end-all and be-all?" Becca didn't get a chance to respond. "Really, what does he contribute?"

Clara watched as her person mulled over the possibilities. "He does have a certain charm," she murmured, earning another dramatic roll of Marcia's large, dark eyes. "I mean, who else?"

Even as she voiced the question, the answer hit her. Larissa might be overbearing and Trent a flirt. But it was Ande who had first told her about the coven's financial irregularities and that Suzanne had been concerned. Becca wanted to trust her coven mate's grudging promise that she would talk to the police. That didn't mean she couldn't check up on the alibi she'd given her.

"Marcia, Ande said she was with you last Saturday, when—" Becca broke off, unable to finish.

"Yeah." The other woman sounded thoughtful, but a trace of a smile lit her face.

Becca paused, taken aback, and then forced herself to go on. "Was Luz with you too?" She winced as she asked the corroborative question, but in the fading light her pained expression was invisible to all but her cat.

"Well, yeah." Marcia chortled. "You can ask her."

"Ask Luz?" Becca turned, confused, only to see Ande approaching.

"I don't think that was canon." The taller witch joined them, in the guise of handing out the paper cups.

"It most certainly wasn't," agreed Marcia. "We were supposed to do a regular circle, invoking the elements, and then toast Suzanne after."

"Hey, guys." Kathy approached, jug of cider in hand.

As she filled their cups, Becca took the opportunity to ask, "Did you think that was odd?"

"What, that?" Kathy turned to look at Larissa, who seemed to be deep in discussion with Trent. "Someone likes to be center stage is all."

"Maybe." Ande and Marcia exchanged looks.

"That's right." Becca nodded. "Weren't you saying there was something off—"

"Ande!" Larissa called. "Do you have those cups?"

"Don't mind her." Kathy took Becca's arm, turning her

away. “She’s a bit—I don’t know—she gets paranoid.”

“Larissa?” Becca gently detached herself from the younger woman’s grasp.

“No, Ande.” Even as Kathy lowered her voice, she gave the name her usual dramatic emphasis. “She can be a little obsessive.” Her voice sank to be quieter still. “I heard what she was saying, but I’m not sure I would believe it. I mean, accusing someone of embezzling? In fact, I wouldn’t be surprised if the police were looking at her, you know.”

Becca only paused a moment before responding. “No, she and Marcia were together that afternoon.”

The redhead’s eyebrows registered her surprise. “Really? Was Luz there too?”

“I…I think so, but I’m not sure.” Becca looked around as if searching for more confirmation, but Kathy was already reaching for her arm once more.

“Come on.” She led her away so quickly that Clara had to scurry to avoid being kicked. “Let’s get some of those cookies before they’re all gone.” She had a point. Marcia was already on her third. A gingerbread spice mix, Clara could tell, as she raised her black leather nose to the air. And even though Trent appeared more interested in the cider, Larissa was pushing a paper plate of the cookies toward him as the other women arrived.

“May I?” Kathy reached over to nab one. “Thanks.”

Becca, Clara observed, had hung back once Kathy had released her arm, and now sidled over to Trent.

“I’m sorry about your amulet.” She kept her voice low and dipped her head. It wouldn’t do to be caught staring at the warlock’s chest. “And about Harriet.”

“Harriet?” His voice rose, puzzled.

"My cat." Even in the growing dark, Clara could see that Becca was blushing, and that her own awareness of her rising color only made the flush worse. "The orange and white one."

"Oh." One hand went to his chest again, and Becca turned away. Clara wished she could tell the shy, sweet girl that her pink cheeks were barely visible to the other humans.

Trent must have sensed something, though, because as Becca moved away, he reached for her, and as if the warmth of his chest was carried through his fingers, she became redder still. "She doesn't usually do things like that," she said. And just for a moment, Clara had to wonder if her person was really talking about her sister cat.

"It was no big deal." Trent's voice was low too, almost as if he were sharing a secret. "It was just the chain for my—that thing."

"Your amulet?" Becca chirped in what Clara thought of as her helpful voice, even as Trent's mouth tightened in dismissal.

"And what are you two up to?" Larissa shoved the plate of cookies between them before he could respond.

"Nothing much." Becca took a cookie. "Thanks."

"Keeping yourself busy?" One dark brow arched in emphasis. The question appeared to be directed to Becca, but even as she spoke, the older woman turned to stare at Trent.

"I'm basically focusing on my research," Becca offered when it became clear that the man at her side would remain silent. When Larissa's brow rose further, she explained. "I'm kind of an amateur genealogist. I mean, I might as well use my research skills for something." More silence, and Becca couldn't avoid the awful suspicion that she was being judged.

Something about those dark eyes and the raven-wing black of those brows. "And I'm looking for work still, of course." Still nothing, and so she ventured on. "I called Graham today."

The other woman blinked at that, so slowly that Clara almost thought she was a cat. "Your friend?" Becca offered.

"My mentor," Larissa corrected her with a nod. "Of course. I'm so glad, dear. I'm sure he'll look after you."

"I hope so." Becca sounded a little anxious. "He agreed to see me, but I'd hate to think that this was just because Suzanne—"

"Nonsense." Now it was the older woman who was patting her arm, her lacquered nails nearly black in the fading light. "I'll talk to him. I'll make sure he knows how special you are."

Becca swallowed so hard that Clara looked up in alarm. Humans didn't have hair balls. She knew that, but the young woman before her was patently unnerved. Her older colleague didn't seem to notice, however. In fact, she'd moved on to Trent and was leading him down toward the water.

"What was that?" Kathy again, her mouth full of cookie.

"Oh, I followed up with that job lead Larissa was telling me about." Becca's gaze followed the older woman as she walked away. "Only, well, I'm wondering if it's a good idea. I'm not sure—" She stopped abruptly, and Clara's ears perked up, the black sensor hairs inside tingling. "I'm not sure what kind of reference she'll give me."

"I get it." Kathy finished the cookie and wiped her mouth on the back of her hand, while Clara studied her human. Becca had changed her mind about what she'd been about to say, and her pet wanted to know why. But Kathy didn't seem to notice. Leaning in, she dropped her usually brassy voice down into a conspiratorial hush. "Larissa uses her purse strings to control everyone, and you don't want to just step into Suzanne's shoes. I mean, talk about bad luck! Hey, why don't you call my boss instead?"

"Oh, I'm sorry." Becca turned, as if seeing the other woman for the first time. "I meant to tell you. I did reach out—Eric Marshfield, right? He said he's not looking for anyone now."

"Oh, gee, that's my fault!" Kathy shook her girlish curls. "I'm so sorry. I meant to speak with him, first. He doesn't know it yet, but one of the girls I work with is about to give notice—"

"I don't know." Becca cut her off.

"No, really." Kathy's smile wrinkled her freckled nose. "Eric needs someone. I'll clear it up and get back to you."

"Thanks." Becca managed a smile. It was nearly full dark by then, and the party had begun to break up. "Do you think we should clean up?"

"Well, the cookies are gone." Kathy seemed to lose interest, but she tagged after Becca as she collected paper plates and napkins into the bag that had transported the cider.

"Thanks, dear." Larissa took the trash from her, folding the bag top over as she drew it close. "Would you like a ride home?" Marcia, Kathy, and Trent had already lined up behind her.

"No, thanks. I'll walk." Becca turned around as if to seek a companion or, perhaps, Clara realized, to continue a discussion. But Ande was already gone.

Chapter 27

Clara woke the next morning with a start. *"Something's burning!"* She mewed over to Harriet, who was still sacked out beside her, and went in search of Laurel and Becca.

"North, south, east…" She found Becca in the living room, waving around a bundle of smoldering twigs. "No, wait, that's west."

Laurel was observing from a safe distance, under the dining room table.

"What's going on?" Clara asked her sister.

A flick of the tail. *"Some spell she looked up to get rid of negativity."* The seal point turned and, leaving the room, whined in pure Siamese fashion. *"More like she wants to get rid of us. That stinks."*

Any further complaint was cut off by a metallic shriek that sent Becca scrambling. After quickly dousing the sage bundle in the sink, she clambered onto a chair to silence the alarm and then opened the apartment's front window.

The noise woke Harriet, who joined Clara and Laurel as their person wandered around the living room, fanning the air with a newspaper. *"It's not right, waking us like that and then not feeding us,"* the sleepy marmalade grumbled with a yawn

"She will," Clara reassured her. *"She always does."*

"Wake me when she does." Harriet settled in for a nap

as Becca, a bit more tousled than usual, began her morning toilette. After watching her oldest sister curl up on the sofa, Clara found Laurel in the bedroom, where Becca was dressing.

It had taken Clara a few moments to understand what her sister was up to, those blue eyes focused so intently as their person rifled through her closet. Only after she'd taken out a halter-top sundress did Clara turn on Laurel with a hiss.

"What?" Laurel's ears flicked back. Any interruption tended to dispel her ability to suggest thoughts. *"You want her to succeed, don't you?"*

"Not like that." Clara did her best not to growl. *"It's not that kind of meeting."*

"They're all *that kind of meeting."* Laurel turned her back on her sister, but despite her feigned nonchalance, that chocolate tail was already whipping back and forth.

Clara, who knew how much was at stake, wasn't going to let this one go. "*Laurel,*" she hissed. No response beyond another flick of those dark ears. "*Laurel!*" The calico had raised her paw to smack her older sister on her café au lait behind when Harriet interrupted.

"Where's our breakfast?" The big marmalade looked around as she lumbered over to the chair, where two discarded outfits had already been tossed—evidence of the battle being waged between her younger siblings. *"Is she—are you two—going to keep this up all day?"*

"No." Turning away, Laurel began grooming, as if the appearance of her own dainty brown booties were all that mattered. *"It's hopeless."*

As Becca pulled a modish—but modest—skirt and matching jacket out of her closet, Clara sighed with relief. She hadn't wanted to fight. Clara didn't think her slinky seal-point sister was jealous of her own particular power—the ease with which she passed through walls and closed doors. But the calico did suspect that her sister would not stand to have her more mischievous wishes thwarted again. Luckily, not even Laurel would start an argument with Harriet about breakfast, and the bigger cat's interruption had already broken her brief spell. No magic was required to remind Becca of her most important of duties, however, and while Harriet and Laurel were still face down in their dishes, Clara snuck out—catching Becca as she headed for her appointment.

***

Maddy was outside, leaning against a concrete pillar and smoking, when Becca got to the Central Square office where she worked.

"I thought you'd quit," said Becca, stepping back after a quick embrace.

"I have, sort of." Her friend stubbed out the butt and fanned the air. "But I wanted to catch you before you went in."

Before Becca could comment on the logic of that particular excuse, her friend had reached out for her again, holding her at arm's length while she surveyed Becca's skirt and floral summer jacket.

"You look good." Maddy nodded. "Too good for this place."

Clara had to agree. As much as she disliked Laurel messing with their person's thoughts, in this case, the lingering effects of her suggestion had been positive. Becca wasn't what one would call stylish, but the skirt and jacket worked together nicely, giving the young woman a more mature, put-together look than what she might have otherwise chosen. If only the acrid smoke didn't insinuate itself into the pretty fabric.

"Thanks." Becca smoothed the already wrinkle-free front of the jacket and threw her shoulders back. "I want to make a good impression."

"If anyone can…" Her friend glanced over at the building's glass doors, shaking her head. "He's in a mood. That's why I wanted to catch you—to warn you."

Becca's brows shot up.

"Well, yeah, and to have a smoke. I mean, it's, what, not even nine thirty and he's already reamed out the entire team."

Becca's perfect posture slumped. "What happened?"

"I don't know." Still watching the door as if afraid of what might come out, Maddy shook her head. "Another fight with his ex, I think. I got in early—we really could use some extra help, you know—and I could hear them. I mean, he was on the phone, with his door closed, and I could *still* hear him. I think she lives in one of his properties and has an untrained dog or something. He was yelling about 'a shorter leash.' I know, it sounds stupid. Remind me to never get married."

Becca opened her mouth to respond and wisely shut it again before her friend could see.

"Anyway, don't mention pets." Her friend turned back to face her, once more taking in Becca's outfit, from shoes to hair. "Though maybe cats would be…no, just don't. And you do look good. This weather, your hair has some curl to it. Once we get you a job, we're going to go out and meet some decent guys."

"But not to marry." Becca raised her hand to cut off her friend's objection, a grin perking her pink cheeks up further. "That'll be great. Though I may have a prospect of my own."

"Oh?" Maddy drew the syllable out till it dripped with

inflection.

"I'll tell you after." Becca took a deep breath and once more brushed down her spotless jacket. In some ways, Clara thought with more than a touch of pride, her person was very like a cat. "Wish me luck!"

Becca certainly moved like a cat as she exited the elevator for the fourth-floor office. A wise cat, that is, who entered an unknown territory with some trepidation.

Head up and back a little stiff, she stepped carefully, craning around to get her bearings as she walked through the open archway marked Reynolds and Associates and looked around.

Maddy had told her about the office's open plan. Beyond the receptionist's desk, cubicles with low dividers filled the floor, while the boss's office sat far in the back. His door was closed, although she could see the balding man pacing through the interior window. And though all around her heads bent over keyboards or focused intently on glowing screens, she—and presumably all the workers who appeared so focused on their terminals—could hear him yell, "Not one more penny!"

Becca swallowed. At least Maddy had warned her. But before she could even contemplate facing the monster beyond, she had to pass the gorgon at the gate.

"May I help you?" The tone got Becca's attention, and she turned to find herself facing a pair of cat-eye glasses. Maddy had warned her about Ms. White. "Reynolds's faithful attack dog," had been her exact words. "If a dog wore sparkly glasses and too much lipstick."

"Yes, please." Becca summoned what she hoped was a

placatory smile, her own lips feeling suddenly dry. “I have an appointment with Mr. Reynolds.”

“Risa, you’re not listening!” bellowed the voice from beyond the front desk.

“I’ll see if he’s in.” The gatekeeper turned, rhinestones sparkling, and made a show of fussing with her phone.

“That’s it! No more!”

In the silence that followed, Becca held her breath, her smile frozen in place. Finally, whether through habit or some change in lighting on the phone that only the gatekeeper could decipher, the bespectacled woman before her looked up again.

“Mr. Reynolds will see you now.” The corners of her crimson mouth wrinkled up slightly. Clara hoped it was in sympathy. “Good luck.”

Muttering what she remembered of the charm against ill fortune under her breath, Becca made her way across the office, skirting the low cubicles and avoiding the inquisitive gaze of the inhabitants who glanced up quickly as she passed, like so many timid mice.

Becca wasn’t feeling any braver by the time she’d crossed the floor and paused to take a deep breath before she knocked on the door. The bark that greeted her—“Who is it?” —didn’t help.

“Mr. Reynolds?” She stepped into what was actually a rather nice office. Although the balding, red-faced man behind the desk was as disheveled as she’d expected, matching the pile of papers scattered before him, the room itself was spacious and lit by the huge window opposite, which looked out on the river and the city beyond. “I’m Becca Colwin.”

Reynolds’ eyebrows bristled like caterpillars as he gestured toward a chair.

"Larissa Fox referred me?" She perched gingerly, back straight and ankles crossed.

"Oh, yeah, Larissa." He looked down at his desk and began to shuffle through the papers there. "One of Larissa's pets, huh?"

He didn't say it like he was expecting an answer, and so Becca held back, waiting until he found what appeared to be a printout of her resumé before proceeding. "As you can see, I'm experienced in research—"

"No master's, though." Reynolds frowned and flipped the page over, though if he hoped to find the answer on the back, Becca knew he'd be disappointed. "I'm looking for someone with an advanced degree."

"I understand." Becca had rehearsed this bit with her cats. "But I'm sure you'll agree that three years of experience conducting multi-platform research has taught me the requisite practical skills that a graduate degree might not.

"Besides…" She paused, and Clara's ears perked up. Usually, she had stopped by this point. "Someone with a graduate degree might not want to get her hands dirty. But I'm not afraid of doing off-site research, digging through any kind of files. City archives, paper, microfiche, you name it. I'm very motivated." She paused again. "I really need this job."

The caterpillars separated as the man before her flashed a grin that was like sunshine through the storm clouds. Even his color began to improve. "And I can pay you less than someone with more letters after their name too, I bet." He didn't wait for an answer. "You've got more grit than my ex, I'll give you that. She expects everything to be given to her, or to her pets."

Clara could tell that Becca was holding her breath.

Maybe Reynolds could too, but he appeared lost in thought.

"Ah, at least you're—wait, you must know that other girl. The one who…" He waved one stubby hand around as if to summon the name from the air around him.

"Maddy Topsic?" Even as she said it, Becca caught herself. Suzanne had worked here too, of course. Clara could almost see the shadow cross his mind. What was it Kathy had said? *"You don't want to just step into Suzanne's shoes."*

But Reynolds accepted her answer. "Maddy, yeah. She's a good kid. Takes too many smoke breaks, but she gets her work done."

Becca's sigh of relief was audible, and the man before her smiled in earnest—and then sniffed audibly. "You smoke too? Never mind." He waved off his own question. "Look, I'm not promising anything. But let me take a look at what's going on, and I'll get back to you."

"Thank you, sir."

His eyebrows went up again at that, but he kept silent. Only as Becca rose to take her leave did he call after her. "Oh, Becca?" She turned and waited. "You might not want to use the name Larissa that much. Her credit around here is kind of used up."

***

Although she must have seen Maddy's eyes peeping over the carpeted cubicle on her way out, Becca kept on walking. Not until she was out on the sidewalk again did she stop, leaning back against the column where she'd found her friend, to take a deep, calming breath. She'd been trembling, Clara realized, and it required all the little cat's discipline to keep from rubbing against her in soft comfort.

She wasn't the only one. As soon as Becca had her

breath, her phone rang.

"How was it?" Maddy was on the line, the sound muffled as if she had her hand over the receiver.

"I think he liked me." Becca sounded surprised.

"Of course he did!" A little louder, before sinking back down again. "But what about the job?"

"He said he'd let me know. I think, maybe, I got it." Becca paused as she reviewed the conversation. "I think he was starting to ask me about Suzanne. Only I kind of spaced when he asked if I knew anyone there. I mean, I only found out she worked with you after she, well, anyway, I just said you."

"Great." Maddy didn't sound like she meant it. "I hope I didn't sink you."

"No, not at all. In fact, he said you were a good worker or something." A snort on the other end of the line. "I don't think Larissa's reference was good for much, though. He made some comment about her."

"It got you in the door, though." Maddy's voice was philosophical. "Maybe she put a spell on him?"

"That's not what we're supposed to use our magic for, Maddy."

Another snort, and her friend asked. "So, what's this about a possible romance? Please tell me you're not giving Jeff another chance."

"No, no way." Becca began walking, her face up to the sun. "This is, well, it's not exactly a date. But I am getting together Sunday with someone I met recently, just to talk."

"You didn't tell me about anyone."

Becca bit her lip. Clara knew she didn't like lying, but what she was doing was close. "He's, well, it's the guy I met the day that Suzanne—the painter. The one I went out for coffee with."

"I don't know, Becca. Going out with someone you met at a crime scene—"

"He's a witness, Maddy, same as I am. He's been trying to help the police too. And I'll be careful." She rushed that last bit in before her friend could interrupt.

"At least it's not Jeff." Maddy's approval was, at best, begrudging. But Becca looked relieved at the change in topic.

"Speaking of, I didn't tell you the latest, Maddy. Jeff's been acting really weird. I think he's trying to throw suspicion on someone in my coven." The line fell silent. "Maddy?"

She paused, waiting for her friend to respond.

"Look, Becca." The humor was gone from Maddy's voice. "You know what I think about Jeff, and I'm sorry I didn't tell you earlier about what a cheating sack of whatever he is. But I'd almost prefer him to some stranger you just met. You're a little too close to this investigation. I know you think you have some insight, but remember, Becca, a girl was murdered, and I wouldn't trust anybody who might have been in the position to hurt her."

Chapter 28

Maddy's warning notwithstanding, over the weekend, Becca settled down to what had become her daily routine of online research. By Sunday, even Clara's sisters were beginning to wonder if their person would ever leave the couch again.

"What's she doing?" Laurel stretched, extending her slim café au lait body along the back of the sofa as she craned over toward Becca's shoulder. *"Doesn't she have a date coming up?"*

"That's hours away. She's doing research." Clara sounded a bit smug as she snuggled against her person's thigh. In truth, the little calico had only the slightest idea what Becca did as she tapped the machine on her lap, but as her person clicked away, she had recognized the family portrait—and her own feline forebear—as it surfaced once more. From that one startling image and from Becca's various comments as she summoned other, similar sights, she'd gleaned that the young woman was once more looking into her own past and, unintentionally, that of the feline sisters. How this slim machine helped her do that might well be Becca's own form of magic, the plump calico mused. Besides, Clara acknowledged as she shifted to make herself even more comfortable, the computer was warm.

"I wonder if I should tell the coven about my family..." Becca stared at the screen. "I mean, it might explain the spell."

Neither Laurel nor Clara knew exactly what she was talking about. And Harriet, snoozing as usual, didn't care. But as Becca scrolled through the pages, she found herself torn. Her latest find—a newspaper clipping from 1926—had been tantalizing in the extreme. A Rebecca Horne Colwin—her own great-grandmother—had "miraculously" survived a fire that had destroyed her house. She'd emerged from the wreckage, the clipping read, clutching her "favorite mouser" to her breast.

"Of course she went back," Becca commented as she scrolled over the scanned clip. "She had to rescue her cat."

Clara and Laurel exchanged a glance. *"Never mind,"* Clara purred softly. *"We know who did the rescuing."*

Becca was too absorbed to notice as the seal point nearly barked in reply. The use of the word "miraculous" was unusual, she thought, as she made a note to check if such speculation would have been common in the newspapers of the day. Maddy had been the documents specialist, back when they were in school. But even as she typed out her query, she found herself wondering if the author—or the authorities—had meant to imply something else. A woman, living alone with her cat, might be suspected of many things, even in the supposedly enlightened twentieth century. Might "miraculous" be interpreted as "suspicious"? If the fire had taken place a hundred and fifty years earlier, would Becca's ancestor have been thrown back in, to be burned as a witch?

"They probably didn't know about arson then." Becca's fingers floated about the keyboard. "But it can't hurt..." With a few strokes, she sent off the query. Maddy might scoff at Becca's interest in Wicca, but surely, she'd help her friend dig into what looked like a particularly interesting bit of family history.

"I wonder if I can make this into a screensaver?" With a tap-tap-tap, she'd enlarged it. "Wow, look at that, Clara." The little cat raised her head to see. "Doesn't that kitty look just like you?"

Laurel stared down as Clara debated her answer. No, she couldn't actually tell their person that, yes, the "famous mouser" in the photo was a foremother of Clara and her two sisters. Nor could she explain Becca's mistake to her—that it wasn't the woman in the photo whose magic had saved her life and her cat's. It was the woman's calico familiar who had managed to extract them both when that earlier Rebecca Colwin's attempts at a warming spell had gone so badly astray during one chilly New England night. That didn't mean she wasn't tempted to try.

"Don't you dare." Laurel reached down, claws extended. Even as the sisters squabbled over how they could use their powers—and both Laurel and Harriet did tend to favor relaxation over rigor—they all were well aware of the cardinal rule: no cat could reveal the basic truth about magic to a human. *"If you think you'll get a pass just because she has the same stupid markings..."*

"I won't." Clara ducked her head and resumed her position, curled against Becca's leg. As much as she wished she could communicate with her person, it was neither possible nor advisable. Still, if she could only get Becca to stop trying out spells, it would be something. As the three cats knew, magic was for felines. And once again, Clara regretted that her oldest sister had not taken more care with her particular skill.

"I wonder..." Becca was looking at the pillow Harriet

had summoned. For once, the fat marmalade wasn't sleeping on it. She'd dropped off while sunning on the sill, instead. But it didn't take magic to understand the import of that glance. Between the clipping and that soft apparition, Becca was thinking of trying a spell again.

When the phone rang, Clara looked up at Laurel. Her sister's blue eyes blinked back, blameless. *"Not me,"* she purred beneath her breath, not that Clara was sure she believed her.

"Becca, it's me." Maddy sounded frazzled. "We've got to talk."

"You know, I was just thinking of you." Becca, on the other hand, seemed inordinately pleased. "In fact, I was wishing you would call. I wonder if perhaps the key to a summoning is—"

"Becca!" Her friend cut her off. "You didn't 'summon' me. I've been meaning to call you, all right? Even before you emailed. I keep thinking of you going out with that painter guy tonight. You're not still thinking of doing that, are you?"

"Yeah, I am. But not—wait, Maddy." Her friend had started to sputter. "Maddy, I should explain: it's not really a *date* date. I have questions for him. Questions that the police might not know to ask."

***

Only after Becca promised that she would meet the cute painter in a public place, and would check in immediately after, did her friend calm down. But whether it was because the cats' determined person was planning some high-level sleuthing or some other reason that Clara couldn't discern, Becca seemed unable to concentrate after her conversation with her friend. Instead, she spent the rest of the afternoon fussing as she hadn't in months, redoing her hair and picking over her clothes, before settling on a perfectly fine outfit that Clara hadn't seen before.

"Don't look at me." Laurel sat beside her younger sister in the bedroom doorway, watching their person get dressed. She flicked her tail in the feline equivalent of a shrug and began to bathe.

"Don't tell me she's going out again." Harriet had joined them on the bedroom rug, having woken from her nap hungry.

"I'm sure she'll remember to feed us," said Clara, who had her own mixed feelings about the evening. *"Besides, she won't be out late."* She'd gathered that much from the phone conversation.

"No matter." Harriet turned. *"I've got things to keep me busy too, you know."*

As Clara watched her stump off, fluffy tail sweeping the air as she walked, she couldn't avoid a niggling tickle of fear. Harriet never had anything more important on her mind than food. Nothing that didn't immediately gratify, at any rate.

But when her sister's exit was followed by the soft thud that indicated she'd landed on the sofa, Clara did her best to turn her focus elsewhere. Harriet wasn't likely to get them into any trouble in one of her favorite napping spots, no more than she already had anyway. It was Becca who was going off to meet a strange man. Never mind that he smelled pleasant—Clara thought of the trees by the river—the painter had been there, at Suzanne's apartment, the day she had met her violent end. And nothing about that scene had ended well for anyone.

Still, Becca had a bounce in her step as she bid the kitties farewell and headed down to the street. Harriet was still nestled into the sofa as she left, but even Laurel didn't try to stop Clara from following her.

"If it were a little darker, I'd join you," said the older cat, licking her cream-colored belly. *"You know I would."*

"Of course," lied Clara, touched by her sister's concern, and then leaped into the growing dusk.

Becca was, as she'd promised, careful. She circled the block twice before entering the little café. Still, Nathan had gotten there before her. Clara heard her sharp intake of breath as he stood and waved with a smile.

"I got here a few minutes early." He reached to pull out Becca's chair, only bumping it into her. "Sorry."

"Not a problem." Becca arranged herself and looked around. "Did you order?"

"I thought I'd wait. Shall I get?" He stood again, but she held out her hand to stop him.

"No, I will." *Good girl!* Clara thought, silently thanking Maddy for her warning. As nice as this man smelled and as harmless as he'd proved to be at that first coffee date, it never paid to take chances. Besides, in five minutes, the pair were seated again, heads together over mugs of mocha.

"I know it's supposed to be a winter drink, but…" Nathan sipped, then licked the foam moustache.

"I know, right?" Becca agreed, appearing to relax. But when he reached forward, as if to place his hand over hers, Becca drew back. "Hey, Nathan, may I ask you about that day?"

"The day your friend was killed?" His voice had gotten serious.

Becca nodded. "I was talking to my ex." Her words sounded rehearsed, and Clara realized that in fact the young woman had been practicing her approach that afternoon. "And he told me that the police seem to suspect my—well, the group of friends that I know Suzanne from."

It wasn't the best explanation, but Nathan appeared to accept it. Clearly, there was more coming.

"I was wondering if you could tell me again in detail what you heard that day. What you saw."

There was no chance of hand holding now. The young man seated opposite her didn't leave or protest. But after taking a deep breath, he stared down into his mug, as if the answer was written there. Then he began to talk.

"You know that I didn't see what happened. Or who," he added quickly. "I mean, yeah, I saw you go in, because I'd noticed you. But otherwise…" Even in the noisy coffeehouse, a silence hung between them.

"But you heard something?" Becca didn't have magical powers. She was, however, a perceptive young woman.

Nathan nodded. "There was that phone call that I told you about. An argument—but that was hours before. And there might have been something else. Right before you came by, I had my music on, but there was a moment between songs. I heard—I thought I heard—that poor woman arguing with someone."

"With who?"

He shook his head, as if disappointed with himself. "I put it wrong. In truth, I only heard her—your friend. I'm pretty sure I recognized her voice. She used to say hi to me." He paused for a shy smile. "So I thought it was her, and that she was yelling at someone—but it was so brief. Just a few words."

Becca stared at him, willing him to go on.

"I told the cops all this. I can't be sure. Something about 'him' and 'tech,' maybe. Or 'protect.' It could have been either. All I know is that she was angry and she was yelling at someone. It was so brief, I wasn't even really sure I heard anything, but in retrospect, maybe I did. Maybe I heard her yelling at someone who was in the room with her."

"Tech?" Becca barely breathed the word. "My ex is in tech." She bit her lip. "If he didn't break up with her, then maybe there was another man. Maybe he knew…" She looked up at the painter, a horrible suspicion dawning on her face.

"But he called you, right?" Nathan interrupted the runaway train of thought. "You said he called and you answered, as you went in?"

"Uh-huh." Becca drew out both syllables. Clara could almost see the thoughts going through her mind: *Maybe it was the other man. Someone else who knew Suzanne. Who knew them all…*

"Well, then he wouldn't—it would've been too obvious." Nathan's answer was overly hearty, as if he were trying to convince himself. "I mean, to call you right after…" The words died out, but his meaning was obvious.

"Unless he saw me and wanted to stop me from going up. From finding her. He said he was at his place, but he didn't want me to come over." A high, nervous note had entered Becca's voice, a sound that made Clara want to draw her away to safety and peace. "Maybe he was really hiding nearby—"

"No, wait." Nathan must have heard it too. He reached across the table and took her wrist. "Don't get ahead of yourself, Becca. You're angry at your ex, so it makes sense you'd suspect him. But be sensible. He's worried about you. He's the one who told the police it might be someone from your coven, right?"

"Yeah." Becca exhaled, the tension easing audibly. And

then just as quickly, she jumped up, pulling her hand back as fast as if he had bitten it.

"Coven?" She barked out the word. "How did you know I was in a coven? Unless you knew it from Suzanne."

"No, wait." Nathan shook his head, as if he could dismiss his error, but it was too late. Becca's chair had already toppled backward as she fled out the door.

Chapter 29

"Becca, what's wrong?" Maddy's anxiety only riled the cats up more. All three had been orbiting Becca since she'd run in, slamming the door behind her, and nothing Clara could do would calm her sisters—or the young woman who panted into the phone. "Are you all right?"

"I'm okay." Becca leaned back on the door. Speaking made her breathe, at least, and that helped to calm her slightly. "Just—Maddy, I think you were right. I think Nathan, the painter, might have murdered Suzanne."

"Wait, what?" The response was so loud, Harriet stopped in her tracks, and Clara almost bumped into her as she stared up at their person. "I knew you shouldn't have gone out with him. Him or that other witch guy. They're both trouble."

"No, Trent is—I don't know what Trent is." The distraction seemed to help Becca too. Stepping over the heap of Harriet, she proceeded into the living room, and Clara jumped to the sofa, hoping to claim the cushion next to their person before Laurel could. To her surprise, it was Harriet who barreled up next to her, shoving her out of the way.

"Mine!" Even before Becca sat down, the big cat had settled, spreading herself over one sofa cushion, while one white paw hooked over its padded edge.

"Never mind." Clara could visualize the other woman

waving off the digression. "Tell me what happened with the painter."

"It was so weird." Becca was still talking as she reached over to stroke Harriet's orange and white fur. "I didn't have any sense—I mean, I trusted him."

Clara eyed her sister. Harriet didn't seem to be enjoying the absentminded stroking that Clara would have reveled in. More than that, however, she seemed intent on holding her place even as Becca shifted.

"Yes, I know he was at Suzanne's building. But the police had questioned him and everything." She turned further as she spoke, but Harriet didn't budge, hanging onto the edge of the sofa cushion with one snowy paw. "It was strange, Maddy. It started off with him telling me something else he heard that day. Something he hadn't told me before. He said he told the cops, but I only have his word for it. And there's something else…"

More high-pitched chatter from the other line.

"He—and, please don't say it—but he knew something he shouldn't." Becca closed her eyes, as if the memory was painful. "When we met, he'd said he didn't know her—that they'd only said hi once or twice. I didn't want him to think I was too flakey, so I'd only told him that Suzanne and I were in a group together. I'm sure of it. But he mentioned the coven, Maddy. He knew Suzanne better than he let on, and, no, I don't think that's the kind of the thing the police would know to ask him about."

Clara didn't have to listen to get the gist of Maddy's response. She agreed that Becca was probably too trusting. What she didn't agree with was that the young woman should probably avoid men for a while. After all, Clara had liked

Nathan's sweet-sharp pine scent and gentle voice as well. But Becca was responding.

"Also, he knows Larissa, which is suspicious. Unless…" She paused, and there was silence on the other end. "Larissa gave him my number. She could have told him about Suzanne, about the coven too. Oh, Maddy, do you think I made a mistake? Do you think I just ran out on a nice guy for no reason?"

"Becca, a woman was killed, and you're worried that you weren't polite?" The answer came back loud and clear, and for once, Clara had to agree.

"I guess you're right." Becca's hand was resting on Harriet's broad back, and Clara waited for her sister to jump down. "At any rate, I should write Larissa a thank you—for the job recommendation, I mean."

"Maybe hold off." Clara barely heard Maddy's response as she focused on her sister. Harriet didn't like steady pressure on any part of her broad anatomy. If she didn't move soon, she was liable to bite. "I asked Reynolds about new hires and he said something about a new guy coming in: a new *guy*."

"Maybe he meant generically?" Becca switched hands on the phone, and Clara breathed a sigh of relief. "A new person?"

"I don't think so. He said something about a fox in the henhouse. I gather the other candidate is coming in next week. I'm sorry, Becca. It's all marketing research anyway. Not the kind of thing you should be doing. I mean, do you really care who is spending more than they can afford?"

Clara longed to lean in and comfort her person. If only Harriet would give way.

"Well, I would have, but it's okay." Becca shrugged.

"That job was a long shot for me anyway."

"Look, I'll see what I can find out." There was an edge in Maddy's voice that made Clara think of Laurel and her dirty tricks. "We're not giving up just yet, kiddo."

Chapter 30

Her friend's words didn't have an immediate effect. Either that, or Laurel was using her powers of suggestion to keep their person nearby, because Becca spent most of the day on the sofa, skimming job sites and the occasional kitten video. But the young woman was too resilient to be thrown for long, and when Tuesday broke with sunny promise, she was up and dressed before any of her cats had finished their morning toilette.

"Another date?" Laurel paused in her routine, paw extended behind her ear.

"I don't think so." Clara tried to hide the worry in her voice. Laurel's plans for their person did not align with what her younger sister saw as Becca's best interest. To cover, she began to lick her paw.

"You just did that one." Laurel's blue eyes didn't miss much. *"What are you hiding?"*

"Bye, kitties!" Becca called. It was a habit, nothing more, but Clara still looked up—and felt a paw weighing down on her tail.

"Talk," said her sister.

"Yeah." Harriet had ambled over. "*Talk.*" From the way the plump orange and white cat was licking her chops, Becca suspected she'd been cleaning the breakfast dishes rather than

her luxurious fur. Still, if she was going to trail Becca, Clara had to rally her sisters to her side and fast.

"I think this has to do with that man she was out with the other night." This was for Laurel, whose tail lashed once, back and forth, in interest. *"He's been texting her. Though it could be a shopping trip."* That was for Harriet. But the plan almost backfired.

"Wait a minute." Harriet wasn't usually that quick on the uptake, but when food was involved she didn't let much get past her. *"You're just saying that..."*

"Look, if you want to join me, you can." Already, Becca's footsteps were growing fainter. *"I'm simply worried about her. And she is our responsibility."*

Harriet looked at Laurel, and Laurel stared back. Clara held her breath, whiskers trembling. Becca was almost out of earshot already. But the little calico had hit on the one truth that all real cats know. Laurel lifted her paw, and in a flash, Clara was out the door, ignoring both its wooden solidity and the latch that had locked it shut.

"Make sure she brings back treats!" Harriet called after her youngest sibling, but she was already gone.

***

Quickly fading her orange patches to grey, Clara did her best to blend in with the morning's shadows. Still, in her haste, she nearly tripped a young mother, busy with her toddler, and had to act fast to dodge a bike messenger cutting across the sidewalk to avoid construction. Her haste paid off, however, as she caught a whiff of Becca's clean, warm scent and—soon after—the sight of her dark curls bobbing through the crowd.

"Maddy's right," she was saying to herself in a voice too soft for any human ear to catch. "I need to get back to work—at least on my own work. It's too easy to rely on web searches, and how can I expect anyone to hire me if I don't keep up with primary sources?"

Her musing and her stride were cut short by the buzz of her phone. For although the young woman kept up her jaunty pace as she fished the device out of her pocket, a quick glance at the screen stopped her cold.

"No!" she exclaimed before even answering. "I'm just—no." She shoved the phone back into her pocket and shut her eyes. By the time she opened them, a few seconds later, her phone had ceased its buzzing. "I'll call them back later," she promised out loud. "Even the police can't expect everyone to take every call."

But it was with a more tentative step that she set out. And when a car drove slowly by, she stopped once more. Black and white at its ends, with a slash of gold in the middle, it resembled nothing so much as a calico like herself, Clara thought. Only the sight of the vehicle—or maybe it was the words written on its side—had Becca gasping.

"They can't…" She paused, her thought unfinished, and turned slowly to check out the road behind her. "Are the police following me?"

Clara had never really envied either of her sisters their particular powers before. Right now, though, she wished she were better at suggestion. Watching her person, frozen with indecision—or could it be fear? —was heartrending. Surely, the appearance of the cruiser, coming right after that rejected call, was coincidental. Besides, she thought, no one could suspect the sweet young woman of murdering her friend, no matter what her unfaithful ex may have suggested to the police.

"Jeff." One word, spit out like a pill, and Becca turned

to walk quite purposefully in the opposite direction. As Clara realized where she was heading, she had to wonder if perhaps she possessed some of Laurel's skill after all.

***

"Jeff Blakey, please." Becca stood at the steel and glass front desk of the Kendall Square startup. Before the purple-haired receptionist could do more than open her mouth, she continued. "Tell him Becca Colwin is here."

"Right away." The receptionist, who couldn't have been much more than Becca's age, bent her over the phone and turned away as much as she dared. "Jeff?" Clara, if not Becca, heard her quite clearly. "There's a girl here to see you. I think she's upset."

"I'm not…" Becca bit back the end of her sentence and began drumming her fingers on the hard surface. "Thank you," she said when the receptionist looked up again, the jewel in her pierced nose glittering.

"He'll be right out." The receptionist blinked and then turned quickly away.

"Maybe he does think I'm dangerous." Becca's faint murmur was nearly drowned out by the tattoo of her drumming, but she kept it up until her ex pushed open a glass door to step into the reception area.

"Becca." He flipped his hair back. "I wasn't—did we have a date?"

"I need to speak with you." Becca pointed to the office exit. "Now."

***

"Why did you think it was someone in the coven?"

Jeff had appeared surprised when Becca stopped immediately outside the tech central building. When she turned to confront him in her sternest voice, he could only blink in astonishment.

"Jeff Blakey, you answer me." Becca had her arms crossed as she questioned her ex and her stance wide, almost as if she would block him from walking on. "What made you think it was one of us?"

"I don't know." The lanky young man looked down, his hair falling once more in his eyes. "I was just talking, I guess."

"Just talking?" Becca's eyes narrowed, rather like Laurel's, her usual smile long gone as her mouth settled in a firm line. "To the police?"

"Well, I told you what Suzanne said." As he spoke, Jeff glanced back at his office, though whether he was afraid of being overheard or hoping for an opportunity to bolt back in was beyond Clara. "You know, about someone following her. And I didn't want the police to think it was me."

"You didn't mind them thinking it was me though." A bitter note had crept into Becca's voice. "And they evidently believed you. Did they just take you at your word?"

"Oh, honey." Instead of answering, he made the mistake of reaching for her. Laurel couldn't have slapped him down that fast. "I'm…I'm sorry, Becca. I wasn't thinking. I thought I was in the clear, and so when they called me in again, I guess I panicked."

At that, Becca stared at him so hard that Clara began to wonder if her person really did possess magical powers.

"Be honest now," she said, folding her arms again. This time, Clara saw her make a discrete sign with her hands that she knew her person had first seen in one of her books. "Did you hurt Suzanne?"

"No, I did not." He actually faced her as he spoke and that, more than any supposedly magical gesture, convinced Clara, if not Becca, that he was most likely telling the truth.

Or at least part of it. "So, why, Jeff? And don't hold back."

The young man before her sighed, as if he could deflate and disappear, and then craned around once in a fruitless search for an escape. "Okay, I hurt her. But not like that!" He rushed to counter Becca's panicked response. "Look, I wasn't the best—I should never have been with her. I was thinking about you, really. And I thought she had picked up on that."

Becca waited, her skepticism showing on her face.

"She said something about how she'd found out something—something unexpected."

"Did it have to do with money?" Becca interrupted. "With funds going missing?"

"Maybe. No. I don't know." Her ex looked thoroughly miserable. He didn't even bother brushing away the hair that fell, limp, over his eyes as he slumped forward. "All I know was that she said she'd stumbled on to something that was supposed to be a secret.

"She never told me what it was." He spoke softly now, as if talking to himself. "I thought it was about me. About something I'd done, and then, adding it together with her saying that someone was following her, I thought that maybe you–"

"A secret. And you thought—" Realization was dawning on Becca as she recounted what her ex had said. "You didn't want me coming over to your place that Saturday. You thought that I might have been stalking Suzanne, and that the cops might have thought you were. And for all your protestations, it seems you must have an alibi that you don't want to tell me about. Jeff Blakey, you were cheating on Suzanne too. Weren't you? That's why she took down all her photos from Facebook. Photos of the two of you. She dumped you—and you, you had another girl at your place on the Saturday that Suzanne was killed. Maybe even when you called me."

"It was all wrong with Suzanne from the start." He didn't even bother to deny it. "I never should have—I missed you, Becca. It just took me all that to realize how much you meant to me. I'm so sorry. I never should have broken up with you. I never should have said anything about you to the cops."

"No, Jeff, you shouldn't have. But you did."

When he reached once more for her hand, she pulled away without any sign of regret.

"Goodbye, Jeff. Take care of yourself." She didn't, thought Clara, even sound that sad.

Chapter 31

Jeff had stood, watching, as Becca walked away without looking back. Her cat had been particularly proud of the way she had strode off, as confident as a tabby in the clear fine day.

But as soon as she'd turned the corner, Becca's shoulders slumped. And while Clara didn't see any tears on her dear person's cheeks, she could tell from the way her lips trembled and how she jammed her hands into her pockets that she was fighting to hold them off.

Once again, Clara wished for Laurel's powers—or at least the freedom to show herself and cheer her person with a head butt and a purr. Maybe some of that translated, however, because before long, Becca was standing straighter. Soon, she even caught herself—looking around as if realizing where she was—and spoke aloud. "Research," she said. "Time to get back to work." And when she turned and began walking with a sense of purpose, Clara trotted along, out of sight but cheered beyond measure.

The word spoken by the young woman meant little to the cat. The idea of research, as well as work, for that matter, is foreign to felines. Clara, like her sisters, had gained her in-depth knowledge of the world through instinct, as much as observation. However, what she did understand as well as she knew her own whiskers were her sacred obligations to the young woman ahead of her, not only as royalty but as a pet. The fact that she also loved Becca, with her earnest intentions and gentle voice, only made these duties more pressing.

Clara knew she had her sisters to turn to if anything were to happen to Becca. But neither the fluffy Harriet nor the sly Laurel could ever replace the petite brunette with the curly hair and the gentle voice, for all her all-too-human bumbling. Clara had spoken the truth when questioned by her sisters. She didn't know what Becca had planned, or where she was going—she certainly could not have anticipated that detour with Jeff. But thinking of that uncomfortable confrontation, Clara felt her apprehension growing, as Becca picked up her pace, pushing along crowded sidewalks and then—with barely a pause—dashing across a busy street. Becca meant well, but her less-than-feline senses didn't pick up the dangers that Clara's did. Her kind heart was too trusting, her manner too open. For a small creature—and the young woman was relatively small in the greater scheme of things—she was positively careless. Or so Clara thought as the young woman turned from the street toward a looming red stone building and trotted up the wide steps as if unafraid of whatever she might find inside.

***

Clara made it in before the heavy door slammed shut, in time to see Becca approach a carved wooden barrier that stood waist-high, barely containing the aged dragon inside.

"Records, please?" Becca approached and the creature looked up, her scowl hinting at unimagined terrors. Amazed at the valor of the young woman she loved, Clara drew back. Only her devotion to the girl kept her from running.

"Third floor," said the dragon, and went back to her newspaper.

Clara watched as Becca began ascending the wide steps. These were a challenge for the cat, as they offered little shadows and no place to hide. And while they weren't as crowded as the city sidewalk, there were plenty of people walking both up and down. A feline, even a magical one, might be noticed here.

Still, when Becca turned onto the landing, Clara knew she had to act. With a mad dash she leaped up the stairs two at a time. "What!" A woman gasped, causing her companion to turn in alarm.

"I thought…" The woman gaped around her, pushing her glasses higher up on her nose. "Never mind," she said. But by then, Clara was gone.

She found Becca one flight up, inside a large room lined with files. Although the flickering blue light of the overhead fluorescents didn't offer much in terms of shadows, this room was at least quieter. Indeed, the blue-haired woman behind the counter appeared to be asleep.

"Excuse me?" Becca's voice was soft. Living with cats, she had practice at gently interrupting a nap. Not until the woman blinked up at her did she continue. "I'd like to make a records search."

Records. Suddenly, it all became clear. Reassured now of her person's purpose, Clara found a corner by the window as Becca filled out paperwork. So this is what her person did at work, Clara thought to herself, watching as Becca took what looked like a large bound journal over to a table and began making notes onto a pad. From the way she tilted her head and bit her lip, it was easy to see the young woman was deeply engaged, and the scratching of her pencil certainly sounded industrious. Watching her, Clara realized that her person had a rich interior life of her own, something her cat had never fully realized. This made her respect Becca and love her even more. It also, if she was being honest, made her a little sleepy.

"Thank you, yes. The family name is Horne—Horne or Horne Colwin." Clara jumped. She must have fallen asleep. Becca was standing before the clerk again, only this time she was handing back the large journal. In its place, the blue-haired woman offered her a box. Even from where she sat, Clara could smell dust and age—and something else as well. A certain familiar spice that drew her over to the table where, once again, Becca sat as she began to go through the papers within.

"Here it is," she muttered to herself as she made another notation in her book. "Marriage and household…1749." Clara's ears pricked up. Cats may not be the best with dates, but some years were not to be forgotten. "Rebecca Horne and…Mistress Greybar?"

Becca pushed her chair back with a squeak that made Clara flinch. "That doesn't make sense." As if she were arguing with herself, she sat up, turning the card over in her hand, and then placed it on the table, drawing another and then a third from the file. "The cat is listed as the principal—" Another card and another soft sigh of exasperation. "Impossible," she said at last. "These records…the transcription…there must be something wrong here."

With another squeak, she stood and carried the file box back to the front desk, but the clerk there was at the far end of her enclosure, in close conference with a conservatively dressed older woman whose hair was done up in a khaki turban. Heads together, they appeared to be speaking softly, and neither noticed the agitated young woman who waited with growing impatience.

Cats don't count time, not as humans do, but the confidential chat did seem to go on for a bit. Even as the clerk tried to draw away, the older woman reached out, holding onto her arm as if loathe to let her go.

Maybe it was that move or the clerk's apparent desire to end the conversation or a certain familiarity to the dark purple nails on the older woman's manicured hand, but something emboldened Becca. "Excuse me," she said, and then repeated herself. "Excuse me," her voice somewhat too loud for politeness's sake.

"I'm sorry." The clerk pulled away, though whether her apology was to the turbaned woman or the client she'd kept waiting was unclear.

"Larissa!" Becca started, for the turbaned woman had looked up as her confidante withdrew. "It's me, Becca."

"Becca, darling." The older witch came forward, a smile spreading across her face, which was much less heavily made up than usual. "My." Those lacquered nails came up to her mouth, as if she had suddenly remembered her appearance. "My dear! Do tell, what brings you here?"

"Research," said Becca. If her colleague's unusually mundane attire surprised her, she didn't let on. "I'm sorry if I—"

"No, no, no." Larissa waved off her objection. "Please, go on."

"It's busywork, really," Becca admitted. "I figure, until I get something else, I might as well keep my skills up, and I've always been interested in genealogy. But I might have just found something that may explain what's been going on."

"What's been going on?" Larissa's brows arched like a cat's back, and Clara felt her own fur rising in response. "Dearest, you have to tell me."

"Please don't." Clara did her best to focus. If only she had her sister's power. If only her person could see how her words appeared to have set the older woman on edge. But no matter how the little calico concentrated, Becca kept on talking.

"I wish I could. I feel like I've gotten so close." Becca sighed, as if the effort cost her. "Only I think that something must have gotten messed up over the years."

"Is it something I can help you with?" The clerk interrupted, and Clara thought she seemed grateful to focus on her other client. "Perhaps if you tell me what happened, we can clear it up."

"It's silly." Realizing she had an audience, Becca gave an embarrassed laugh. "But are you sure that these are careful transcriptions of the original records?"

"Of course. This office houses family records—births, deaths, and marriages—back to 1635, as well as documentation of financial transactions in the public record." She sounded quite proud. "In fact, I was just telling your friend here—"

"It's not important." Larissa slipped around the counter and took Becca's arm. "Just a fancy."

"Well, good." The clerk sounded relieved. "Because these are public records, ma'am. That's the point of our office."

"Of course they are." With a grin like a Cheshire cat's, Larissa dismissed the clerk and led Becca away from the desk. "So please, dear girl, tell me more about what you've discovered."

Clara watched in horror as the older woman led her

person away with a grip on her upper arm as firm as a new mother's on a kitten.

"It's just…odd." Once Becca was into her work, Clara remembered with dismay, she lost sight of anything else. "I've been tracing my family history. Did I tell you, one of my ancestors was reported to be a witch?"

"Woman of power, *please*." Larissa winced but kept walking, propelling Becca toward the exit. "So, you're researching your family?"

"Yes." Becca pulled back. "That's why I joined the coven in the first place. I mean, I was interested, of course, but—"

"Of course," Larissa burst out. "I remember now. How fascinating. My own family history is shrouded in shadow. I believe we may have Native American ancestry—the name Fox, of course."

"I see." Becca didn't look like she did. "Is that what you were asking the clerk about?"

"What? No, nothing like that." Without the flowing sleeves, Larissa's dramatic dismissal resembled a flailing fledgling.

Maybe that's what brought Becca back. "I'm sorry I didn't see you at first." Becca took in her colleague as if seeing her for the first time. "I've been kind of caught up—and I should get back."

"But I've wanted to speak with you." Larissa leaned in close enough for Becca to note the fine lines around her eyes. "Alone." A dramatic pause as she batted those eyes. "Have you noticed anything odd about Ande? She seems to have become fixated."

"Ande?" Becca examined the woman in front of her,

as if the answer to her query would be written on those black brows or the hawk-like nose between them. "Fixated—on what?"

"On Trent, of course." Larissa's voice had dropped to a whisper. "You know she has a crush on him."

"No, she said—" Rather than finish her sentence, Becca extricated her arm. "I'm sorry. I need to get back."

Larissa reached for her once again, and Clara saw her opening. As Becca stepped back toward the records, the cat ducked her head and jumped. Landing a beat behind her person, the agile feline arched her back and hissed. It wasn't enough—the toe of Larissa's shoe still caught her in the belly as she stepped forward—but at least it was the rounded toe of a running shoe rather than her usual pointy number. Plus, the impact did cause the other woman to stumble and pause as she righted herself. And with that, Clara dashed off after Becca, slipping into the records room just as the door swung closed.

"Hang on!" Becca called out. The clerk was in the process of lifting the journal off her desk. "I'm sorry. My friend wanted to talk with me."

"I'm sorry as well." The blue-haired woman put the journal back down with care. "I hope I didn't lose your place. Too many patrons don't bother to bring the materials back, you see."

"No, it's fine." Becca glanced down at the open book. "I'm almost done, anyway. There's just one thing in here I don't understand."

Cat-shaped glasses tipped, waiting. "Maybe I'm reading this wrong," said Becca. "But this lists the residents of this house as Mistress Rebecca Horne, widow, and Mistress Greybar. I'd come to believe that Mistress Greybar was

Rebecca Horne's cat."

The eyes behind those glasses stared back. "And?"

"Well, doesn't it seem odd to you that her cat is given the same standing as her owner?"

"I don't know what to tell you." The blue-haired woman sniffed. "I'd read that as this Mistress Greybar being a member of the family. I can tell you that our records have not been altered in any way. Though perhaps there was an error. Your friend…" She shook her head.

"I'm sorry." Becca's voice softened. "She can be a bit imperious. Did she think you—or your office—had done something wrong?"

"Not really." Another shake. "I shouldn't be discussing other clients' issues anyway."

"I understand." Becca lowered her voice, but there was a note in it that let Clara know she was hatching a plan. "I'm actually wondering if you can help me with something else—something that might be related. I'm not sure what she told you, but my friend and I both belong to a group, and I believe its financial records might be on file here."

"If you're incorporated here in the city, or have applied for a license, they are." If Becca had hoped the bespectacled clerk would reveal Larissa's request, she was to be disappointed. However, before she could come up with another query, the clerk retreated to the desk and so Becca followed. "What name is your organization incorporated under?"

"Oh." Becca stared down, as if the answer would appear on the counter before her. "I don't know if we're incorporated."

"Do you hold a license? Pay municipal taxes?"

"No." Becca drew the word out while she thought. "I

know, why don't you look up licenses under the name of our founder, Larissa Fox."

"Would you write that down?"

Becca filled out the proffered form and returned it to the clerk, who took it back to her files, tut-tutting as she walked. While she waited, Becca stared at the door. Questions about Larissa were palpably weighing on her. But before she could do anything about them, the cat-eye glasses were staring back at her.

"Are you confident about these names?"

"Yes, though not the spelling—"

The clerk cut her off. "I tried alternative spellings, including double X and a PH for Fox. It didn't change anything. I don't have any records of ownership or licenses in this city for anyone named Larissa Fox."

Chapter 32

"Maddy, it's the strangest thing." Becca reached her friend as she made her way home. "I wouldn't have even thought of asking, only Larissa was going on about Ande, like she'd done something wrong, and then I remembered that Ande was the reason that Suzanne was asking about the coven's money. She said we were down a few thousand dollars, and—"

"Becca, do you hear yourself?" Maddy's patience was running thin. "Bad enough you're in this crazy group, now you're getting involved in its finances?"

"But that's just it." Becca had been mulling this over. "This might be why Suzanne was killed. After all, if Suzanne thought that somebody was embezzling—"

"Becca! Stop it! This is a police matter, okay?" When Maddy yelled, her voice was audible even to the people on the street. "Leave it to them, please."

"But the police don't really understand about the coven." Becca had to make Maddy understand. "They're not going to know how we all relate to each other, and they wouldn't have heard about the funds going missing."

"Didn't you say this Ande was going to tell them?"

Becca bit back her retort. "She promised to, but she didn't seem to think it was a big deal."

"Okay, then you've got to tell them—" Maddy stopped

herself.

"You just said that I should stay out of it." Becca was nothing if not reasonable.

"No, you're right." Maddy was obviously making plans. "I'm sorry I even said anything. You've got to stay as far away from this as you can. I'm sorry you're even still talking to anyone in that coven of yours. Besides, like you said, if this Ande was the whistleblower and even she didn't think it was a big deal, then it wasn't, I'm sure."

"But Larissa was definitely hiding something," Becca said, as much to herself as her friend. "She didn't want me to hear what she was looking for in the records. She tried to hustle me out of there."

"She's a weird old lady, from what you've told me." Maddy wasn't giving up. "She was probably just hoping to find out she had a witch in her background too."

"Maybe." Becca had to agree. "She did go on a bit about her heritage. Though between you and me, I think Fox might be a made-up name."

The burst of laughter made her draw back from the phone. "You think?" Clara could picture Becca's friend wiping away the tears. "Hey, kiddo, I think I may have found out something about the other candidate for the Reynolds job."

"Yeah?" Becca's cheer suddenly dissipated. "Let me guess, he's got a master's."

"No, but he seems to be very chummy with Reynolds. The old buzzard walked him out, and I heard him say something about 'your mother.' Friend of the family, I'm guessing."

"Great." Clara didn't really understand sarcasm. Cats don't need it. But even she could tell that Becca's response didn't reflect her true feelings. "Well, without an advanced degree, I was a long shot for that position anyway."

"I'm sorry. I'd have loved to have you here. Even though this Nathan is kinda dishy."

"Wait—Nathan?" Becca stopped cold, earning a nasty look from a passing shopper

"Yeah, didn't I tell you? He breezed right past Ms. White, so I asked. His name's Nathan Raposa."

* * *

Maddy hadn't managed to calm her friend down by the time Becca got home. But Clara was grateful for the other girl's attempts.

"I'll come by as soon as I'm sprung," Maddy had said, signing off. "I'll bring wine—and chocolate."

Clara didn't have a chance to warn her sisters, as Becca clomped into the house in a mixture of anger and despair.

"I can't even…" was all she said as the three cats circled in wordless sympathy. Clara had, by then, unmasked herself to join the throng. "And now, you!" This, alas, was to Harriet, who hadn't moved quite quickly enough and nearly tripped their person.

"Harriet!" Clara head butted her older sister out of the way. *"Watch it! Becca's had a bad shock."*

"Becca? What about me?" Harriet sat and began to groom, but at least this time Becca saw her and managed to step around her. *"Clearly nobody cares about me or what I want."*

"Quit grumbling." Laurel rubbed against Becca's shins and, as their person stopped to reach down and stroke her silky fur, took in her scent with a black leather nose. "*Interesting,"* said the Siamese. *"Jeff, and—what's this?—I'm getting a whiff*

of patchouli, or is that pine?"

Clara looked on in dismay, unsure what to do. She'd already lost her chance at the best place next to Becca on the sofa. A soft grunt announced that Harriet had once again taken over that middle cushion, and she now surveyed her sisters as if challenging them to try to unseat her.

"Don't you dare..." A low growl underlined that stare. *"Mine."*

"Fine." Clara settled on the rug as Becca made her way to the sofa.

"Oh, kitties." Becca sat with an exasperated sigh. "You don't know the half of it."

"If the clown here would tell us, we would." Laurel sidled up to her sister.

"I will, I promise." Clara kept her voice low. It would do her person good to sleep. A nap, as all cats know, is always a sensible option.

But before Becca could drift off into a healing slumber, the doorbell rang and she sat up with a jerk. "Maddy!" At least she was smiling as she approached the door, although when she opened it, that smile disappeared. "Kathy?"

"Hi, am I disturbing you?" The perky redhead beamed up at her. "I'd been meaning to give you a call about Eric. I know you said he blew you off, but, believe me, he's going to be looking for someone soon—if he isn't already—and so I thought I'd drop by."

"Oh, thanks." Becca sounded more confused than grateful, but she stood aside to invite the other woman in. "Did you just get off work?"

"I was in the area." That eager smile. "Anyway, about the job. We're short now, even if Eric's too cheap to admit it.

I know Larissa's friend is looking for someone too. But you didn't sound too keen about that, and since I know one of the other girls I work with is going to give notice at the end of the week…well, my boss will definitely need someone, and we're almost like family."

Walking into the living room as she rambled on, Kathy eyed Harriet and then took Becca's place on the sofa. Wisely, she didn't reach for Harriet's pillow.

"So, have you talked to Trent much?" Settling in, she leaned back to address her hostess. "I mean, since the whole thing with Suzanne?"

"What? No." Becca passed behind her into the kitchen. "I still have trouble believing it—and I, well, I was there."

Kathy fell uncharacteristically silent, her round face drawn with concern.

"I'm sorry." Becca leaned back into the room "Would you like something to drink? I still have some of that wine."

"Oh, no, thanks." Kathy managed a smile again. "I'd take a Diet Coke, if you have it?"

"Coming up." As Becca fussed in the kitchen, Kathy looked around. Harriet threw a protective paw over her pillow. The other, Clara noticed, stayed on the edge of the cushion. A nasty premonition began to make the fur rise along her back.

"Harriet..."

"I'm sorry, you were asking—were you close to Suzanne?" Becca returned with their drinks. "I gather she and Ande were into something together."

"I didn't really keep up with Suzanne, but Ande, I just don't know." Kathy took a sip, but her wide brown eyes stayed focused on Becca. "She's been bad mouthing Trent, you know. No sense of loyalty."

"Really?" Becca paused. "I thought they were on good terms."

Kathy shook her head. "Not since she made that play for him. I don't know what she was thinking, but she's not his type, if you know what I mean. Same thing happened with Marcia, a little while before you joined."

"Ah."

Maybe it was that wordless exhalation or maybe Kathy saw something on Becca's face, because hers grew suddenly concerned.

"Oh, dear! What is it?" She leaned in, her eyes wide with sympathy.

"Nothing major." Becca shook her head, eager to stem the younger woman's gossip. "It's me," she said at last. "I had a weird date with someone over the weekend. Another Mr. Wrong."

Kathy giggled and sat back, as if waiting for the story. "Tell me about it," she said. "But really, slandering someone is not the way to go."

"I didn't—" Becca sat up.

"Not you, silly." To Becca's surprise, Kathy stood to go. "I meant Ande. But hey, I'm glad I caught you. You really should send a resume over to Eric. Or—do you want me to?"

"If you wouldn't mind. He kind of gave me the cold shoulder. Hang on." Becca went to get her laptop, nudging the pillow as she rose. In response, Harriet slammed a paw down—but not so fast that Clara didn't see something glitter.

Clara's fur rose further.

"What's that, kitty?" Kathy had seen it too, and as Clara looked on in horror, the guest reached over. Harriet, torn between guarding her pillow and the shiny toy, started to growl.

"No!" Despite the growing danger, Kathy wasn't addressing the cats. Instead, she was looking at the small, gold object in her hand. A perfect replica of Trent's amulet.

"*What did you do?*" Clara was standing, back arched as she stared at her sister.

"*That's mine!*" Harriet had struggled to her feet. Ignoring her sister, she turned to the invader, her growl growing to a high-pitched whine.

"Kitties! What's the—" Becca had returned, laptop in hand. "Kathy, watch—"

Too late, Harriet had already coiled—an orange and white fury with one goal in sight. Launching herself, she wrapped her paws around Kathy's hand and sunk her teeth into the soft flesh of her thumb.

"Ow!" Pulling her hand back, the redhead freed herself with a jerk that sent the amulet flying to the floor. That's when Clara saw her moment. With one leap, she landed on the gold replica and—hearing the thud as her sister hit the floor beside her—sent it flying.

"Kathy, are you okay?" Becca was kneeling on the sofa beside her visitor, examining the bite marks on her hand. "It doesn't look like she drew blood."

"I'm fine." The redhead snapped, pulling her hand back to cradle it against her body.

"I'm sorry, really." Becca looked mortified. "Sometimes they fight, but they've never…" She broke off. "I'm sorry."

"Don't sweat it." Kathy was already rising. "Good luck with that guy you're seeing." And with that she was gone.

"Harriet, Clara, really!" The slamming of the door had frozen both cats in their tracks. Clara looked up at her person in dismay. Harriet was still glaring at her sister. That lucky shot had set the little gold piece skidding under Becca's big armchair—where the original had ended up after Harriet first grabbed it and where the marmalade was too stout to follow. "What got into you?"

Clara rose and approached her person carefully. Tail down, in dismay, it was all she could do to gently rub her head against Becca's outstretched hand. To try to explain about Harriet's ability—and her selfish decision to recreate the amulet that she had so envied—was beyond her. Even if she could manage the language skills, to let a human in on the powers they all shared was forbidden. Not to mention how hurt Becca would be if she ever found out that it was her plump feline who had managed that original summoning, rather than herself. Becca was just beginning to have faith in herself once more. Even if she could, Clara would do nothing to discourage her now.

Chapter 33

By the time Maddy came by, Becca had rallied. Harriet was still upset, of course, and had already boxed Clara's ears twice. Laurel, perhaps wisely, was staying out of this particular squabble. She sat on top of the bookshelf, observing the proceedings with her cool blue eyes.

"I think everyone in that coven of yours is crazy." Instead of cookies, Maddy had brought a bottle of wine, and after pouring them both healthy glasses, she had plopped down on the sofa and listened to Becca's story once again. "And I'm glad you walked out on this Nathan—that's definitely the same guy." She paused to pour herself more. "Do you think he could be Suzanne's stalker?"

"I don't know." Becca looked into her own nearly full glass as if it held the answer. "He keeps texting me now too."

"What does he say?" Maddy sidled up to her friend, as if she expected her to pull the phone out right then.

"Well, he started off worried about me, asking why I ran off." Becca raised her glass and twirled it before taking a tentative sip. "Then he asked if he'd done anything wrong."

"Anything wrong—like stalking you." Maddy sat back, set on her conclusion. "I mean, first he calls out of nowhere and asks questions about you, and then he takes what should have been your job."

"It wasn't actually out of nowhere," Becca began to protest, but her friend cut her off.

"But you said you didn't tell him about the coven, and he knew about that, right?"

"Yeah, but he does know Larissa, so she probably told him." Becca had had time to think. "Maybe Larissa recommended him for the job too. If he also has a family connection, it makes sense."

"Stalker." Maddy seemed to be relishing this. "And a creep. But I blame that Larissa too. I mean, she said she'd refer you for that job."

"Yeah, but…" Becca looked at her friend, as if she weren't sure if she should continue.

"Becca?" Sensing something good, Maddy put her drink down.

"Something someone said—I think Larissa might, you know, keep her boyfriends."

"Keep, as in retain?"

"Not exactly." Becca lowered her voice, although neither Harriet nor Laurel were listening. "Keep as in pay for. And that first time I ran into Nathan he said he was visiting a relative but …"

"Ah." Maddy sat back, resting her wine glass on Harriet's pillow. Clara, who had been paying attention, thought the plump woman did not appear overly surprised. "And suddenly the handsome painter gets a referral to a cush office job. Though he's not going to keep that lovely sun-kissed look if he comes to work for us."

"But why would Reynolds hire him?" Becca hugged her knees to her chest, like she did when she was thinking, and turned to face her friend. "I mean, to be honest, he didn't seem particularly pleased when I said Larissa had sent me—he even told me that she'd used up her credit, or words to that effect."

"Well, maybe you're in luck, then, kiddo." Maddy shifted to face her, moving her glass back to the table, much to Clara's relief. "Maybe you're still in the running. Maybe this wasn't even a real interview. He wasn't in there for long."

"Maybe." Becca looked doubtful, and Harriet used that moment to swat once more at Clara.

"What's up with your cats?" Maddy looked at them as if seeing them for the first time.

"They've been fighting." Another shake of the head. "I don't know why. I think Clara stole a toy. I saw something go flying."

"Don't you dare!" Clara hissed, and immediately regretted it. Only after the words were out of her mouth did she realize that her sister hadn't been paying attention.

"*Meow!"* Too late now. With her most plaintive mew, Harriet drew all eyes to her as she lay down and stretched her paw under the armchair. *"Please!"*

"Oh, poor kitty." Becca was up in a moment. "Hang on."

While Maddy watched, Becca tilted the chair back, revealing a well-chewed catnip mouse, a wad of aluminum foil that Laurel had become obsessed with over a month before. And, yes, the replica of Trent's golden amulet.

"What is that?" Maddy was on the shiny piece before Harriet could right herself, carrying it to the kitchen to examine it in better light. Short though she was, once she stood up, she was out of the cat's reach.

"That's—no, that's impossible." Becca seemed as stunned as Kathy had been.

"Becca?" Maddy looked from the trinket to her friend.

"That's Trent's. From my coven, the, uh, warlock." Maddy's brows went up, but she kept silent. "He came back after the coven meeting, and we were sitting on the sofa." The color in Becca's cheeks only made Maddy's brows rise higher. "He had that on a chain and it must have been swinging and, well, you know how cats are with moving objects. Anyway, Harriet took a swipe at it and broke the chain. But I thought he'd picked it up."

"You've been busy." She fixed her friend with a quizzical stare. "So it wasn't all painter boy?"

"It wasn't like that." Becca looked down, her cheeks positively scarlet. "Well, it might have been. Only, I didn't expect it. I mean, he's been flirty, but, Maddy, I think he's flirty with all the women. Anyway, he had just kissed me when that—when Harriet intervened. She scratched him too. Not intentionally, I don't think. Just that her claw got caught. Anyway, that, ah, broke the mood, and he left soon after."

"You'd almost think your cat was looking out for you." Maddy was still smiling, but her face grew serious as she looked at the amulet again. "This feels like real gold. And he just left it?"

"I was sure he'd taken it. I thought I saw him put it in his pocket." She shook her head. "I mean, he didn't ask me to look for it or anything."

"Is he rich?" Maddy was rolling the amulet between her thumb and forefinger. Harriet, Clara suspected, had made the piece heavier than the original. Maybe slightly larger too—those plush paws weren't as dexterous as human fingers.

"I don't think I've ever heard him talk about a job," Becca admitted.

With a sigh, Maddy handed over the piece. "I don't know, Becca. Between a rich playboy and a stalker-y creep, I think you've got to meet some new guys. But, hey, if you're really okay, I think I'm going to crash."

Becca didn't argue as she escorted her friend to the door, examining the piece as she walked. "What is it?" her friend asked.

"I'm not sure." Becca was examining the back of the amulet. "Only, I thought there was something engraved on the back. I remember reaching for it, and Trent kind of pulled it away. That's what caught Harriet's eye, I think. And this piece? It's blank."

"I'd say your mind was on something else that night," said her friend. "I mean, there it is, solid in your hand."

***

"How could you?" Clara turned on her oldest sister in fury. Never mind protocol, Harriet was endangering them all.

The big marmalade knew it. *"It's just a small thing,"* she pouted. *"And so shiny. And now I have to make another."*

"Don't you dare!" Clara was positively spitting, she was so mad. *"Don't you see what you've done? Now there are two of them. And Becca is going to return it to that Trent—and then they'll know!"*

"Return it?" Harriet's fluffy face screwed up in confusion, her nose pulling in like a pedigreed Persian. *"But it's mine."*

"Don't be dense." Laurel landed with a thud between them. *"Both of you. This is going to make things interesting. Becca's going to bring that Trent around again now. She'll have to."*

Clara sat, her tail curled around her fore paws, and

brooded. Although she was unable to explain why to her sisters, she knew from her whiskers to her tail tip that none of this boded well.

Chapter 34

The text messages continued, as did the calls. Clara could tell from the beeps and buzzes Becca's phone made, even as she left it on the table. In part, Clara thought, her person was ignoring the tiny machine, despite the tantalizing way it vibrated. In part, she feared, Becca was trying to make sense of the amulet—doing her best to reconcile her memory with the palpable reality she now held in her palm.

Deprived of her toy, Harriet turned her attention to the device. Perched on a chair, she reached one paw up, intending to hook it and send it flying. Laurel looked on, mildly amused, until another vibration sent her back to the apartment door. Clara, catching the same emanation a moment later, froze—torn between her person and that infernal device, and the interruption about to occur.

"What?" Becca looked up seconds later, as a loud rapping sounded on her door. The faint scent of pine, as well as Laurel's satisfied smirk, alerted Clara to the visitor's identity, but Becca, oblivious to such subtle clues, opened it, only to jump back with a start.

"Nathan!" She moved to shut the door. His work boot, splashed with paint, blocked it.

"Becca, please. I can explain."

She looked up at him, mouth agape, and relaxed her hold on the door—just as he pulled his foot out.

"I'm sorry," he said. She was leaning on the door—ready to slam it shut. Only, she didn't, which Clara thought curious. "I'll stay here," he said, seemingly chastened.

Becca looked at him, and for a moment Clara wondered if she did indeed have magical skills. The way she studied his face seemed to be seeking something in his eyes. Something deep. Finally, tilting her head, she spoke again. "Tell me," she said, "how did you find out where I live?"

"Larissa," he responded, spitting the name out as if it tasted bad. "I mean, she'd already given me your number."

"And about the coven?" She was relaxing—Clara could hear it—but she waited while he nodded.

"Larissa again." He gave up the name with a sigh. "And I'm sorry, I should've told you—I'm sorry I scared you. For what it's worth, I've had enough. I'm not going to cover for her anymore."

"Cover?" Becca, intrigued, didn't shut the door. She didn't move to open it up any further either. Instead, she stood, one arm on the frame.

He nodded. "She thinks she can control everything. But I'm through with that."

Becca waited, but it didn't take any particular skill to see that she was factoring in what she'd heard about the older woman—and about younger men. Her "pets."

"The job." Her voice was flat. "My friend Maddy saw you today. I know Larissa is setting you up. Getting you that job."

"What? No, I have a job. I paint houses."

"Right." Clara had never heard Becca sound so angry.

She glanced over at her sister. Laurel's eyes were wide. "Look, I get it. This is an expensive city, and Larissa is generous. Larissa likes to help people. Larissa likes her 'pets,' especially young, good-looking men."

"Larissa," Nathan cut her off before she could go any further, "is my mother."

***

Ten minutes later, the two were sitting on the sofa, Laurel curled and purring between them. Clara, for her part, was trying to make sense of all she'd heard. So, for that matter, was Becca.

"I'm sorry I let it go on so long," the handsome painter was saying. "She gave me your number and then she told me where you live. She seemed to really like the idea of us getting to know each other, and, no, she didn't tell me you were in the coven together. She didn't have to—as soon as I heard you say 'Larissa,' I knew. She only uses that name for her so-called 'mystical' endeavors. To everyone else, she's plain old Risa."

"Risa?" Becca tried to reconcile the old-fashioned name with the woman she knew. The jet-black hair. The scarves and the perfume. "Larissa is Risa. Your mother. That's why you were bringing flowers over. But why Fox?"

"Just a translation." He smiled, as if at a private joke. "Raposa means fox in Portuguese. So, yeah, Risa Raposa. I guess it's better than what my father did."

Becca's confusion showed in her face.

"He anglicized it. Well, sort of. Reynolds was his version. I think someone told him that fox in French was renard, and he either misheard or thought that still sounded too foreign."

"Reynolds—like Reynolds and Associates?"

"Yeah, you know them?"

"That's the job—the one I thought Larissa—your mother—was setting you up for." She couldn't hide the humor in her voice. "Suzanne worked there, and my friend Maddy does too. She saw you at the office and thought you were there for an interview."

"No." He dismissed the idea, shaking his head. "I pity anybody who has to work for my father. I mean, no—you can't think…"

"I don't." Becca finished his thought. "In fact, I'm trying to leave all that to the police, but I haven't heard anything that would imply he's involved."

"Good." A sigh of relief. "He's not a bad guy, but, wait, you want to work for him?"

"Yeah." Becca nodded. "Well, I've applied for a position there. Thought I had it too. Reynolds—your father—seemed to like me. But then Maddy heard that someone else was being interviewed—one of Larissa—*Risa's*—pets. So…"

Before she could spell it out, Nathan interrupted with a laugh. A nice laugh, thought Clara. Not too loud, but it came from his belly like a purr. "No wonder you thought I was her boy toy!"

Becca didn't comment. She didn't have to.

"Believe me, I know about my mother. So does my father. It's part of her whole thing—wanting to be young forever. It's probably why she got into the whole magic thing."

"Huh." Becca fell silent, lost in thought.

"I'm sorry, I don't mean to downplay your group, if it works for you." Nathan leaned back, unburdened. "I mean, I understand about Wicca having spiritual aspects and everything…"

Becca wasn't listening. "Maybe that's why Trent didn't look harder," she said to herself. Nathan looked at her inquisitively, but she shook him off. "It's nothing. A small thing that was puzzling me. That's all. So, if it wasn't about the job, why were you at the office today, if you don't mind me asking?"

"Hey, I feel like you have the right to ask anything." He grinned a bit sheepishly. "He wanted me to drop by. I thought it was about finishing up that triple-decker. Yeah, he's a landlord—and the source of most of my referrals, I've got to admit. Turns out, he wanted to talk to me about doing an intervention. They fight like cats and dogs, but at some level he still loves my mom. She probably still loves him too, but he's worried. She's spending way too much money, and he thinks she's being ripped off."

"That fits with something Ande—another member of our group—said." Becca was thinking out loud. "Only, I had the impression that it was our group finances that were going missing."

Nathan's face said it all.

"The group finances are really Larissa's—Risa's." The reality kicked in as Becca pieced together everything she'd heard. "Despite what we chip in, we're just a pet project for her, aren't we?"

"Hey, she can afford it." Nathan was making nice. "I mean, Dad's done well and she has a good income. Only, it's not unlimited, and he's getting sick of bailing her out."

"Did you tell the cops all this?" Another, darker thought was clouding Becca's brow. "I mean, about your mother and the money and all?"

"Of course." He sounded concerned. "But she's not—I

mean, she can be pretty nutty and everything but she's not a killer."

Becca held back from saying the obvious—that somebody was. Nathan must have missed the look on her face, because he kept talking.

"Which, all things considered, is a good thing," he was saying. "Because I know she had a real grudge against that girl, though I guess that's over now."

As soon as the words were out of his mouth, he stopped. "You can't think—" He gasped. "She's—no, Becca, we're talking about my mother."

"I'm sure the police will get to the bottom of it," said Becca, doing her best to sound encouraging. But Clara knew what was going through her mind—that the police had already suspected someone in their coven, and that her person believed herself to be a prime suspect because of her connection with Jeff. "They have to. I wonder if they know…"

"No." Nathan sounded horrified. "Becca…"

"Suzanne was seeing my ex, Jeff. But before then, she'd gone out with Trent, at least a few times." Becca laid out the points, as if talking to herself. "At least, I think so. I don't know if Larissa—Risa—your mom knew, but I think maybe she and Trent might have something going. And I think Suzanne found out that Jeff cheated on her, so I'm wondering if she might have run back to Trent. Or maybe she had been stepping out on Jeff. Or even—"

"Becca, please." The man beside her was pleading. "This is all crazy."

"You're right. I should leave it all to the police." Becca stopped and managed a smile. "This is all…this is a lot to think about." She rose and walked back to the door, turning to

Nathan as he followed. "I believe you about what happened with us, and I'm sorry for running out on you," she said.

"Of course." He made his own brave attempt at a smile. "And I'm sorry I scared you, coming over like this and everything. Only, you wouldn't take my calls."

"No, it's okay." Becca took his hand, and for a moment it seemed like he would say something more. But then he turned and left

Laurel seemed pleased as punch with the visit, purring as Becca stood there, leaning her head against the door. Clara, however, kept her eyes on her person, willing her to ask the questions that were rising in her own mind.

"Don't you think it was a little odd?" she asked her sister. *"Him dropping by like that?"*

"He likes her," purred Laurel. *"He's insistent."*

"I hope she checks on his story." Clara couldn't keep her tail still. Something was wrong, only she couldn't quite put her paw on it.

"It's that mother of his, if anything." Laurel jumped onto the tabletop and began to bathe. *"Becca should steer clear of that one. I bet she's jealous, our girl being so young and pretty. And that she lives with us too."*

"Maybe," said Clara, half to herself. It was difficult to carry on a conversation with Laurel when her sister was up on the table, and she weighed making the leap herself. Becca preferred the cats not to sit there, but she had basically given up on disciplining them. Besides, their person had wandered off into the bedroom, apparently lost in thought as she rummaged through the papers on her desk and then her bureau top as if seeking an elusive prey. Nothing seemed to be stirring though, and so with a wiggle of her behind, Clara prepared to leap up.

That was one advantage of being the smallest. Why Harriet couldn't even—

Then it hit her. Where was Harriet? She craned around, scanning the table as she did so. The amulet—the replica that her oldest sister had summoned for her own amusement, the piece that Becca was clearly searching for—that was missing too. Clara scooted over to where Becca had left it when she'd heard the knocking on the door. Closing her green eyes in despair, Clara felt her ears and whiskers sag. Harriet had been so upset, but because her bulk made jumping up to the tabletop unlikely, Clara hadn't thought she'd be able to do anything about it. Now she remembered her sister, sitting on the chair, one paw hooked up over the surface.

What had happened was obvious. The big white and orange cat had managed to fish it off the table while none of them was looking, and now she and the crucial gold piece were gone.

Chapter 35

Becca was too honest not to call Trent to tell him what she—or Harriet—had found. She wasn't sure what else, exactly, she would say to him, she told Clara the next morning as she continued to search the apartment. After all, it wasn't that he'd lied to her—not exactly. He may simply have chosen not to reveal some aspects of his relationship with Larissa.

"And we're not even sure of that," she said as she peered under the sofa for the umpteenth time. Clara looked over at Laurel, but her sister had grown bored and tuned out, her café au lait side gently rising and falling as she napped.

"I mean, okay, it's likely." Becca, kneeling, looked around. "But it's their business, not mine. Unless…" She bit her lip, and Clara knew she was thinking of Suzanne—and of possible motive. "At any rate, I need to tell him that pendant of his is here, somewhere. If only I could find it."

Just then, Harriet came strolling into the living room. It was certainly close to lunchtime, but considering that her oldest sister had been in the bedroom, Clara wasn't sure why she was licking her chops. And then it hit her.

"*You ate it? That little gold toy you summoned?*" She jumped off the sofa and approached her sister, reaching up to sniff at her whiskers.

"Yes, I did!" Harriet sounded quite pleased with herself as her sister proceeded with her examination. "*So now you can get off my case about it,"* she said smugly.

Clara sat back, waiting.

"I used a treat as a base." Harriet couldn't resist explaining. *"Because it was something I wanted. So when I realized what Becca was looking for, I just turned it back and—yum. It had gotten a little stale, though."*

Clara could have hissed, she was so upset. *"But now Becca will never find it!"*

Harriet's own ears flicked in annoyance. *"Make up your mind, why don't you?"* her words a near snarl as she walked past her sister toward the kitchen. *"First you tell me to get rid of it. Now you're all hissy.*"

"He must be frantic." Becca's words could have described her own state of mind, except for the gender. In fact, over the next hour, she did her best impersonation of an animal on a rampage, her search ramping up as she swiped papers off surfaces and tipped furniture over in a growing frenzy. By the time she had all the sofa cushions up, all three cats were seeking shelter on the windowsill. Quite unfairly, both Laurel and Harriet blamed their youngest sibling.

"I'm not the one who summoned a version of that thing!" Clara defended herself as best she could. She knew what those cold stares could mean, and she had no desire to have her ears boxed or her whiskers pulled. And if Harriet sat on her again… *"I asked you not to do that anymore!"*

It was hopeless. Harriet looked briefly at Laurel, who puffed herself up ever so slightly. Then, both turned to face Clara.

"It has come to our attention that you seem to think

you're the only magical cat in this household." When Harriet spoke in that tone of voice, Clara knew better than to argue, even though her sister was being horribly unfair. *"Time and again, recently, you've countered our quite natural desires to use our skills to entertain ourselves. And—"* Clara couldn't help herself and opened her mouth to object. One raised paw, claws just showing through the white fluff, stopped her, as Harriet continued. *"And thwarted our natural desire to improve the life of our person, as is our duty."*

Biting down hard, Clara kept herself silent. Harriet was reciting the cats' canon law.

"*Instead, you seem to believe that you are the only one who can aid our human in her pursuits, or that you have some kind of special bond with her."*

With that, Harriet turned to Laurel, who stared at her little sister so hard that she began to go cross-eyed. That was the Siamese in her. *"You don't,"* she added, her voice a growly undercurrent to Harriet's pompous mew. The double vision was distracting, Clara knew, and silently thanked their mixed genetics for cutting the lecture short.

"She must be punished." Harriet, still peeved about Clara's interference and the loss of her toy, was not going to let the lesson go that easily. *"I'm out a toy—and a treat!"*

"You ate the treat." Clara couldn't help herself. Harriet turned on her with a snarl.

"Kitties, what is it?" Becca looked up from the floor, where she had surrounded herself with the sofa's cushions, including—Clara noticed—Harriet's tasseled creation. "You're picking up on my mood, I guess. I'm sorry."

She sat back with a sigh that made Clara yearn to go to her. Laurel must have noticed her posture, or maybe it was the way her rump rose as she readied to leap, because suddenly she felt a paw come down on her tail. *"We're not done yet, missy!"*

This was too much. Clara turned and hissed, raising her paw—claws out—to her sister. Nothing was going to keep her from Becca! Only just then, the muted ring of the phone interrupted them.

"Oh no!" Becca jumped up and turned, tossing pillows as she searched frantically. "Where did I leave it?"

Seeing her moment, Clara pulled free and jumped down to the floor. Her superior hearing had already identified the location of the humming device, and with a nudge at Harriet's pillow, she was able to uncover it.

Becca grabbed it up with a smile that was worth all the treats in the bag to the calico. "Bother." She sounded a bit breathless from the search, but still she reached out to stroke Clara's mottled back. "Well, at least there's a message."

Clara leaned in and closed her eyes. Her sisters would make her pay for her interference, but right then she didn't care. Becca's hand was warm and she pressed just hard enough to make Clara stretch as she worked her way from shoulders to tail and then—froze.

"Oh no." Becca barely choked out the words. "I can't believe I forgot to call the detective back," she whispered in horror. "And now they're asking me to come down to the station."

Chapter 36

"Don't say it!" Clara glared at her sisters as she waited by the door. There would be a reckoning, but no way was she letting Becca talk to the police by herself. Not that she was sure what, exactly, she could do.

"Maybe I can convince her to run for it." Laurel had picked up on their person's distress and was stalking back and forth while Becca hurriedly changed her shirt. In all the tumult, it had gotten quite dusty.

"I could bring the amulet back." Harriet hiccupped, her shoulders bouncing in an alarming fashion.

"No, please." Clara did her best to keep her tone polite. *"You don't have to."* She ducked her head in the feline equivalent of a curtsy to both Harriet and Laurel. *"I think it's best if she just tells them the truth—what happened without any magic. I'll report back."* Becca had emerged from her bedroom, smoothing her hair back as if she were indeed feline, and now she was reaching for the door. *"I promise!"*

***

Clara stayed close to her person as she hurried through the busy streets. In a way, Becca's distraction helped—there was no way she was looking around for one small, shaded cat, even one with an orange patch over one eye. It helped that the day had progressed as well, giving Clara her choice of afternoon shadows to choose from as she leaped and darted to keep up with her person's progress.

It was only when Becca neared the stairs to the Cambridge precinct that Clara held back. That tall, stone building, with its heavy doors, was too much like a cage for her liking. And truth be told, what could she do if the people inside were to hold Becca against her will?

Maybe she did have some of Laurel's power, because Becca paused, as if constrained by the same fears. As Clara watched, Becca stepped off the sidewalk, almost as if she too could disappear in the shade of the sickly maple that grew out of the pavement nearby.

"Blessed goddess, hear my plea…" Clara caught the words, barely audible, of a protective spell, one that the coven had recited only weeks before. Becca didn't seem to remember that Suzanne had been the one who found it—and had been rather expert at reciting it. Maybe, thought the cat, as she watched her person make a complicated gesture behind her back, it was just as well humans didn't have any real power. If only she had a way of telling Becca that at least one of her pets was watching out for her. Standing there, murmuring—these people seemed to believe that everything had to be repeated three times—she looked so anxious that Clara longed to jump up into her arms.

She couldn't, of course. To do so would not only break the rules, it would unnerve the young woman, and the plump feline suspected that Becca would need all of her wits in the interrogation to come. Thus, the loyal feline was forced to hang back, in the shadow of that maple, and watch as Becca, looking as uncomfortable as a cat in the rain, finished the spell. At least, Clara thought she did—as she watched, her person wrung her hands in what could only be understood as an attempt to stroke herself back into good humor. Clearly, she was trying to muster the courage to enter the building that loomed before her.

Perhaps it was unfair of Clara to blame Harriet, but the calico couldn't help it. Her big sister's carelessness had set in motion a chain of events that at least had disconcerted their beloved person, and then her selfishness had exacerbated the situation. Of course, none of that would have mattered if Becca hadn't gotten involved in the coven or ever flirted with the dashing warlock.

"Trent!" Clara blinked up as Becca called out. Sure enough, there was the warlock—coming down the steps of the precinct. Could it be, she wondered, that her person *had* in fact summoned him? "Over here!"

"Becca?" The bearded man who turned toward her was nearly unrecognizable. His usually sleek dark hair hung lank, his darkly shining eyes looked tired, set deep into shadowed sockets. Even his usual open-necked blouse had been replaced by ratty sweats, the droopy pants pulled up to reveal bunched white socks above worn sneakers. "Is that you?"

She stepped forward, into the light, and Trent rushed over to her. He would have taken her hands, Clara thought, only, at the last moment, her person stepped back. In response, he raised one hand to his oily hair, pushing it back from a forehead that Clara could now see was quite lined.

It wasn't the hair though, or even his overall appearance that held her back.

"Are you okay?" said Becca, her voice low, her gaze shifting over to the building he had just left.

"Of course. What brings you here?" As he spoke, he stood up straighter and attempted a smile. To the observant cat, his teeth looked like fangs. “Are you—” His eyes darted nervously as he spoke, as if checking to make sure nobody had come from the police station behind him. But even as his scanned the street, he seemed to gather himself, his voice lowering into the confident baritone Becca knew well. “Are you going in to chat with the detectives again?”

“They called me,” Becca admitted, her face pinching up. “Twice. But why are you back here? Did something happen?”

“Not at all.” The smile stiffened as two uniformed officers descended the stairs, and he paused until they had walked by. “I gather there have been some developments, and I came in to offer my assistance, of course.”

“You volunteered?” Becca glanced down at his sweatshirt, the sweat pants, and sneakers. “Trent, if you don’t mind me asking, do you have a job?”

“Not you too.” For a moment, his face contorted in anguish, the sharp planes of his cheeks becoming drawn and desperate. Then, just as quickly, he recovered. “I do have a promising prospect—or I did.” He licked dry lips. “It’s nothing I’m at liberty to talk about right now. Of course, I do have other projects ongoing. A few investments.”

Becca didn’t appear convinced, to her cat’s clear-eyed gaze. Instead, it seemed like she was formulating a follow-up question, when he chuckled.

“Oh, is it my outfit?” He struck a pose, even as his grin wobbled. “I was working out, and after a run by the river, I found myself nearby the precinct.”

“You found yourself…? That’s right!” Becca’s eyes went wide as whatever query she’d been about to pose was eclipsed. “Your amulet! I found it. I mean, I thought you had already found it, but then it turned up, and I was going to call you. Only, I lost it again."

"What are you talking about?" The fake smile was gone.

"The one you dropped when my cat broke the chain." A rushed whisper of explanation.

"That's crazy." Trent shook his head, and the greasy locks fell back over his forehead.

"Ms. Colwin?" a voice called out. The rumpled detective was standing on the stairs. "Is that you?"

She ignored him in her rush to explain. "I thought maybe you didn't care that much. I mean, it looks like an expensive piece, but maybe—"

"I don't know what you're talking about." Trent's hand went to the neckline of his dirty sweatshirt and pulled out a chain. "I have it. I took it with me—you saw that. I only had to put it on a different chain."

"Rebecca Colwin?" The detective again.

Clara could only look on in sympathy as Becca stared in mute horror at the amulet in Trent's hand. "See?"

Chapter 37

"This makes no sense." Three minutes later, Becca was still rooted to the spot by the impossibility of what she had seen. Trent, whose confidence began to crumble as more uniforms strolled by, had taken off with a brittle giggle and a promise to be in touch. By then, the rumpled detective had finished his smoke and returned inside.

Only after one of those passing officers had paused on the walk beside Becca, turning as if to question her, did she move on. Even then, she could have been sleepwalking, her mind reeling with confusion. It was all too much, and when she rounded the corner, she leaned back against a brick wall, closing her eyes as she slid to the ground, desperate to gather her thoughts.

"Miss, are you all right?" a bearded stranger, his panting Labrador looking on placidly, asked with concern.

"I'm fine, thanks." Becca bounced back to her feet but could only produce a feeble attempt at a smile. "I've just had a shock."

"Do you have a friend you can call?" The good Samaritan looked ready to move along. "Someone you can talk to?"

She had held the amulet in her hand. Maddy had seen it. It didn't make sense. Unfortunately, what did make sense was

Trent's appearance, here at the police station. The warlock had been called back—she didn't buy his story about volunteering for a second—and he'd just as clearly been questioned about his finances. That meant somebody had made a call. Maybe Ande had said something. Only, Kathy had said that Ande was out to get Trent. Which seemed odd in that Ande had been so reluctant to come forward, despite Becca's urging—and despite her knowing that the group's bank account had been plundered. Was this all connected somehow? Was Ande behind it all—or Larissa, with her money? Suzanne had wanted to talk to Becca about the group's finances. She, not Ande, had been alarmed about the money going missing. But before she could explain, she'd been killed.

"I'm not sure," said Becca to the concerned stranger, and then she got up and walked away.

***

"Ande? Please call me back." Becca had been calling as she walked, pacing the city streets like an anxious cat. With each new voice message, she'd become more annoyed—and more certain that everything was indeed interconnected. Yes, Ande had been the one to note the financial disparities. She'd also been the one to downplay them—only a few thousand, she had said—to Becca and, possibly, to Suzanne as well. But if she couldn't reach the wiccan accountant, she was going to have to tell the police detective all she knew. Only, she was hoping to have a little more information before she bearded that particular rumpled lion in his den.

"Ande, if I don't hear from you soon, I'm going to tell the cops everything. I have to." Even as she spoke, she had another thought. "And, I'm sorry. I know you told me stuff in confidence, but I'm going to tell them about Larissa too." She paused. "Please, call me."

It wasn't merely that she didn't want to betray Ande's trust. The idea of crossing the older woman by herself was scary. Larissa liked to be in control, and she certainly wouldn't want to hear that her finances had been discussed—by the coven's resident accountant no less. Still, whatever was going on with the older woman's investment into their little group, it was looking more and more like it was connected to Suzanne's murder. And the fact that Becca had been asked to talk to the police once more gave her reason—and license, Becca figured—to seek some answers. After all, she couldn't avoid going into the precinct for much longer.

Phone in hand, she continued walking—not back home, as Clara had hoped, but toward the riverfront tower where Larissa had her condo. The shadows had grown longer by then, as the afternoon progressed with more calls and more messages left. While this made Clara's path easier, it didn't mean she worried less. Becca should be withdrawing from conflict. Heading home to where her sisters waited, Clara thought. Instead, she was marching toward a confrontation.

Half a block away, she was stopped by the sound of her phone.

"Becca?" Ande's voice rang out from the little device. "I'm sorry I missed your calls. I've been crazy busy."

"It's okay. Thanks for getting back to me." Becca paused and turned away from the glass-fronted tower, as if those windows were eyes that could see her here, out on the walk. "I'm sorry—I'll get right to it. Did you talk to the police?"

"Excuse me?" Ande's confusion sounded real, but Clara crept closer to hear what she could.

"The police," Becca repeated. "Did you tell them what you told me about the coven's finances—or maybe they're really Larissa's?" Becca stared up at a tree, as if the details of that earlier conversation could be found in the new leaves. "And did you say anything about Trent?"

"Trent? No. Look, all I know is that Suzanne said she'd found something," Ande corrected her. "That last night we were all together, before the meeting. I don't know if she really did, poor thing. But why are you harping on this? Surely, a couple of grand one way or another isn't motive for murder."

Becca's mouth opened, but she didn't speak. Clara knew why. Most cats wouldn't understand the ins and out of finance, and, in truth, Clara couldn't have balanced a checkbook if her kibble depended on it. But she did understand how carefully her person was watching her pennies. Yes, she suspected, to some people a few thousand dollars might be motive—and it seemed quite apparent that Becca was thinking along the same lines.

"It's not me who's doing the asking," she said at last. Ande probably couldn't hear the dying note in Becca's voice—part sad, part rueful—but Clara could. The woman on the other end of the line couldn't miss the urgency with which Becca repeated her initial question, though. "What did you tell the police, Ande?"

"I didn't tell them anything," her friend insisted. "I haven't spoken to them. I'm sorry, I know I said I would, but I haven't had time."

"You haven't had time?"

"I've been—look, it's not just work, Becca. I've got other obligations to other friends." The other woman was beginning to get defensive. "I want them to catch whoever did it. But I don't think I've got some great insight into what happened. It's not like Suzanne and I were close. I mean, outside the coven. I didn't even know she'd gone out with Trent before I did—that is, before she met her new guy."

Jeff. Becca winced. "Yeah, well, the police are looking into it—and they want to talk to me again. I need to make sure they have all the facts." Becca turned to take in the modern tower. Inside the glass foyer, the light flickered. An elevator opened, and a swirl of color stepped into the lobby. "I'm going to make Larissa tell me what's going on. I know she doesn't like to talk about money, but this is serious."

***

Inside the lobby, another figure appeared. A man in jeans and white shirt rose and greeted the colorful arrival.

"Please don't." A note of anxiety—or could it be fear? "Becca, you know how private she is. I don't want her to be angry at me for speaking out of turn, not to mention that she did kind of consult with me in my professional capacity."

"I'm sorry, Ande. Look, I ran into Larissa when I went to the records room at city hall, and she wouldn't tell me what she was working on. I'll try to make it sound like I'm following up on that. I'm sick of all the secrets." Becca turned away as the doors opened, discharging the woman and her waiting date. "They need to know if someone was embezzling—"

"Wait, what?" Ande interrupted. "Becca, I never said—"

"Look, I've got to go—and I'm sorry." Becca dropped her voice, cupping her phone in her hand as the couple's laughter got closer. "Just—you should know—I've also been hearing things. Like, that you were maybe trying to frame Trent."

"Me? Trent?" Ande's voice squeaked as Becca looked up in time to see the bearded warlock himself, showered and dressed once more in his usual open-necked shirt, escorting a laughing Larissa down the walk.

Chapter 38

"Maddy, there's something going on here." Becca made her next call to her friend, hitting the number even as she emerged from her hiding place behind a hedge. "Ande says she hasn't talked to the police yet. And Trent and Larissa are definitely a couple."

"Becca, do you hear yourself?" Her friend was leaving work. Becca could hear the traffic noise as she neared the T. "A woman was murdered, and you're playing detective?"

"I'm not playing." Becca stopped herself and pulled a bit of boxwood from her hair. "Maddy, the police want to talk to me again. They've been calling, and everybody knows I'm out of work and I need money—and that Jeff dumped me for Suzanne." Before her friend could interject, she rushed on. "Someone's been talking to the police, and I'm worried that they're not getting the full story. I'll go in and talk to them, I promise. But I want to figure out what's going on first. I only came over here to talk to Larissa, and now…seeing her with Trent…"

Maddy snorted. "Well, at least I know why Reynolds is always in such a mood. I can't imagine he's thrilled with how his ex is spending his money."

"Maddy, that's not fair." Becca felt a little bad that she'd texted Nathan's revelation to her friend the night before.

She'd been so overjoyed to find out that the handsome painter was neither job competition nor Larissa's love interest that she'd probably revealed more than she meant to. Now Ande's words came back to her. "You never know what's going on in someone else's relationship."

Another snort. "Maybe not in theirs—but that Trent? Oh, come on."

Becca bit her lip. Maddy was touching on the conclusion that she herself had reached. "There's also—Maddy, I don't think I told you, but I spoke with Jeff—"

"Oh, Becca!"

"No, we're not getting back together—don't worry about that. Only he brought up that Suzanne had thought someone was stalking her again. He thought it was me, but she'd also gone out with Trent and she had a necklace that she loved but that she never wanted to wear when she came to the group."

"That coven of yours…" Her friend's censure chilled the phone line. "And this is the guy you went out with too?"

"I didn't really." Becca caught herself. "Okay, maybe I did, but he's been out with everyone. Ande as well as Suzanne, and I think Kathy has a crush on him too. Only seeing him with Larissa makes me wonder."

"Becca, you're not making sense."

"I am!" Becca insisted. "She had this necklace—a crystal teardrop. I think Trent gave it to her, and that Larissa knew." The image of her colleague, lying lifeless on the floor, came back—the horror of it. The streak of blood already growing dark. The knife protruding from Suzanne's bare throat. "Maddy, I think the killer took the necklace."

"Please, Becca," her friend entreated. "This is a job

for the police. You need to stop this—you need to tell them everything that's going on."

"I can't, Maddy—not just yet. They must already think I'm involved, or else why would they be asking me to come in again? And, well, I don't know, do I? Maybe she'd just taken it off. And the whole thing could be totally innocent."

"Yeah? Well, who killed her, then?"

Becca didn't have an answer for that one, and her friend knew it.

"I'm sorry, kiddo." Maddy was fading as she descended into the subway. "Look, I'll go with you tomorrow, first thing before work, okay? And tonight—do you want to come over? We can watch a movie or something."

"I'd love to." Relief suffused Becca's voice, and for the first time since she'd left the house, Clara relaxed. "Oh, but, no, I can't."

Clara's ears pricked up. As, it seemed, did Maddy's. "No? Not another date?"

"Oh, I wish." Exhaustion—or exasperation—drained the life out of Becca's voice. "I can't believe I forgot, Maddy. And now it's too late to cancel."

Silence on the line. Then, "Becca?"

"The coven is meeting tonight, Maddy! That must be where Larissa and Trent were heading, and I've got to rush home and clean up."

***

In truth, Becca had over an hour before the group was scheduled to convene. That left her plenty of time to get home and pick up what was generally a fairly neat apartment. True, Laurel and Harriet had been bored in her absence, and had made their point by knocking several small objects off the bookshelf. The point, Laurel said, was to keep Becca busy while they debriefed Clara, a task for which the seal-point feline seemed to have more enthusiasm than their oldest sister, who had made herself scarce.

"Can't this wait?" Clara looked on in sympathy as Becca frantically rushed around, picking up pens and paperweights. *"Becca is in a tizzy."*

"How do you think we felt?" Laurel's ears flicked backward, revealing a bit of temper. *"You run out to talk to the police, and we don't hear from you for hours."*

"I know, but we never got there."

Becca was on her hands and knees, looking under the sofa. Searching once more, Clara realized, for the amulet.

"She ran into that Trent, and he showed her that he still has his pendant," she explained.

"*Good.*" Harriet had ambled in from her nap. *"Then I can make another. So you owe me a treat!"*

It was useless. Clara's spirits sunk, as did her tail, and she turned from her sisters to watch her person's frenzied quest.

"Listen up!" A sharp slap to the side of her head brought her back. Laurel, her blue eyes blazing. *"You act like you're the only one who cares, but we want to do what's best for her too. But you've got to tell us what you know—and quickly too! Those cookie eaters are on their way."*

"Cookie eaters?" Harriet looked toward the door.

"Harriet, focus!" Clara looked from one sister to another. She'd never heard Laurel speak this way, not to Harriet. Even the big marmalade seemed somewhat taken aback and sat blinking under that blue glare.

"I know I've been a bit lax." Laurel had the grace to dip her head. Cats see a direct stare as an offensive move, and

once she had their attention, the middle sister seemed ready to shift into a conciliatory fashion. *"This has been a comfortable perch. But you do know our family history, don't you?"*

Harriet blinked and turned to Clara, who tilted her head inquisitively. *"I know we have a duty to our people and that we come from a long line of witch cats."*

"And what happens when we don't pay attention?" Laurel's tone had become a bit schoolmarmish—only with an edge that worried Clara and set her spine tingling. *"What happens when we aren't careful?"*

"We don't get treats?" Harriet offered the most serious punishment she could imagine.

"*Our people—the women we are bound to serve—are taken as witches in our place."* Laurel was practically hissing. *"They're taken away away and burned."*

"They don't do that anymore." Harriet looked to Clara for support. *"Do they?"*

"I don't think so." Clara wracked her brain. She hadn't heard of anything like that. *"But the police haven't been very kind to our Becca,"* she added, her soft mew growing more thoughtful. *"And she's worried that they do suspect her of something. They do keep calling."*

"You see?" Laurel said, turning. *"Tails and whiskers up!"* And just then, the doorbell rang.

***

"Hey, Marcia. Come in." Becca did a good job of hiding her disappointment, but Clara heard it in her voice, in the dying fall as she opened the door for the first arrival. "Oh, is that a cake?"

"Banana bread." Marcia looked around, her large eyes widening dramatically. "What's up with your cats?"

Clara turned. Harriet and Laurel were both staring at the diminutive woman, and even a human must have been able to feel the suspicion—and, in Harriet's case, hunger—in their gaze.

"I was out for a lot of the day." Becca was improvising. "I think they were lonely."

"Okay, then." Marcia gave the sisters a wide berth as she passed into the apartment. "I'm the first one here?"

"Yes." Becca ran past her to replace the sofa cushions, which she'd piled on the table. "Sorry, I was…I was doing a little cleaning. Shall I take that?"

"Sure." Marcia leaned in slightly, and Clara had the distinct impression that the shorter woman was about to confide. Only just then, the doorbell rang again. "Never mind. I'm going to get a knife."

"Becca, I've been thinking." Ande stepped in before her host could say anything. "Maybe she was down at city hall because she's filing a suit for fraud?"

"Who was?" Marcia emerged from the kitchen with a bread knife—and the obvious question for a paralegal. "What's the suit?"

"Oh." Ande blinked, at a loss for an answer.

"It's nothing," Becca covered. "I was doing research on something, and I ran into a roadblock. I think someone was trying to keep some information private."

"Who's the claimant? Of course, I don't know if anyone could keep a fraud suit private," Marcia opined as she sliced. "We deal with those all the time, and it really depends if it's criminal or civil—and that can get complicated. It's not like a bankruptcy, where you can get the records sealed like that."

As Marcia snapped her fingers, the doorbell rang again,

and when Clara saw Larissa in the doorway, she looked over at Laurel. If only her sister would use her powers of suggestion to change the subject. Laurel, however, had had enough of the doorbell and retreated to the sofa. Harriet, meanwhile, was nowhere to be seen.

"Darling, so nice to see you again." Luckily, Larissa was as self-involved as usual. "I trust you were able to get your work done?" She took Becca's arm as she entered, almost spinning her around. "I was working on a little project of my own, you see." As she leaned in, Clara got a whiff of patchouli that almost made her dizzy. "I might have good news for you later, but let's not share anything yet. Are we agreed?"

Becca tried to step back, but the older woman held her tight. "Yes, I would like to talk later," she said, peering over her shoulder. "I have some questions too."

"Yes, yes, later." Larissa was already moving on, releasing her and progressing into the living room, as Kathy came to the door.

"Is Trent here?" She looked around.

"Sorry." Marcia's voice had an edge in it that made Becca turn. Before she could say anything, the bell rang again. Their warlock had arrived.

***

An hour later, the banana bread was gone and Becca, as well as her cats, were more than ready for the convocation to be over. Becca was too polite to rush anyone, of course, but the usual rituals simply grated this night and she had felt a headache coming on as soon as the group was seated, though that could have been because of the patchouli. The cats were less patient, particularly once the treats had been eaten. All three had been staring at the coven members with a concentration that no sensitive human should have missed.

But if Becca had hoped to move things along—and to be able to corner Larissa—she was out of luck.

"I was thinking," said Marcia during a pause in the readings. "Maybe it would be good to go around and speak of Suzanne. I feel like maybe I wasn't as somber as I should have been during the memorial, and I want to explain—and give her the proper respect."

Ande, on her left, squeezed her hand, murmuring something about it all being understandable. But Larissa seemed to hear the proposal as a challenge.

"Excellent suggestion, my dear." She tossed her hair for emphasis, and then held forth for a good fifteen minutes about the "promise" she had seen in the young woman.

Ande kept her tribute shorter, and Kathy basically passed. "I didn't really know her," she said. "I only ever saw her here." When Trent began to expound—something about inner beauty and manifestations of the goddess—Becca winced.

"Trent, darling." Larissa must have noticed her hostess's pained expression, Clara thought. Either that, or Laurel's powers were finally having an effect. "Do you think we could possibly move on to the final benediction?"

"But I didn't—I mean, I'd like to make an announcement first," said Marcia, turning from the goateed warlock to address the rest of the table. "That is, if Becca doesn't mind?"

"Not at all." Becca managed a smile. Her headache was getting worse.

"Thanks." Marcia's voice was warm, at least. "First, I'd like to thank Becca for having us. Luz and I were wondering if perhaps this was too soon. Especially for Becca." She held up a hand to stop Larissa before she could complain. "Becca was the person who found our departed sister, after all."

"We are all grateful, Becca," Trent broke in. "Aren't we? I was just saying—"

It was too much. "I'm sorry." Becca stood. "Trent, Marcia, can this wait? I feel like my head's about to split open."

Ande rose and followed her into the kitchen, where she filled a glass with water.

"It's the stress," said Ande, pressing the glass into Becca's hand. "I mean, the police and all."

"Police?" Larissa came in as Becca drank, stinky teapot in hand. "You were talking to the police again?"

"I was supposed to." Becca leaned back against the sink, felled by the combined stench of that brew and Larissa's perfume. She had no more energy to dissemble. "They called me back. Trent too."

"Well, I'm sure it was nothing." Larissa raised her arms, her sleeves flapping like wings as she shooed the other coven member back into the living room. "Now, Ande, why don't we give her some space?"

"I don't need space." Becca sounded so tired, Clara wished she could simply rest. "I need answers."

Marcia peeked in, only to be dismissed with a wave of Larissa's hand. "I don't know what you're talking about." The older woman's volume had sunk dramatically.

"Yes, you do."

Clara watched, transfixed. She'd never seen her person so serious.

"Clara! They're scattering!" Laurel's yowl carried

from the living room. Larissa started, her eyes going wide.

"That's just my cat." Becca brought her attention back. "Larissa, I get it. You were trying to have the records sealed. The bankruptcy records. It all makes sense."

"What? No." Another yowl, and Clara resisted the urge to respond. Couldn't her sisters take care of anything?

"Are you okay?" Ande stuck her head back in, nearly stepping on Clara's tail. "Otherwise, I'm going to head out."

"Everything is fine," Larissa hissed, and Ande withdrew, as if the older woman had indeed been a snake.

"Larissa, it's over." Becca looked up at the older woman, trying to see the person beneath the mascara and the scarves. Clara could hear Ande and Marcia talking softly in the living room. "I know that you've been keeping Trent—and that you're overdrawn." The older woman's mouth dropped open. "That's what you and your ex were arguing about, wasn't it? Just tell me one thing, Larissa. Did you kill Suzanne because she and Trent were involved, or because she found out your little secret?"

"That's crazy." Chin high, Larissa dismissed the idea.

Becca, however, was not cowed. "The records room?"

A sniff.

"You couldn't turn him down." Becca thought back to what Jeff had said about "bad juju." What Maddy had overheard at the office, and the laughing couple she herself had seen earlier that evening. "You were obsessed with him, and so you were trying to have your bankruptcy records sealed, so nobody would know how much you've been giving Trent."

"I was *not* looking to have any financial records sealed. Not that it's any of your business." Her mouth closed so tight, the lines showed her age.

"I'm sure the police will disagree…"

"It was my divorce proceedings, if you must know." Larissa spat out the words. "I knew you were poking about, and I didn't want anyone finding out about Graham, and about, well, you know…"

"Your adult son, Nathan?" Becca's brows went up. "The police still have motive. Suzanne was involved with Trent, and you know it."

"So what?" A toss of the hair, but not a denial.

"You were jealous," said Becca. "She was pretty—and younger. Maybe you didn't mean to kill her when you lashed out. Obsession can be dangerous."

To her surprise, the older woman laughed. "Obsessed? Are you kidding? Was my little fancy supposed to make me lash out?"

"Who's lashing out?" Trent walked in. "And what are you two still doing in here? I thought we were leaving, Larissa. Is everything all right?"

"It's fine." Larissa brooked no argument.

"No, it's not." Becca lifted her heavy head to take in Trent. "Larissa found out about Suzanne. She saw the pendant you'd given her—here, when Suzanne wore it by mistake. The crystal teardrop."

"What? No." Trent giggled, a high, nervous sound. "That's crazy. I would never—"

"That's why you went to Suzanne's, wasn't it?"

The warlock blinked as if he'd been slapped. "No, I—no," he stammered, the color leaving his face.

Becca's voice was flat. But even exhausted, she was relentless. "You wanted that necklace back, before it cost you your place."

"Suzanne liked that crystal better than she did me." His whisper was barely perceptible. "She said it was more real."

Becca ignored him. "You're lucky the parking meter alibi'd you, but you must have wondered. That's why you ran to Larissa as soon as the police had released you. Why she was the first person to call me—even before my mother. She wanted to find out what I knew. What I'd figured out."

"I didn't think Larissa had hurt Suzanne." Trent was growing desperate. "I never thought …"

A beringed hand flicked the back of his head.

"Oh, stuff it, Trent," Larissa cut him off, then turned back to Becca. "I knew about Suzanne. Just as I knew about his fling with Ande and his little flirtation with you. Those dalliances mean nothing. He always comes back to me."

Trent's mouth opened and closed, like a beached fish, but neither of the women were watching.

"You can't prove that." Becca considered, and for the first time, Clara heard doubt in her voice.

"As a matter of fact." Larissa beckoned and Trent stepped toward her, his face unreadable. With one long claw, she hooked the chain around his neck and pulled it forward, forcing him to bend. Taking the amulet between two fingers, she briefly examined it—flipping it over to its backside before holding it out to Becca. "Read," she commanded.

"Love renewed," Becca read aloud, "under the Flower Moon." The inscription ended with the date of the coven meeting—the Wednesday before Suzanne's murder.

"What was that?" As Becca stood silent, trying to make sense of what she'd read, Clara turned to Harriet for an answer. The calico didn't need to remind her sister that this inscription hadn't been duplicated on her summoned facsimile.

"I didn't see any words when I grabbed it." Harriet blinked. *"Besides, who cares about words? I wanted the pretty shininess of it."*

"Trent's a boy." Larissa addressed the stunned Becca, as if the man she was referring to weren't there. As if she wasn't holding him, literally, on a chain. "But he's a good boy. He knows who owns him."

"What's going on here?" Marcia poked her head in, her Sox cap already in place. "I thought we needed to get going."

"Just cleaning up." Trent pulled back as Larissa released him. His voice was unnaturally high, and the shorter woman looked at him, puzzled. Turning his back on his mistress, he moved toward Marcia, the fingertips of one hand playing down her arm. "But we're about done, if you want to get out of here, Marcia."

Only Clara and Harriet could see the leer on his face, but surely Becca could hear the insinuation in his voice. "In fact, Marcia." His voice sank to its sexy lower register. "I've been wondering if you'd ever thought of spending some time with me." He moved to usher her out of the kitchen, his voice like warm honey. "You've got the darkest eyes…"

Clara glanced back at Becca, concerned. Her person had once been interested in this man not that long before.

"Gross." Marcia's retort broke through his murmurings. "Just…no, Trent. No. Are you clueless?"

She stepped back. Away to face him. Even Ande, who'd been fussing with her bag, was looking at her now.

"I never got to make my announcement." Exasperation gave Marcia's voice an edge. "Luz and I are getting married. We wanted to invite the coven to our ceremony. Maybe even have a hand-fasting or something. But forget it. You're gross, you…you second-rate lothario."

As she turned away, Trent burst into tears.

All hell broke loose after that. Larissa pushed by Becca to cradle the crying man in her bosom, and Harriet and Clara had to scurry to avoid being stepped on. Ande stood, transfixed, as Marcia stormed out of the apartment, without even taking her loaf pan. Becca, meanwhile, just sank into a kitchen chair and put her head down on her folded arms.

It was up to Clara to make sense of the scene: Trent, Marcia, even Ande were accounted for, and Larissa had faced Becca's accusation unfazed. Still, something was wrong. She'd been so sure that Becca had uncovered a hidden truth. She looked around. *"Where's Kathy?"* she asked her oldest sister.

"Here!" Another howl came out of Becca's bedroom, and the cats ran to their litter mate, who was staring at a closed door. *"She's in there,"* Laurel explained.

"Enough of that!" Harriet threw her bulk against the door and they all heard the gasp of the startled young woman as the big marmalade tumbled into the bathroom.

"She's going to throw her out." Clara turned to Laurel.

"*This is my house!"* Harriet grumbled, her aggrieved mew echoing on the tile. "*Besides, this is what cats do!"*

Clara looked back toward the kitchen. Becca still hadn't emerged, and her pet was growing concerned.

"Hey, what the...?"

Laurel's ears pricked up and she nosed the door. Clara joined her and soon they were all inside the tiny room with the young woman who was, Clara noted, fully dressed. Ignoring the two cats who had just barged in to join their sister, she was kneeling by the toilet paper roll, as if changing it. Only she seemed to be fussing more than Becca ever had.

"What's she doing?" Laurel asked her older sister.

"She's got something." Harriet craned to look. But by then Kathy was washing her hands and had stepped back into the bedroom. *"Something shiny..."*

Standing on her hind legs, Harriet knocked the roll off its perch—and as the paper unfurled, something clattered to the tile floor. Clara gasped as it glittered and rolled, making a wide arc that stopped at her front paws. Clear as water, with a silver clasp at one end—it was Suzanne's crystal teardrop. The one she'd been wearing the last time she'd been here.

"Hello?" Kathy was still in the bedroom. Clara's ear flicked back to catch what she was saying. "Cambridge police? I can't talk for long, but I think Rebecca Colwin is involved in the murder of Suzanne Liddle. I just found something that belonged to the victim in her apartment, and I'm now in fear for my life."

Chapter 39

The three cats glared at each other. This was exactly what Laurel had warned them about. What Clara had feared, without understanding how it could come to be. An anonymous tip, and in the living room, Kathy was now urging Ande to leave. Larissa could be heard clunking down the stairwell, giving Trent directions as she led him out to the street.

"Let's let poor Becca be," Kathy was saying as she ushered Ande toward the door.

"What can we do?" Clara looked at her sisters.

"I have to make her wonder about Kathy..." Laurel began to concentrate, a furrow appearing in her café au lait brow. Ande, meanwhile, was calling out her farewell. Clearly, Becca was not seeing her friends out.

"She's getting away." Clara was panicking. *"The police are going to find that thing. And Becca is just sitting there."*

"Not on my watch," said Harriet, and with that she nosed the crystal teardrop and with one quick dab of her tongue, slurped it up.

"Harriet!" Clara bounced back in surprise. *"What did you do?"*

"No evidence, no worries, right?" The fluffy marmalade licked her chops.

"But—are you going to be all right?"

"I think so." Harriet hiccupped, lifting one paw as if to cover her mouth. In the hall, they could hear Ande asking Kathy to wait.

"Becca, you okay?" Ande called to their hostess.

"Yeah, I'm fine." Becca roused herself and headed toward the door, where Kathy was visibly fidgeting.

"Poor guy." Ande was chuckling a bit as Clara emerged from the bedroom. "I told you, you never know what's going on in anyone else's relationship."

"Yeah, I guess." Becca gave the taller woman a quick peck on the cheek. "I hope Marcia doesn't give up on the rest of us. I mean, she's the only one—sorry." That was for Kathy, who was staring at the closed door as if she, too, were a cat.

Ande reached for the knob. "I hope you feel better," she said. "Get some sleep."

"Kathy, do you have a moment?" Becca stopped the redhead as she would have followed. "I just…I've got something I want to talk to you about."

"Well, I—" Visibly torn, the other woman stepped back into the apartment. "Sure."

"I was hoping you could clear something up." Becca looked puzzled as she wandered back toward the kitchen, picking up the stacked plates on her way, Clara in tow. Harriet, of course, came trotting along too. Her older sister really had earned her treats tonight.

But first the dishes. As all three cats lined up to watch, Becca fussed with a sponge.

"What's up?" Kathy was fidgeting. "'Cause I should be off too. And you really should get some rest."

Becca squirted soap on the dish pile and stared at the translucent bubbles that formed as if they held the key to everything. "I was wondering about something," she said. "You knew that Suzanne was working for Reynolds—for Larissa's ex."

"I did?" A shrug. Beneath her freckles, the redhead's cheeks had gone pale.

"Yes." Becca nodded as she reviewed some internal script. "I'm sure of it. You said something about me 'stepping into Suzanne's shoes' when I went to interview with Reynolds."

Another shrug as Kathy eyed the door.

"But you denied knowing her outside of the coven just now."

Kathy's mouth went wide. "I was—you had a headache—and—"

Without waiting for her to finish, Becca kept talking. "And what's going on with you and Ande?"

"Me and…Ande?" Kathy swallowed hard.

"Yeah, you seem really down on her." She raised her voice to be heard as she ran the water. "You were the one who first told me she went out with Trent, but recently you've been talking about her setting him up. It almost sounds like you want me to suspect her—and now you're all friendly again. Did you two have a falling out?"

"No." The younger woman barked the word with scorn. "It's *Marcia* who's got the problem. I mean, lashing out at Trent like that?"

Becca turned and regarded her curiously, then started on the mugs.

"I kind of think Marcia had a point." She sounded thoughtful as she squeezed out her sponge. "And, well, I guess this means you were wrong about her wanting to go out with

Trent."

"Well, I picked up that she had something against him," Kathy blustered. "I was right about that!"

Becca didn't respond. Instead, she kept talking as she added more soap. "Come to think of it, Marcia was the one who told me that Suzanne wanted to do a casting out—that there was a problem in the coven. When I brought that up, you pointed out that Suzanne was going to blow the whistle about the coven finances." She could have been talking to the dishes, but Clara's ears pricked forward. "You said that Ande had told her someone was embezzling, but Ande didn't say that. She knew the numbers were off by a few grand, but she assumed Larissa had been sloppy."

Kathy forced out a laugh that sounded a lot harsher than her usual giggle and stepped closer to the counter, where the loaf pan sat.

"Ande thought a few grand would be small change to Larissa, and when Larissa didn't say anything about malfeasance, she figured she was right. But, of course, Larissa wouldn't have complained. She was protecting Trent." Becca was shaking her head. "And Suzanne never got a chance to tell me what—or who—she suspected. I've been trying to figure it out, and it seems that the only person who you haven't cast aspersions on is the one person who probably did make off with some of the coven money: Trent."

As Clara looked on in horror, Kathy reached toward the pan—and past it, for the bread knife that Marcia had used to cut the sweet loaf.

"Do something!" The cry came out as high and plaintive mew.

"Hang on, kitties." Becca was up to her elbows in

suds. "You'll get your treats. Kathy, can you grab that little canister?"

"Yeah, sure." But the other woman was holding the knife, not the cat treats, as she took a step closer.

"Until tonight, I kind of thought Larissa might have, well, done something." Becca turned on the tap to rinse her hands. "Only—"

Clara opened her mouth to howl again, but stopped herself. If Becca turned now, without knowing what was going on…

A sudden pounding on the door did the trick. Both women turned. "Police!" A male voice, deep and insistent. "Open up!"

"Coming!" Becca reached for a dish towel as Kathy stepped back, sliding the knife back onto the counter. But even as Becca turned away from the sink, she stopped in horror. Harriet, front paws spread, was huffing, as if short of breath. Her stout body jerked once, twice, and then with a sound reminiscent of a stopped drain opening, she urped up the crystal teardrop.

"Kitty!" Ignoring the pounding that continued on the door, Becca knelt. With one hand on the plump marmalade, who sat up and licked her chops, she looked down at the little puddle—and the pendant lying there.

"What?" She reached for it, still kneeling. "Suzanne's necklace?" And whether it was because of the accumulated evidence or that Laurel's furious concentration had finally gotten through to her, she looked up, then, at Kathy. "Kathy?" Her voice was sad rather than angry. Solemn, rather than scared. "Why?"

The other woman only shook her head. "She was going

to ruin him," she said, as if her conclusion were obvious, her voice barely above a whisper. "She was going to ruin Trent! He's special. You know how precious he is. She was going to expose him. Tell everybody that he was writing checks on Larissa's account—taking her money to buy presents for his other little chippies."

"Oh, Kathy." Sorrow infused Becca's voice. "She wouldn't have ruined him. She couldn't have. He and Larissa have an understanding. She'd have forgiven him. She already has."

"Police!" The pounding more insistent. "We're coming in!"

"Hang on!" Pendant in hand, Becca rose, heading toward the door. "I'm sorry, Kathy," she said. She didn't see the other woman reach once again for the knife.

"*Becca!*" Clara mewed one last time, but her soft cry was drowned out by the pounding on the door. Laurel, by then, was concentrating so hard her ears stood out sideways and her blue eyes crossed. Even Clara could feel the vibrations emanating from the determined seal point—urging Becca to turn. To look.

For a moment, Laurel's thought bomb seemed to be working. Becca paused, as if confused, her hand on the front door even as the cops called out one more time. But it was too late. Kathy was coming up behind her, knife raised. So Clara, shading herself as quickly as she could, dashed in front of the onrushing woman, sending Kathy flying and the knife clattering down. And Harriet, who knew in her proud marmalade heart that she had done quite enough with her normal digestive processes, did not deign to provide a pillow and simply sat and watched as Kathy fell sprawling to the floor.

Chapter 40

What happened next was hectic, and—their jobs done—the cats did their best to scurry out of the way. With a gasp, Becca turned, having unlatched the door. Two uniformed officers pushed in.

"Are you all right, miss?" The first officer bent to help Kathy to her knees. "We received your call. Are you the victim of an assault?"

"Bruce, wait." His partner nodded toward the knife, which was still spinning on the floor, just out of reach of the prone woman's hand, and then to Becca, who was backing away in horror.

"Ma'am?" The second officer reached to support her as she collapsed against the wall. She looked up, stunned, then held out her open palm—revealing the crystal teardrop.

"This was Suzanne's. It's kind of sticky." She apologized as a look of wonder came over here. "Did you—did I summon you?"

Clara closed her eyes, even as Laurel yowled in protest. Harriet, meanwhile, waddled over to the sofa, where she settled on her pillow, as proud as could be.

***

Twenty minutes later, the events of the last few minutes had been sorted. Becca still had the wet dishcloth in hand, and

Kathy wasn't even denying what she'd done.

Instead, as she was escorted down to the waiting cruiser, she seemed to be attempting a justification for her actions—from the murder of Suzanne to her attack on Becca.

"You don't understand!" The redhead could be heard through the open window. "I did it for Trent."

Her voice faded as the cruiser took her away. But as Becca turned back toward her dishes, a shadow fell across the floor. The rumpled detective stood in her open doorway, scowling.

"Ms. Colwin?"

Becca gasped, and the cats looked up.

"Detective Abrams!" She spoke quickly, before she, too, could be cuffed and escorted out. "I'm so sorry I didn't call you back!" Reacting to her agitation, Clara approached and circled, determined to do whatever was necessary to protect her person from this latest threat. "I got your messages, and I meant to get back to you, honest."

"Excuse me?" The detective asked, a puzzled expression creasing his lined face further. "What are you talking about?"

"You, or your office, kept calling me and I never picked up. I knew I had more information, but I wanted…" Becca stopped, unsure of how to proceed. "I thought I could find out more. That is, before I came in."

The edge of the detective's mouth twitched. "Before you came in?"

"I never meant to evade justice." Becca swallowed hard and stared in amazement as that twitch evolved from the ghost of a smile into a full-fledged grin. "I should have called back."

"You mean, you should have responded to my

secretary." He nodded, as if suddenly everything had become clear. "Yes, you should have. She was getting desperate to reach you. We've had your hat for over a week now, and this beautiful spring weather can't last forever."

***

The resolution of the case was sad, but not surprising, and Becca kept her pets informed by reading aloud the daily updates in the news.

At first, Kathy, on the advice of her attorney, claimed self-defense. She argued that Suzanne had attacked her when she'd gone to talk to her about her "ridiculous" suspicions and that she'd simply wanted to reason with the other woman, whom she accused of slandering the man she described as their coven leader. It was a reasonable defense, Becca mused as she read. Although no eyewitness had placed her in the Cambridgeport walkup, a plethora of evidence—including, Becca read, smudged fingerprints on the cake knife—had already made her a suspect, and the district attorney had been in the process of building the case when she had called from Becca's apartment.

"They could have said," Becca muttered. Clara, for once, was grateful for her own inability to respond.

Of course, the fact that the redhead had lunged for Becca under a similar circumstance made that defense a little less plausible, and soon after, she had her lawyer claiming temporary insanity—and citing the hot-bed atmosphere of the coven and its unhealthy influence on its youngest member as a contributing factor.

That accusation more than anything else had served to bring the coven back together. Marcia forgave Trent his ill-timed pass, and the handsome warlock appeared to have recovered from his humiliating exposure. It helped that Larissa had given him a new gift—an intricate chain for his amulet.

But it wasn't Trent, ultimately, who had prompted Suzanne's request that last night. At least, that's what Becca concluded.

"Suzanne wanted a casting out spell because of Kathy." Becca had pieced it together in the intervening weeks. "She knew about Trent—about the money—but it was Kathy who was spreading rumors. Setting us all against each other. Suzanne might not have known who was stalking her. She certainly didn't know how dangerous Kathy was, but she knew the coven 'pet' was a bad influence, and she wanted her gone."

"Makes sense to me." Ande had joined her friend over tea—mint, this time—to debrief her as the case unfolded. The accountant had been giving testimony about what she'd found in the coven's accounts and had come over after the trial had adjourned for the day to find Becca and all three cats waiting for the latest.

"I didn't know the half of it, but working for Reynolds, Suzanne must have figured out the connection," Ande explained as the cats looked on. Laurel's mouth opened slightly, taking in the tea's aroma, while Harriet began to shift, eager for the talk to give way to eating. "She heard enough to know that Larissa was Reynolds's ex and that she was desperate for money. Reynolds had been telling her in no uncertain terms that she had to get rid of her 'boy toy' before he'd give her any more. I guess Larissa was claiming that she'd been ripped off because she was embarrassed."

Becca mulled that over as she waited for her tea to cool. The woman who had yanked her lover's chain didn't seem the type to embarrass easily. "Maybe she just thought she could get more money out of her ex that way?"

"Or maybe she really didn't know how much Trent was taking, forging her checks and all?" Ande asked. "I should've known, the few times we went out. He definitely acted like he had something to prove."

Becca kept silent, but from the slight rise in her color, Clara knew she was thinking of a misadventure on the sofa—and how the intercession of her cats may have saved her from a bigger mistake. To hide the blush—or maybe because of Laurel's intense concentration—she broke off a piece of almond cookie and held it down for her cats to lick.

"So what are you wearing to Marcia and Luz's wedding?" Ande was polite enough not to comment. Not even when Harriet body-checked Laurel out of the way.

"I don't know." Becca was grateful for the change in subject. "I've got to go shopping. I'll tell you, though, it would be nice to have money again."

"Reynolds owes you, big time." Ande nodded. "I mean, I'm sure you're great for the job—but you also helped keep Larissa out of prison."

Becca's color deepened as she broke another cookie for the cats. "I don't think it would've come to that. Nobody really thought she'd done it."

Her guest cracked a grin. "I don't know. You thought so."

Becca nodded, growing thoughtful again. "I even wondered if you were involved."

"Well, yeah." Ande's smile widened. "I was so caught up in the wedding planning, I kind of missed that maybe it wasn't the best time to be all secretive. So who are you bringing?" Ande's smile widened. "The old guy or the new?"

Becca's cheeks were flaming now. "He's not my new guy."

"You're bringing the boss's son! Excellent." Ande pushed back from the table, startling the cats. "Anyway, it hasn't all been nuptial—I really do have a load of work waiting for me. And you have to get ready for your new job."

"Maybe." Becca looked over at Clara, almost as if she could read the calico's green eyes. "We'll see."

***

Despite Reynolds's repeated entreaties, Becca kept stalling.

She needed some time, she said. She had her own research project to finish up. Even after repeated visits back to the city records hall and hours poring over documents, she still couldn't understand exactly what she'd found. At night, she studied her copies and checked her notes, reading everything she could find about Rebecca Horne and her cat. Was it possible that a feline could have had legal standing in the early days of the Commonwealth?

What, she kept asking, was the relationship between her ancestor and her cat?

Neither Clara, Harriet, nor Laurel chose to enlighten her. On that, the three sisters were agreed. Their brief moment of solidarity had passed, otherwise, and by the time the high summer had come around, Harriet was once more ignoring her youngest sister, while Laurel had taken to teasing her.

"I'm the head of this family," Harriet announced as she shoved her siblings. *"Without me, we would have no more Becca to serve us."*

"You wish, chubby," Laurel snarled, just a bit. Clara, who knew her middle sister was still self-conscious about

being seen cross-eyed, kept quiet. She didn't even interrupt when Laurel suggested a dress for the upcoming wedding. The slinky number might have been a daring choice for the young researcher, but Clara had to admit, Becca looked good in it.

***

As it was, Becca was running late the day of the ceremony, a midsummer hand-fasting down by the river. She'd spent the morning at the records hall, again, trying to track down another possible branch of her family when one of the clerks had interrupted her.

"Excuse me, are you Becca Colwin?"

She'd looked up to see a round face with round glasses that should have looked jolly but was instead tense with worry.

"I am." She glanced at the papers before her. "Is there a problem?"

"Oh, not with your research. Not at all." The woman's voice dropped to a whisper. "It's only—I hear you're the witch who solved that murder last month?"

"Well, I'm not sure." Becca couldn't hide her smile, though it had more to do with being recognized for her magic than for her role in exposing Suzanne's killer.

"I have a friend who could use some help." The other woman didn't wait for Becca to explain. "She's in trouble, you see. And, well, she needs someone who can draw on other powers…"

***

"I don't know if anything will come of it." She told Clara about it as soon as she got home. "I mean, I really haven't done anything since the pillow."

She shimmied into the dress as she spoke and looked at herself in the mirror.

"But even if the police were already building a case against poor Kathy, I did help." She reached for a necklace and paused, looking at the beaded choker she'd chosen as if it reminded her of something else. "Besides, it would be nice to earn a living doing something I really care about." She turned her head this way and that, letting the beads sparkle in the light. "Helping people with my magic—and my research skills too."

Just then, Laurel came in, and suddenly, Becca was lifting her hair off her neck and reaching for a clip.

"Nice," the seal point purred. Clara glanced over, but held her tongue. Becca did look good with her hair up. More sophisticated.

"What?" Harriet ambled in, in time to see Becca putting on her earrings. *"No treats?"*

"I don't think you'd want to eat those," Clara ribbed her sister as Becca rose and addressed the three of them.

"So, yeah, kitties, I think I'm going to turn down Reynolds's offer after all, not that it wasn't nice of him, and set out on my own. Becca Colwin, Witch Detective. Do you like the sound of that?"

"Oh no!" Clara protested, while Laurel's ears went out sideways in consternation.

"Or, Colwin and Cats? Maybe that." She turned one last time before the mirror and then smiled down at her flabbergasted pets.

"Now don't you think for a minute I don't know what's on your minds," she said as she reached for a pretty lace shawl. "Of course I'm giving you dinner before I go out. And, yes, Harriet, treats too."

Acknowledgements

So many friends and readers helped bring this new series to life. Karen Schlosberg, Brett Milano, and Lisa Susser were early readers, and Sophie Garelick, Frank Garelick, and Lisa Jones have always been incredibly supportive. My agent Colleen Mohyde got the book to my brand new editor Jason Pinter, making magic for me along the way. And Jon S. Garelick not only read multiple versions but put up with some very late dinners, too. Purrs out to you, my dears. Purrs out.

ABOUT THE AUTHOR

A former journalist and music critic, Clea Simon wrote three nonfiction books, including the *Boston Globe* bestseller The Feline Mystique (St. Martin's Press), before turning to a life of crime (fiction). Her more than two dozen mysterious usually involve cats or rock and roll, or some combination thereof. A native of New York, she moved to Massachussetts to attend Harvard and now lives nearby in Somerville.

Visit her at www.CleaSimon.com or at @CleaSimon.

Available now from Clea Simon

and Polis Books

The new Witch Cats of Cambridge Mystery!

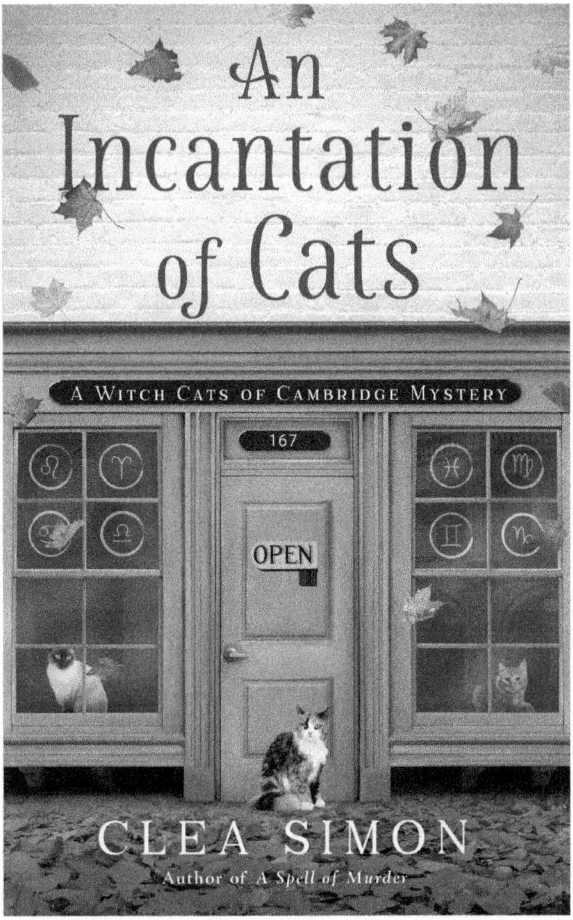